RETURN OF THE INQUISITION

The seven people sat around a polished stone table in conference. All were dressed in magenta drapesuits, except for the old man at the head of the table.

"The theology is clear," one said. "It has been established for centuries. The Gorboducs themselves have shown by their behavior that they are perversions, not true humans."

At last the old man spoke. "It confirms my suspicion that this was only a hoax on the part of a sworn enemy. I believe the Gorbie must be sacrificed publicly."

"You mean executed?"

"Exactly. He's done too much damage already."

By Paul O. Williams
Published by Ballantine Books:

THE PELBAR CYCLE

THE GIFTS OF THE GORBODUC VANDAL

The Gifts of the Gorboduc Vandal

Paul O. Williams

A Del Rey Book

BALLANTINE BOOKS ● NEW YORK

A Del Rey Book
Published by Ballantine Books

Copyright © 1989 by Paul O. Williams

Library of Congress Catalog Card Number: 88-92847

ISBN 0-345-35597-0

Manufactured in the United States of America

First Edition: May 1989

Cover Art by Paul Alexander

For Portia and Bill Blau

☐ Prologue

As Umber Trreggevthann moved among the racks of clear cocoons containing his charges, a bored, guttural voice from the command room announced over an all-ship speaker, "Approaching Landsdrum system. Occupied planet. Will pass above system plane, three hundred million *kizzdroggz* off. Stage seven alert."

Umber sighed and turned to Atel, who glided down the far aisle of the vital cargo bay checking life supports. "What's wrong?" she called across to him.

"A feeling. I wish Alayynr was awake. I wish it were a full alert."

"Stage one? Why? These feelings of yours—ever since Klluum. Droc pile. Put steel in your backbone again, Umber. You once were—"

"Yes. You've said," he snapped, turning to the monitor as she pushed off and glided across the pod to him. She stopped herself by grasping his massive shoulders and slowly settled in the faint gravity produced by the slow rotation of the chamber. Umber covered her hand with one of his as he touched in an information code on the console and examined the commonly known data on Landsdrum. They studied it in silence for some time.

"Another droc planet," Atel said.

Umber nodded. "I wish we could tell them," he murmured.

"They've been raided. They wouldn't listen now."

"Klluum will find a way. They have a long year. Seven hundred twenty-two point six-eight days. Must be almost two Esstrremadrrian years. Even so, looks like it's late in the plague cycle."

"You said it was hard to tell."

"It is. But it has to be late. Look. Native life is almost all in the sea. Poor land biology and massive erosion. They've made no attempt to check it. That's the problem with drocs, they're too easy a food supply. Those people don't even know how bad things are. They were too long in space and forgot about planetary life, or perhaps just don't care. What some grrrazz would do for them." Umber moved his finger across the Landsdrum holo floating in the hazescreen.

"Typical droc planet," Atel said flatly. "You can't save them all. Think of saving us, maybe."

"I think of what we could do even with the few species on board," Umber returned. "It's a largish colony. Must be five million. Miners. Look at that list of metals. They make freight hulls, too, and it looks like they mine elsewhere in the system —moons and asteroids. Religious music is an export industry. That's got to be the last stages of decadence."

"Decadence?"

"Religious decadence. Look. They're Starstream Emigrants. They've got some variation of Godworship."

"Too bad. Stuffy bigots. Every colony a variation of the same, and every one thinking it's got the only ultimate truth."

"Some of it's not bad. Says here they patrol the system and might even have passive buoy monitors. What's wrong with the captain, cutting through here?"

"Fuel, Umber. And our speed is necessary because of the droc cycle. Don't be nervous. It's only an alien-monitoring system for trade."

"Not only. Look at that coding. It's early warning for Dark Sector Raiders. Droc pile! We'd better veer off."

The speaker clicked. "Stage three alert," a voice said, less bored. "We are being monitored by a Landsdrum vessel. Enlarging. Armed patrol ship, Whank class, Starstream type. Attention. Attention. Stage two. They have locked on us."

Umber and Atel stared at each other. "Alayynr," she gasped. "He's in cool sleep. We'd never wake him."

"*Dazzrrnn*," Umber swore. "This bag of old metal'll never make it through an attack. Any at all and Alayynr's done, Atel." They stared at each other.

Umber touched the command center code. "Yes?" a voice replied.

"Commander Trreggevthann," Umber said. "I know it's not in regulations, but if we send them a standard routing and basic lading, we may prevent an attack."

After a pause, they heard a subdued growl. "Trrreggevthann," a voice bellowed, rolling the guttural "r" to show his anger. "I'll see to your trial when we get home. The code is clear. Gorboducs choose their contacts. No one forces us. I despise you for a Fantine swamp and all its pestilence."

Umber shrugged. "Yes, Captain, I would not have suggested it but for the enormous importance of the vital cargo. Can that not be in your considerations? I request it."

"Stuff it. We're busy, slime. At your trial."

"We have to survive to have a trial. I welcome any trial and will demand it be by combat."

"With pleasure," came a curt reply. "Droc pile. Do your duty in silence."

"Certainly, Captain," Umber said. "And may your warts multiply and so improve your face."

Atel looked at him in horror. Umber shrugged. "It's talk," he said. "It'll fire him up. Do his job better."

"Spying on Klluum has ruined you. *Dazzrrnn*, I'm so ashamed."

"You could be right. But the cargo. And the numbers."

"*Gllatts Burgiinn*, Umber, the numbers! Should we send them?"

"No. Never. Better it's all lost than the Dark Sector gets it. But . . ."

"What?"

"If there's an attack, I'm going to make for the landing pod and try to get to the planet surface. You should come."

"Never. That would be dishonorable. There would be no chance of survival and even if you *did* survive, what if they captured you?"

"I'd endure it."

"Your honor. Your basic honor. I—I'd renounce you. I'd have to. Everything would demand it."

Umber stared at her. "At that point it'd make little difference. The numbers, Atel. They're the best chance for Esstrremadrr. The best yet."

"They'd tap your memory and draw them out. That's vile."

Umber laughed. "No. I erased the memory plant. I've memorized it the ancient way, and—"

"The whole list? Impossible."

"I did it, Atel, while you were in cool sleep, and I put a block on it. If they did draw it out, it'd be so full of chance images and dreck they'd never sort it out."

"You'll forget."

"Never, I—"

"Attention all personnel," the speaker barked. "This is the captain. We are under attack—beams and missiles. Our calculations show we cannot respond successfully to such massive fire. This is the end for us. It remains only to expend ourselves dearly. We are now at stage one. Off-watch crew report to your stations. Abandon cargo pods. I expect all citizens to perform their duty to the fullest and act with absolute resolve. We are true Gorboducs. We have our honor. Somehow we will make the scum feel the bitterness of their act. I regret the loss of the mission, but our duty is clear. I salute you all—except the slime, Trreggevthann. Farewell."

Atel cried out. "Alayynr. He's lost."

Umber tightened his mouth. "And the specimens," he shot back. "Stick the duty station. Come on. The landing pod. I'll grab a few species."

"What's the matter with you? We can't do that to a planet!"

Umber glared. "I won't hurt the planet. It's a mess now anyway with species from at least five systems on it. I . . . want to save—" The huge cargo pod suddenly rocked and twisted. They glanced at each other and raced for space gear. "Just food plants and some ancient mammals . . ." Umber yelled as they ran, his voice fading in the thinning atmosphere.

☐ 1 Encounter

DAME Dyann Penne stared at the analysis of her new pottery glaze, frowning. It had the same constituents and proportions as a previous batch, but the results looked different. She sighed and murmured, "Things are seldom what they seem, Gy."

Dal Gyro Penne jerked out of his dreaming and replied, "Quite so. Quite so." Then he resumed a vacant stare at the wall of his wife's pottery shop.

An orange blinking, with a wrist tickler, jarred Dame Penne. She touched message control and heard, "First warning. First warning. Gorboduc ship in-system. Only one detected. This is a first warning. We are handling."

"It's been years," Dame Penne said. "Now trouble. Probably nothing."

"Quite so . . . not," Gyro Penne responded.

"Nonetheless, we'd better haul Pell in from the marshes and notify everybody. I wish Rad wasn't up there now. He's a little reckless." She rose and with one knotted old hand smoothed her husband's scant gray hair. He looked up in semicomprehension. She took his hand and coaxed him to his feet.

At LSCP Downside Command, Admiral Zonne stood at the bridge of the monitor-ship *Unyielding*, hands behind his back. "Distance from Landsdrum?" he asked.

"Two hundred forty-seven million kilospans, sir," the hunched aide replied from a monitor.

"Our distance?"

"One hundred four million, sir."

5

"Course angles?"

"One hundred seven planet relative, eighteen from orbital plane, sir."

"Eighteen?"

"Yes, sir."

"Type again?"

"Gorboduc cargo vessel, type 3927, with a pod line, discontinued 277 BP, sir."

The admiral strode over and glanced at the diagram, frowning.

"Speed?"

"Point five three six lightspeed, sir."

"Headed home, it would seem. Still, we have a standing order. It is in-system. They're always up to something. Prepare to engage."

The aide repeated the order. Zonne watched the schematics of the automatic preparations march across his screen.

"Lock on solid clusters," he said. The aide repeated the order, though only for form since the ship system had reacted to the voice command.

"Fire perimeter pattern," he said, feeling the jolt through the ship even as the aide repeated the order.

"In three ponders fire particle beams," he intoned, adding, "Send ahead scout squadron, full power."

The aide hesitated only a moment, with the slightest frown, before repeating the order. Zonne shot her a look and found her face bland.

"Tracking and following?" he asked.

"Yes, sir," the aide replied.

The admiral buckled down, drumming his fingers and watching the monitors. He punched up a steaming tube of cerre, popped off the tip, and sipped at it tentatively as the enormous distances brought the action to a nerve-rasping slowness. As the tracks from the *Unyielding* followed the Gorboduc vessel, it at first seemed asleep, then after several measures burst into a line of lights.

"Hostile missiles," the monitor chanted rhythmically.

"What kind?"

"Solid. Dividing. Style of that vessel."

Zonne shook his head. "Engage with defense pods," he ordered, and as the aide replayed it, he added, "I don't understand. All that is ancient technology."

"Pods away, sir," the aide said.

The admiral could see the long line of pods, firing loose from the core of the Gorboduc ship, then dividing themselves and subdividing. He frowned, saw his own solid missiles dividing and subdividing, each cluster deploying and picking a target, and smiled again. He knew that he had at least a hundred impacts for each small section of Gorboduc pod. They were not heavily shielded, and at least one projectile would get through their defense lasers. If the ship was typically Gorboduc, too, the hulls themselves would be explosive. The enemy did not compromise. It was difficult to put together much information about them.

"Pod jettisons have accelerated the core section to point five eight eight LS, sir," the aide said.

"Have the particle beams been pulsing?"

"Yes, sir."

"Well, we merely have to wait, then. I don't understand. It's like herding rock crawlers in the shallows. They have to be up to something."

As the great distances and remarkable speeds began to play out their game, the admiral and the bridge crew watched their own missiles being destroyed by the Gorboduc defenses. They saw the vessel core brighten and break up as the particle beams bored through its shielding. Then they saw pod sections fragment one by one, leaving a drift of wreckage in space. It all seemed so easy. Still, they tried to close and examine all the remains. It was really impossible, even with the help of the deployed scouts, because the speed at which debris bloomed out into space spun the pieces apart too fast.

The admiral eventually retired to his quarters, asking to be called if anything should come up. Something felt wrong. Had they just picked off a stray old cargo vessel going home from an impossibly long journey? Was that all? The Gorboducs were always full of surprises, none of them pleasant.

As he lay there, hands behind his head, calculating, Admiral Zonne received his first surprise. The speaker by his bed clicked and said, "Admiral Zonne?"

"Yes," he replied.

"Scout ship 223 holed, crew feared lost."

"How?"

"Automatic launcher on a platform of debris, sir. So they say."

"Thank you. I'll be right there," he replied. He unbuckled, sat up on the bunk, holding the grips, and sighed. "What next?" he asked himself aloud.

"Sir?" the speaker asked.

"Nothing. Oh. Who captained that ship?"

"A new graduate, Subadvocate Rad Newstrom, sir."

"Family?"

"None himself. He's married to a Penne, sir."

"Thank you," the admiral said, thinking to himself, Well, the Pennes had once had some power, but today they don't mean much. That, at least, is good. They could have gotten Franchesco. That would have been some trouble.

☐ II Capture

DYANN Penne had followed the news with sharp-eyed anxiety, and when she heard about the casualties, she glanced quickly at Gyro. He was asleep. She closed her eyes wearily, then sat back and stared at the phone monitor. Eventually a military face came on.

Before the man could say anything, she said, "Rad, then."

"You've been informed?"

"No. I divined it. How?"

"I'm sorry, Dame Penne. The luck of the draw. He got too

close to a drifting piece of wreckage. It had a residual weapon attached. An old Vandal trick."

"Rad was always one to open the kiln before it cooled," she replied, her eyes brimming. "Have you notified his wife?"

"We've left word. She's deep underground now in new workings and cannot be quickly reached. We have sent word for a station officer on Garre to tell her personally as well."

"I see. Thank you. Is it all over, then?"

"For now, yes. It appeared to be only a single ship."

"Did it send a databurst?"

"Yes."

"Then it is not all over, is it? Well, we'll have to be ready."

"True, Dame Penne. Thank you for understanding. We regret . . ."

"Never mind, young man. It was his duty. We all have our duties." She glanced at Gyro, once a Dal, a full-planet legislator, brilliant and forceful, now still asleep. "Good day, then."

"Again, our regrets, Dame Penne." The screen blinked out.

Dyann Penne looked at her old hands. Pell, her grandson, only seven revolutions old, was living with them since both his parents were off-planet. She would have to tell him about his father. She squeezed her eyes shut for a moment, then rose to seek him out.

Three eightdays later a ground monitor routinely tracing approaching debris noted one larger piece and checked its course. Her supervisor watched over her shoulder. "It will miss atmosphere by two thousand kilospans," she concluded.

"What of ship warnings?"

"They've been sent. Should we capture it?"

"No. Most of the debris is explosive. A nice Gorboduc touch. If it blew, who knows where it would go? Its course will carry it out of the system—to join all the other junk cruising around out there."

The ground monitor had time and enlarged the tumbling chunk of the ship. "Super, come look at this," she called. "It has real bulk. Shape. It isn't just a scrap of hull."

The two stared for a time at the wreckage. "I don't like

this," the supervisor murmured. "It's too big. Call LSHQ on it, Kai."

They placed the call, reaching a bored scanner who said that they knew all about it and that it meant nothing. She was not interested in notifying a superior. Nor did she want civilian advice. Just before she signed off, the ground monitor gave a little gasp, then turned and unaccountably pushed her superior slightly aside.

"Do help us, please, with one thing. We really would like your advice. At least I would," she said sweetly.

The scanner shrugged. She was chewing something. "What?" she asked.

"I am so new. I don't understand how the debris has just managed to accelerate, and coherently, even though it is tumbling like that."

"Gravity, of course," the scanner said with a twist of her mouth.

"Perhaps that explains, too, the course change out of programmed parameters. Our monitor is blinking all sorts of warnings. Probably it's out of order."

The scanner shifted her gaze, turned pale, and muttered, "Oh, my father's fat belly, what—" The link went dead.

The supervisor did not stop to chastise the monitor. She had also turned pale and rushed to the monitor. "That's not debris. That's an escape pod or some missile," she shouted, slamming her fist on the console. "Now, we want all planned notifications." The monitor keyed in the code. Circuit told circuit until a thousand wrist ticklers set off their alarms at once.

At Defense Central LSS, Sarn fired off a squadron of pursuers. Groundarmy could not get its new model skimmers to work. They had to send six sleek officers' liaison ships, only lightly armed, cursing the fact that Lower Space Service would get there first.

The Gorboduc vessel, jagged and twisted like a shard of torn hull, angled into the atmosphere and heated up over the sparsely settled Matted Plain district, near Purple Lake, a brackish arm of the Sea of Cruel Mouths.

As she was herding Gyro and Pell down into the never-used, dank, sour-smelling shelter, Dyann Penne heard the heavy *crump* of the Gorboduc craft's sonic boom. She turned and stared at the empty sky, feeling a thrill of fear and strange exhilaration. "Grayma, come on," Pell called from below. As she descended, she heard the six booms of the pursuers, close and loud, as they swept overhead and began to spread to wide formation.

As they settled in the narrow shelter with seven silent rank drocherders, they felt a single pulse as the ground jumped. Pell began to tremble. "It crashed is all," one of the herders said. "The end of that."

"Wait," Dame Penne said.

The Gorboduc craft had glowed visibly as it burned through the atmosphere, shedding a trail of white hot chunks of its jagged hull. The Lower Space in-atmosphere patrol vessels could see it had given up its pretense of tumbling and, as it slowed, jettisoned pieces of its ungainly shell to become an oval escape pod recognizable in many space cultures.

As the LS ships streaked in toward it, the pod skimmed over the west shoals and salt swamps that lay far off Matted Plain and separated the wide expanse of the Sea of Cruel Mouths from the deep open ocean beyond.

"Take it before it reaches the Matted Plain, laserman," Admiral Sarn commanded, but the spears of light lancing out at the pod had no apparent effect.

"Can't, sir," the man said. "Too heavily shielded."

"Hold fire, then," Sarn replied through gritted teeth. "They intend to land. Communicator, notify Groundarmy of all the Gorbie's movements."

"I'm sending a running position report, sir," the officer replied, tossing her head slightly.

"Hold back, all. We don't want to overrun them. They'll have to decelerate."

"Braking, sir," came the pilot's reply, as the pod and its pursuers flashed over the shallow sea and approached the wide marshes and matweed flatlands of Matted Plain. Beyond, they could see the erosion-gouged slopes of the Vulftrok Mountains, which ran like a spine down the long North Island.

"They're slowing, sir," the pilot shouted, tension in his voice.

"Keep formation, stay above and behind," Sarn said. "I don't see their point—unless they mean to poison the planet. Curse it that we let this happen. I can't believe it." He slammed his fist into his left palm. Communications flicked a glance at him.

Ahead, the Gorboduc pod skimmed the water surface, then touched it, lifted, skipped again, and lifted just enough to rise over the beach and slice a groove into the flat expanse of matweed beyond it near the Crescent Vine Tangles about two kilospans north of the city. At last it plowed over onto its nose and lay steaming as the LS ships arrived and hovered in a circle. Small fires smoked and burned around the pod. It gleamed dully, lying on an angle, about thirty spans long— less than the average cargo landroller.

"Settle in a perimeter, one hundred spans," said Sarn.

"Our command, Admiral," a voice said over the monitor.

"I assume you are Groundarmy," Sarn replied.

"Overadvocate Alfan Domat, Groundarmy Sector Command."

"We will withdraw when you arrive GSC," said Sarn with a hint of amusement. "Figures emerging," he added. "Eleven so far, suited for space. Staggering."

"Amazing. They haven't destroyed themselves. Have you lasered them?"

"No. Waiting for you. They look wholly disoriented. Two have collapsed. Now three. One is firing a handlaser at a ship. Good old Gorbies. The others are dragging the fallen ones toward the lake. They have reached the lakeside ship and are ignoring it. Now they're moving beyond and forming a defense line, but they look to be in bad shape."

"Domat again. You'd better back away. They may be flashing their ship. We've got them now."

The Groundarmy vessels slid in behind the LS perimeter and settled. One limping figure moved toward a liaison ship, flattened against it, and exploded, driving a hole in it. Men poured out as Domat said, "Release disabling gas. Now. Keep away from them. We want them alive."

"They have in-suit atmosphere, OA. The gas just gets our men."

At that point all the aliens lay down, and their vessel exploded in a blaze of consuming white flame. The fleeing Groundarmy men went down. Only three got up and ran on.

In the shelter at Potsherd Sump they felt the ground jump again. Dyann Penne said, "They're making a muck of it there."

"Why don't they just kill them all?" Pell whined.

"Now we got casualties, they have to," a drocherder said.

"The information may be worth the casualties if we can capture them," Dame Penne replied.

"So long as you're not the casualties," the man returned.

On the scene GOA Domat said, "We'll have to resort to individual stundarts. Proceed."

At that point the capture became routine, the stundarts piercing each suit with its pulse of simple high voltage and complex sleep drug. Domat was the first to exit his ship as the LS vessels lifted back from their perimeter, made formation, and moved eastward with a heavy roar.

Domat glanced after them, then spit. "All right. Careful, now. Treat them like bombs. Defusers first. Deploy now and examine the area with scanners. We don't want any more casualties. Watch for scattered antipersonnel devices shed by that ship of theirs."

The remaining Gorboduc survivors proved simple to handle. The bomb squad defused their self-detonation devices easily, stripped off their silver suits, and found their bodies thin to the point of emaciation and obviously dehydrated.

As they were being redrugged and loaded on a shuttle for Matted Plain Base, GOA Domat's bonereceiver crackled to life. "Overadvocate, this is FS Tomma. We see barefoot tracks here by the tangle, heading in. A very big person. What—"

"Follow instantly. It has to be a Gorbie. Use bodyscanners. Take all available people. He won't get far with the sharpweed up. Crimeaters, be careful. He'll be armed. Use full suitarmor."

FS Tomma watched the shuttle lift off with Domat. "Fine. Hot, slathering crimeaters, go get him. All right. All suit up. We have to dig this one out."

Not far into the tangles Tomma saw a spot of blood, then another. "Domat was right," he said. "Sharpweed'll stop him. Look bright, now. Any body scan?"

"Not yet in this heat, sir," the scanner replied. "Wait. Over that way. Moving toward the lake."

"Hurry. If he gets there, we'll lose him."

"Give some leatherarm a stomachache, sir."

"Ground Command, send us a vessel to hover at the shore," Tomma called into his wristmitter. "We have a signal working that way."

"He's stopped, sir," the scanner said.

"All right. Move in."

They found the Gorboduc desperately trying to fasten strips of vineskin to his bloody feet. He was using an ancient-style hand knife. As they came, he stood and faced them with it. He shouted something no one could understand. He was dressed only in ragged fiber shorts. A yawning recruit put a dart into him, and he collapsed.

"See the size of him," another recruit said. "Too bad you stunned him. Now we have to carry him out, I suppose."

"Only to the spot clearing. We'll lower a wand from a supportship."

"Crimesniffer. He's ugly. Look at him. Look at that long hair. Must be point three measures. Crime. Look at those blue freaky eyes. Blue."

"Looks human to me," Tomma said. "Medic, spray his feet before he bleeds to death. Arms, too. He's been through a garbush or two."

A short while later, as they watched the nearly naked, limp man rise in his sling and hum away, hanging from the supportship by a line, they felt some relief. Even unconscious, the man was imposing by his size and muscular build.

"I hadn't really thought of Gorbies as human, sir," the medic remarked.

"They're only imitations. The devil's imitations," a recruit remarked.

"For the superstitious. He's human. I've worked on a few of them," the medic replied. "Pieces of them," he added.

▭ III Face to Face

CASIO Polon, the Matted Plain Rep, drummed his fingers. Then he held his stylus between the tips of his forefingers. He squinted with one eye, lining up the top of the stylus with the line on the opposite wall. "Oh, crime," he muttered, and touched the code for Sectorparty.

An aide's face winked on. "Sir?" he asked.

"Give me Dal Baats, please."

"Sir, he is conferring at the moment. May I—"

"No. This is Dal Polon in a matter of whitecode urgency. I must talk with him."

"I . . . yes, sir. I'll speak to him."

Polon picked up the stylus again and sighted with it. Soon a corpulent face against a light blue background appeared. "Yes, Polon. How is it with the Gorbies?"

"They're recovered, sir. They abuse everything and spit at everyone. They rail in Gorboduc—even the woman. We have them clipped to pipeframes. The region claims jurisdiction. It wants to execute them."

"Have you managed to communicate with them?"

"No. They seem not to understand Molod or Westsector."

"What about the naked one? The long hair?"

"He's a little different. Quieter. He doesn't spit. His railings are interspersed with derisive laughter."

"I don't understand, Polon. How is it he got out undetected? Why was he not suited?"

"The theory here is that he was to be a spy and hoped to lose himself in the vines."

"That's foolish."

"Yes, sir."

"We can't imprison them very well, Polon, even if that were desirable. The word would get out. It would invite an invasion, even as far out as we are. But you know all that."

"Yes, sir. The region council has an idea of their own—that we give them the Matted Plain murderer's option: choice of execution or a vow of slavery to one of the principal families. The Dal families."

"That's an ancient law—unused. And what if one of them chooses to do that?"

"They think they can't choose slavery, sir. From what they know of Gorbie Vandals—"

"Which isn't much."

"Yes. From what they know, though, they think they'll all choose execution, and a problem will be solved. No Gorbies will be coming for them. And it would be their choice. Less guilt that way."

"There was a databurst, Polon. They'll come for their revenge."

"But we can handle that, can't we?"

"Possibly. We'll have to try. We assume they'll come eventually, anyway."

"Region council also thinks that if any one of them were to choose slavery and the Gorbies found out about it, they'd want to execute him anyhow."

"And us, Polon. Especially Matted Plain. I don't understand why they want to take that on."

"I advised against it, sir. I took up the party position that they should be put in slow life, loaded on a small ship, and shot toward Oryxx."

Dal Baats laughed. "Poor Oryxx. Do we detest them that much? But I imagine the region sees some glory in the possibility of having the first Gorbie slave."

"Or executing them and being rid of them. But a slave would certainly confer distinction on this brackish backwater."

"Please, Dal. You are speaking of your own region." Baats looked away a moment. "You handle it, Dal Polon. We have discussed it, and the law is clear. Region council, unfortunately perhaps, has the jurisdiction. We appreciate your proposing our views. Let's at least hope for execution. Cheaper that way, too."

Polon hesitated a moment. "Yes, Dal Baats. Thank you. I appreciate your advice."

Baats smiled slightly and nodded even more slightly. His face winked out. "Crime. Crime on a crutch," Polon muttered. He knew Baats had counted on him to prevail over the region council. This would not go well for him. Well, he would try again.

But Casio Polon failed. As a consequence, an eightday later a great crowd gathered at Matted Plain to see the aliens. The square filled with people, and they fringed the surrounding poured-stone buildings and leaned on every balcony. In the center of the square around the market platform a set of barricades held back the people, and a hoverskimmer lowered the twelve Gorbies onto it, still clamped to their pipeframes. They were fastened to a rectangular lightalloy platform, which clanged down on the stone.

The aliens yelled and spit. No one could understand them. They laughed among themselves, made faces, and moved to imitate citizens in the forefront of the crowd as much as their tight clamps would permit.

The crowd stood strangely silent. Perhaps it was the imposing size of the Gorboducs, perhaps their tight, athletic faces, the close-cropped heads of all but one, or the palpable hostility that radiated from them. Perhaps it was curiosity, since hardly any of those people had ever been off-planet, and they seldom went to Truncated Mountain, where most of the trading aliens came. As the region council had anticipated, dislike grew in the crowd with the animus from the Gorboducs. They began to stir. A kind of voiceless growl rose from the crowd.

"Get it over with," one man shouted.

"Kill the droc slime," a woman shrilled.

Dal Polon held up his hands for silence. It was slow in coming from the crowd. The Gorboducs blew over vibrating tongues at him and burst into sarcastic guffaws.

Polon explained to the crowd what all knew. The prisoners had the choice of death or slavery for the crime of invasion and murder. They had their choice of the Dal families present, recognizable by their blue coats, as masters. Polon addressed them in Molod. They shouted in Gorboduc. Polon waited.

Finally, one Gorboduc, an older man, replied in Molod.

"I have explained to them what you have said, droc pile. They say they choose death, and it cannot come soon enough to relieve them of the vile presence of so many neverwashed mullock worms. We promise you now that twenty of you will shrivel for every one of us you touch. Not that twenty of you are worth much. A poor bargain for us. It ought to be thirty. At least thirty. We'll have no trouble with that, either. It will come. You chinless tremblers have only to wait."

A translator droned out what the man had said. The crowd surged at the barricade. Somebody started a chant, "Kill them, kill them, kill them, kill them." The Gorboduc took it up, shouting and laughing.

Polon again called for silence. Once more it was a long time in coming. "You have heard—" he began.

"No. Wait. Me be slave," the one long-haired Gorboduc said. "Me agree you. Me slave that man." He nodded in the direction of Gyro Penne, who stood with his wife and grandson in the forefront of the crowd. He spoke in Westsector, the language of Landsdrum.

For a moment the crowd stood transfixed. Somebody shouted, "No. It's a trick. Kill him, too. Kill the filthy murderer." The crowd took up that chant. Polon hesitated a few moments, then motioned the guards to stand between the Gorboduc and the crowd. The prisoners started spitting at their backs—except for the long-haired one, who stood still, head down. The prisoners near him spit at him, too, turning their heads. The curses they hurled at him contained more fury than anything the crowd had received.

Polon had the other prisoners gagged. Then he addressed the long-haired one. "Why do you want this, this slavery?"

"Me coward," the man responded. "Not want die."

The crowd erupted in laughter at him. He made faces at them.

"You can't do that as a slave," Polon said.

"Sorry," the man said.

"What is your name?"

"Umber. Me Umber."

"Where did you learn Westsector?"

"Met man knew it."

"Where?"

"Far off. Far system. He taught."

"Not very well, it would seem. Well, you'll have to choose another family. That one has no active Dals."

"No. That one or none."

"None? That means we will kill you, too?"

"Not want. No. Yes."

"A moment, Dal Polon. According to the murderer's option, he has the choice of Gyro. I've read the law."

Polon turned. Dyann Penne had stepped under the barricade and was addressing him. No one stopped her.

"We prefer—" he began.

"The law is the law," a man shouted up at him. Someone in the crowd began, "The law is the law is the law." The crowd laughed and began that chant. Others began, "Kill them all, kill them all, kill them all." The crowd again grew restless.

Polon touched up the speaker volume. "Silence!" he shouted. "We will have silence!" Groundarmy skimmers rose and hovered over the crowd. Gradually the crowd quieted. Polon felt the pulse in his neck surging. "We will obey the law," he boomed. "Release that man, and if he goes to Gyro Penne, kneels to him, and accepts the collar, he will be his slave forever and will live." Gyro looked around, puzzled. The guards released the Gorboduc, Umber, led him to Gyro and made him kneel. They slipped a kill collar around his neck and handed the control box to Dyann Penne. Umber's long hair hung down, shrouding his face as he knelt.

"Young man, you are ours now," Dame Penne said. "You will haul clay and tend drocs and make up for the loss you caused."

"Me? Loss?" Umber mumbled.

"The loss of my son-in-law from your incursion."

Umber chuckled. "We kill one?"

Dame Penne's hand tightened slightly on the control box.

A guard pointed at an orange button. "That one is for discipline," he said. Dame Penne pressed it. Umber cried out briefly, then shuddered in silence.

"What did you say?"

"We kill one?" Umber repeated.

Dame Penne hit the button again. Umber shuddered slightly, his head straightening. Then he gasped.

"What did you say?" she repeated.

"We kill one?" Umber gritted out.

Dame Penne hit the button again. Again Umber stiffened. Someone from the crowd shouted out, "That's the way with the Dals. Love hurting people. Love it. The bastards. Especially when they're defenseless."

"They deserve it!" somebody else shouted.

Polon boomed, "All right. We will take the Gorbies to Matted Plain Base and their requested execution. Dame Penne, perhaps you could take care of discipline at home. Groundarmy, lift this platform."

All watched as the large hoverskimmer hummed down and took the platform hook. Umber turned to watch as the platform rose. The eleven Gorboducs all glared at him from behind their gags and writhed, twisting in their bonds as they were jerked skyward. As they cleared the crowd and soared out high over Purple Lake, a strong laser speared out from behind the buildings and severed the cable that held them.

The crowd roared as the heavy platform tumbled down through the air and hit the water with a heavy splash. Umber, still kneeling, let out a single wail, shuddered, and then hung his head in complete stillness as the crowd left the square, running down the avenues to the water's edge, where several waterskimmers already had set out toward the widening circle of ripples. Two Groundarmy hoverskimmers rose to seek the origin of the laser.

Pell Penne and his grandmother stood by the kneeling Umber, regarding him. "Why did you do that, Grayma?" Pell asked.

"I . . . don't quite know," she said. "Seemed a waste to just kill them."

"Give me that, then," he said, reaching for the control box.

"I'm afraid it is sensitive to my touch only," she replied.

"Murderer!" the boy cried out.

"What that?" Umber said, nodding toward the lake.

"You killed my father."

"You kill wife, son."

"Where?"

Umber nodded in the direction of Purple Lake.

"There were no boys there."

"Boy die before. Space."

"You invaded us."

"We more far than sun. Going by. It done now. All work lost."

"All what work?" Dame Penne asked.

"All work my life," Umber said, gazing straight at her.

"What work was that?" she asked.

Umber's jaw tightened, but he did not reply.

☐ IV Testing

UMBER woke slowly in a dim, bare room. It was painted an even blue, the blue of the sky of Klluum on a clear summer day. He lay strapped lightly to a padded table, a fabric over his midsection. Gently testing his bonds, he felt the sensors fabricated into them. He paused, testing his strength, his feelings, trying to detect what drugs the Landsdrum examiners had pumped into his body. He could identify none of them.

He sighed, felt his thirst, wet his lips with his tongue, breathed deeply three times, then surged against the bonds, holding his muscles tight, his whole frame trembling. Then he deepened the strain. Three orderlies rushed into the room to restrain him.

"Good you come," Umber said. "Need water."

"You can't break those bonds. Even if you did, we'd be right here, you scummy Gorbie," the older man said.

"Good. Now need water."

"You'll get water on schedule. Be quiet or we'll quiet you," the same man said.

"Good. Be quiet. My schedule now. For water."

"Oh, crime. Give him some water, Elber. The man is thirsty," the other orderly said.

"Me wild. Wild man drink when thirsty, not from schedule," Umber said.

"Both of you shut up. On schedule, I said. You come on, Restin."

"Good-bye, Restin," Umber said.

The younger orderly paused, then glanced at Elber and turned away, saying nothing. The two left.

Umber strained again against his bonds, again holding his body against them until he had to lie back panting. This time no orderlies burst through the door. He shouted in Gorboduc, then lapsed into a long, despairing laugh. Again no one came. Then he used the bonds for exercise, flexing all his muscle groups in order, then running through them once more. It was almost like being back in space, he mused.

The door whisked open, his table whirred upright, and Restin appeared by him with a beaker of water. "Quick," the orderly said. "Drink this. It isn't on the schedule." He tilted the beaker slowly, his hand trembling slightly, and Umber drank rapidly to keep up with him. "Not a word, now," Restin said, turning away.

"Thank," Umber said. "Better."

Casio Polon was irritated. The Gorboduc had psych-blocks that prevented even the veridicals from loosening his tongue. They had kept him several days, but they knew little more about him now than they had initially. And Dyann Penne repeatedly called for information about "her slave." So far he had ignored her, refusing calls or using the adroitness of his secretaries to turn her aside.

Still, he was not prepared to answer for the delay in court or to avoid reddening at the indignity of being served notice by an armed commoner. A quiet fury swelled his neck. He snapped the summons out of the man's hand and said through gritted teeth, "Now get out."

The man smiled slightly with one side of his mouth and said, "That would be normal," turning slowly to leave.

Polon leapt up and shouted, "Get out of here!"

The man turned again and regarded him. "If you are resisting the summons, I shall add a charge of my own," he said evenly.

Polon sank back in his bodyfit chair and muttered, "No. I am not resisting. Stay all afternoon if you like." Then he rose and strode out a private door, which unwound to receive him.

Dyann Penne was in the midst of a slab pot when Polon's face appeared on the visiscreen. "Yes?" she asked, dipping her clay-caked hands in a jar of water.

"There is no need to take me to court," he said. "You will receive your Gorbie in due time."

"Now is due time, Casio. Overdue time. I've heard how you've been treating him. If anybody treats him badly, it will be me, since he is Gyro's."

"Perhaps you could come in and talk about it."

"If you want to talk, you can do so either now or in court, Casio. I know the relevant law."

Polon shook his head. "Very well," he said, sighing. "If there's no help for it. But you must understand the folly of this. An alien raider out living with an old woman and a man barely able to take care of himself. And a boy."

"And some workers and servants. And wearing a kill collar, which I may choose to activate."

"He's been long in space. Our tests show it. He isn't a clod, a wild man, as he calls himself. He's a highly educated enemy. You may be no match for him."

"Perhaps not, Casio. But he's better out here than in some city. And when he's tended drocs for a year or two, he may decide he is a wild man."

"He'll arrive tomorrow, then, if you will drop your suit."

"Tonight, Casio, or I will push it ahead." Dame Penne rubbed a wisp of hair away with the back of a wrist, her hands still smeared with wet clay. Dal Polon noted with a vague satisfaction that her face was smudged anyway.

He raised his hands and dropped them. "Tonight, then." He cut the picture. "Crime," he mumbled. "Tall, hard crime."

Later that evening Gyro and Dame Penne heard the main entrance sounder. Dame Penne motioned their servant, Phant, to answer, and soon Casio Polon appeared with Umber, who looked thinner and pale. Polon handed the kill command to

Dame Penne. It lay black and glistening in her wrinkled palm. Umber watched nonchalantly as she moved her forefingertip over the controls.

She glared at him. "I'm not afraid to use this," she said. "One wrong move."

"No need," Umber replied. "Me meek. Smell droc outside. Good with droc. Know much. Help."

"You'll be smelling drocs a long time, Gorbie," Dyann Penne replied.

"Good. Good with droc."

Casio Polon rolled his eyes. "Now, if I might have two words, Dame Penne. Perhaps you could dismiss your new servant for the time."

"Slave," Pell said.

"Pell, mind your tongue. We will have courtesy in this estate," Dame Penne said. "Uji, take the servant to the droc swamp and show him his platform," she added, nodding to an old man in a clean herder's smock. Uji jerked his head, and Umber dutifully followed, stooping slightly under the doorway.

"Yes?" Dame Penne asked.

"We need careful records kept of this man," Polon said, pacing the room. "So careful, you must detect any slightest action that may be useful to us."

"You mean if he picks his nose?"

"Don't be angry with me. This is a matter of planet security. There is no telling what he may do or be."

"What did the bone scan show? How much time in space?"

"A great deal. He must be twice as old as you—if that can have a meaning. Much slow life."

"What of battle scars, evidence of combat service?"

"Little. His scars are easily explainable except two sets, one a row of three diagonally across his back, the other two scars on his head. But none seems to have been combat-caused."

"On his head? Implants?"

"No evidence of any implants."

"No Gorbie-trial scars, then?"

"No. But we know little of what that means."

"Maybe it means he was the cook."

"Please. In the interest of the planet."

"You need not fear. I have the interest of the planet at heart. So does Dal Penne." She looked across at him. He was asleep, his mouth slightly open. "In his lucid moments," she added. "Uji will watch him and record everything. I'll send you regular reports. No need to be surprised. I just don't think everything is to be learned by analyzing his body fluids and poking at him with this instrument or that. Now, will you have some tea? Varjan tea, from Steek."

Dal Polon bowed slightly. "No, but thank you," he said. "It's been a long day. You will drop your case, I trust."

"Of course."

"Leda . . . how is she? Is she coming home?"

Dyann Penne smiled slightly. "I suppose. Now that Rad's gone."

"That didn't . . . work out, then."

"No, but you needn't be so pleased."

Polon dropped his eyes. "I'm not. But it was hard on her."

"No tea? Is it good evening, then?" She bowed just barely and gave him a slight, wrinkled smile.

Polon looked a little baffled. "Good evening, then," he said, turning to go.

On a platform in the droc swamp, the acrid smell of the creatures feeding below him heavy in his lungs, Umber composed himself for sleep. The hard platform he lay on conducted the night cold through the old sleep-fabric quilt they had dug out for him. He sighed and brushed his eyes. It all seemed so strange, even for a far traveler. He thought for a moment of Atel and the others falling with the platform, and again a choked cry came from him. Would to Being I had never been born, he thought. This, too, has to be endured. I will endure it. I must. I must, he insisted to himself. "Oh, Atel, my Atel," he said aloud. "And Alayynr, my son. My son." Then he steeled himself again, and before sleeping he went over the numbers again, slowly, deliberately, each in the sequence falling through his memory like rain pouring from the cliffs at Sound of Water, in Far Cloud Province, at home when he was a boy.

☐ V Potsherd Sump

THE planetary colony of Landsdrum as a whole had not thrived as some had. Landsdrum was out of the way, off the vast highways of nothingness that marked the best routes from known speck to known speck in the wide-flung outposts of human colonization and trade. Most of the nearest viable planets had been colonized by people of other cultures, other language groups, and the clannish Starstream Emigrants had taken a long time in setting up trade with any of them. Then, too, the Gorboduc Raiders had found them, though they lay on the perimeter of the Gorboduc tribute sphere, and the expense of defense and tribute had bled the colony twice in the previous Landsdrum century.

Though Landsdrum was largely ocean-covered, the massive islands made largely of igneous rock, had eroded, in places ferociously, into wide alluvial plains containing many minerals, including unusual quantities of gold, silver, titanium, chromium, nickel, copper, and a huge deposit of platinum, as well as the usual iron and aluminum. These the Landsdrum colony mined for their own use and for some interplanetary trade, assembling freight hulls and orbiting strings of them for sale to several mineral-poor Starstream Emigrant colonies, and a few other venturers willing to make the remarkable journey to get them.

In return, Landsdrum took other rare metals and minerals, a variety of organic products, including dried exotic foods, large weights of cellulose manufactures, as well as intricately crafted art pieces traded from the far distant, pastoral worlds of Klluum and Razzool. They also brought in technical knowledge and literature from a few far worlds, all of which was outdated by the time it reached Landsdrum, and all of which was studied in detail by the Godworship Councils before it was released to the public.

The more waggish workers lamented that half of the income from the great hull strings that left Landsdrum paid for fires in cathedral undercrofts, warming the hands of the censors with the accumulated sins of the universe. Landsdrum had little secular art because of the influence of the colonial religion, and, strangely enough, even most religious art was not encouraged—except for music, which was varied and complex, forming one of the chief public attractions to general worship meetings.

The colony was rich in some things—some of the Dal class had built silver summer houses, and many had plated their roofs with gold. But the commoners lived mundanely—mining, working in droc husbandry, tending automated factories, or idling. Religious education occupied a great deal of time, though the average Landsdrum citizen had little real enthusiasm for it. It was just there, and managed to encourage a strange passivity among the common people, who entertained themselves with what was available. They spent many evenings in the wrang-juice houses, drinking and quietly playing games. Godworship controlled and regulated the more flamboyant recreations, and the usual sins, with a noose that did not choke them off so completely that the people would rebel, but that was tight enough to make the average person do a little gasping in the fulfilling of desires.

The Dals, from whom all government flowed, were excepted, of course, though they were Godworship trained. Still, rumored excesses of the Dals of Choicity, the one big urban area of the colony, caused winks and jealous murmurs in the evening gatherings of the ordinary. Some of these stories were even true.

The ancestral home of the Pennes, an old but often overlooked Dal family, lay on the west side of the long North Island. It stretched out on an alluvial fan below the naked foothills of the Vulftrok Mountains largely in a swampy flat produced when the River of Good Intent braided and broadened into sluggish ponds and marshes, slowed by the shore rises north of Purple Lake, which was really a semienclosed arm of the Sea of Cruel Mouths to the west.

On their arrival on the planet of Landsdrum, the Star-streamers had found corkscrew vine, plate leaf, and sky suckers well established and a thriving colony of wild drocs awaiting exploitation and husbandry. Potsherd Sump was one of the oldest settlements on the planet, but its remote location kept it and the nearby settlement of Matted Plain from growing as the settlements to the southeast had.

It was precisely the kind of place Dyann Penne would thrive in. Marriage to Gyro had brought her a dignity she wore casually, yet enjoyed. It also had brought her the leisure to pursue her passion for ceramics as well as a good supply of clays from the alluvium and a place to spread her kilns and stacks of products, broken and whole, with the abandon common in rural areas. Now that she was old and Gyro was no longer fit for political discourse, she did not care about even a pretense of neatness in her potshop.

Neither of the Pennes had ever taken a deep interest in droc husbandry but let the workers tend the beasts as they always had, feeding, herding, gathering and nurturing their seeds, slaughtering, and preparing for market. It was a messy, odorous business as well as slightly dangerous. These knobby, cross-shaped, swamp animals could grow to more than a man's weight. They were gregarious and could often be observed lifting a pliant arm or two above the ooze and touching each other in elaborate patterns. The droc herders called this cuddling or stroking and paid little attention to it, though they recognized it as a basic grooming or socializing behavior.

Though drocs did not move very fast, they could move in concert and with purpose, and the several horny beaks along the underside of each of the four limbs that made up most of their bodies could nip out a large chunk of flesh with ease. Two or three large drocs coming on a sleeping person could pin and feed on him, in a short time leaving only bone. Such things seldom happened, in part because of the precautions drocherders took, in part because the drocs themselves seemed only occasionally inclined to be aggressive. But it had been noted that when humans were eaten, the first beaked arm to touch the person almost invariably fell across the mouth and throat of the victim. Clearly drocs had intelligence and memory, though no one on the planet had bothered to research the matter.

Drocherders were not highly respected on Landsdrum. In fact, to call someone a drocherder was to call that person stupid. And many fights had arisen because of it, especially in the mind-altering lounges of the cities.

Uji, though, was mildly proud of being a drocherder, probably because the Pennes dealt with him democratically and fairly and neither shuddered nor turned away because of the pervasive odor that proximity to drocs left on their tenders.

The sun had not quite risen when Uji knocked on a post of the droc watch platform on which Umber had been sleeping. Umber rolled over and looked down. Uji waved his slabvine cane. "This is no vacation, Gorbie," he yelled. "Up. Time to move the easternmost herd to fresh forage. Get your thigh-boots. Food in this sack. Move, now. Move."

Umber sat up, shook his long hair, and dropped to the muddy ground barefoot. "Where food?" he asked.

Uji silently handed him a fabric sack. The Gorboduc un-clipped the top and peered in. He made a face but reached in and stuffed a large fruitball in his mouth. Uji was disgusted.

"You've worked drocs, I hear," he said.

"Many time. Show you want. Me do."

Uji pointed to the broad droc pan in which a cluster of the X-shaped animals had fed on the *Platus platinus* until their blue leaves were gnawed down to nubs. "You want droc led there?" Umber asked, gesturing at a berm separating the drocs from a freshly restored pan beyond.

"I'll help you with the ramp, and then you wade the pan and herd them. I'll give you a tickler prod."

Umber frowned. "No need. That bother droc. Me herd. You see."

Uji threw up his hands. "Suit yourself, Gorbie. It's your body they'll snip. Cinch up your underpants."

Umber grinned slightly at the ancient interplanetary joke.

"True," he replied in a high voice.

After they had set the ramp, Umber startled his new boss by wading into the pan bare-legged, circling around the drocs but moving astonishingly close. Uji frowned but kept silent, watching. Umber reached out to the rearmost, caught a leg, and rubbed its top ridge with his fingertips. The droc held up his leg as the Gorboduc sidled into the notch between two legs, stroking the ridge toward the hub. The droc gently lowered that limb and lifted another. Umber repeated the process, then reached across the droc and caressed the farther legs. The droc slowly wrapped its nearer legs around Umber's waist, but the Gorboduc did not resist. Instead he massaged the small knobs where the leg ridges ran into the high hub ridge as he waded through the deep, smelly mud to the ramp, avoiding the other drocs. On the berm he gently rubbed the droc's leg tips with a forefinger, and the beast released him and slipped to the ground with a wet slap.

Umber then walked around in front of the animal and made slight air-kissing sounds. The droc replied with similar ones, moving slowly forward toward the new pan. Uji noticed to his astonishment that the other drocs were slowly following, heading directly toward the ramp. As they reached its top, in a line, Umber caressed each on its leg ridges, stopping it and examining it briefly. He looked particularly at the leg tips, at length hefting and swinging a large one aside, stilling it with a deft manipulation of its hub. When the last droc was headed down the ramp to the fresh pan, Umber stooped to the one animal he had set aside as Uji, still astonished, came up to him. "What are you doing?" he demanded.

"Old species. Unimproved," Umber said. "Look. Hook tip. This can get plague."

"Plague? You believe that old nonsense about droc plague."

"Plague true. Worry. This need care. See split?" Umber held up one limb of the still-relaxed animal.

"Oh. That'll go away. They get that. It'll heal."

"We heal. It grow better. No hurt. Where droc station?"

Uji, a little nonplussed, gestured. "All right. I'll show you. But don't hurt it. And if you get nipped, it isn't my doing."

"No nip," Umber said. "I put asleep." He heaved the droc onto his shoulder and started ahead of Uji, who regarded him with a slight frown.

In the droc station, Umber gently laid the droc on a table, took a small knife Uji held out for him, and expertly slit, flushed, and closed the small split on the animal's leg tip, removing the small bone from the hook as he did. Uji moved the wound fuser across the incision as Umber massaged its hub.

"What are you doing this for?" Dyann Penne said from the doorway. "I thought you were going to have the slave move the pan thirty-two drocs?"

"They're moved, Dame Penne," Uji said. "This one had a wound. We've been fixing it."

"What did you give it? Those anesthetics are expensive. Better to let it heal naturally."

"No anesthetic, Dame Penne. The Gorbie hypnotized it some way. Look. It's still asleep."

"Need place for it couple day. Dry. Got place?" Umber asked.

"It will shrink, lose muscle. Put it back with the others," Uji said.

"If let, me bring leaf plates, feed. While tip heal. No trouble."

"We can't baby each droc, servant. There's other work to do. Uji, didn't you give him boots?"

"No need," Umber said.

Dyann Penne hesitated a long moment. "You are unfamiliar with the mud pests?" she asked.

Umber frowned. "Droc worm here?" he asked.

"No, thank good sense. A native parasite. Go wash, now. Uji, give him the sand soap. Wash your . . . everything. Scrub. Uji, why did you let him—"

"He doesn't listen well, Dame Penne. He was in it before I could stop him. You. Gorbie. Follow me."

After they left, Dyann Penne strolled out on the berm system and saw to her astonishment that the drocs indeed had all moved and were fanning slowly out across the new pan, feeding contentedly.

That night she reported to Casio Polon. After she finished, he mused a moment. "Droc plague? He told Uji that? Unimproved species? I don't know. All that has been shown to be a myth. You'll have to watch him. I admit I'm astonished, though. You say the hurt droc greeted him?"

"That's what it looked like, Dal. And he took the leg it lifted and held it unmolested."

"But he didn't know the mud pest."

"No. We injected him for inserted seeds. He is a little sick from that now. If there were any, he'll be a lot sicker. Oh, and he wanted to see one. I projected one for him while he lay still from the injection. He looked at it a long time, frowning. He even forgot I was there. He looked at me a little startled when he realized where he was. Then he said, 'Not native. Fantine System, but changed.'"

After the communication, Casio Polon stared at the wall a long time, called up a report on the *Drusculla metoxens*, or mud pest, and searched the Dal library call-up for information on the Fantine System. There was little, and none of it had anything to do with parasites. Fantine IV was a droc planet, however.

☐ VI   Various Vines, Various Tangles

DEEP in the vine tangle at the tip of the delta of the River of Good Intent, on the shores of Purple Lake, strange spears of green lanced upward among the corkscrew vine and the broad plates of the young slabvines of that season.

Nearby, on a plain mud shore of one smaller braided stream, an intricate vegetative fist muscled upward through the dirt. Up a slight rise on one of the river islands, a careful viewer could see a hole beneath two wedged boulders tumbled there by some forgotten winter flood. The dirt in front of the hole showed prints like tiny hands.

A drunk had noticed prints like those near the stream in the vine tangle as his world had begun to level out. He had rubbed his eyes and shuddered, then stumbled out of the tangle in the direction of Matted Plain, vowing to stay off the wrang juice.

At Potsherd Sump, after several eightdays, local curiosity about the Gorboduc had waned. He seemed like a morose, large man with horribly long hair, a shambling man who was always dirty, a man whose droc smell seemed more intense than it was on the creatures themselves, a mumbler whose talk was primitive.

But the presence of Umber had roused Gyro Penne occasionally out of his passiveness. He would ask questions about the man of anyone nearby. No one had many answers. One day, at sunset, he suddenly threw on his waycloak, took his slabvine cane, and walked out the door, heading for the droc pens. Dyann Penne motioned Pell to follow him, and the boy did, his breath quickened by a slight fear, though he knew the alien was confined to his platform by a set kill line that would trigger his deadly collar.

Dal Penne walked with purpose and some speed, his grandson following. As he neared the platform in the dusk, he could hear the Gorboduc chanting softly. He stopped.

"What are you doing?" he asked sharply.

Umber jumped a little. "Sit here," he said.

"That sound. What was that?"

"Sing. I sing."

"Well, I forbid it. It was awful."

"What mean 'forbid'?"

"You can't do it anymore. I don't want it."

"What when you not here?"

"Even then I forbid it."

Umber said nothing but drew the old quilt closer around him.

"Why do you stink so? Why don't you wash?"

"Wash? Where? No one let."

Gyro pondered that. "Why is your hair so long?" he asked. "The others had short hair."

"Hair? For Bbydjrygurr."

"For what? What is a budgerigger?"

Umber burst into a sudden laugh and sustained it, rolling off the platform and landing lightly on the ground. He continued to laugh until Gyro stepped forward and hit him sharply with his cane across the shoulders. Pell ran forward and drew his grandfather back behind the kill line.

"He's your master, and he asked a question," Pell said, realizing that he had never spoken to the alien before.

Umber burst into another laugh and held up his hands when Gyro raised his cane again. "No hit," he said. "Bbydjrygurr animal. We take. Like that." Umber held up a little finger. "Need long thing for nest. I grow Bbydjrygurr nests. They come in hair, bite off, take for nest. Not have nest on ship. I give nest." He held up his long hair.

"Lies!" Gyro Penne said.

"Truth!" Umber replied. "Now need hair keep warm. Live outside. Cold."

"What is a budgerigger for?" Pell asked.

Umber again burst into a loud, sustained laugh, then stopped suddenly. "Bbydjrygurr for self. You for self, right? So Bbydjrygurr. But we use. Take for Rrysarr. Bbydjrygurr eat vine like your. Rrysarr eat Bbydjrygurr. We eat Rrysarr. Nobody eat we."

"Lies," Gyro said again, but more softly.

"What is a ryzar?" Pell asked.

"Animal. Long like hand. Fly. Live in plant. Eat small thing."

"Like the budgeriggers?"

"We hope. Take to see."

"Did you bring some of them here?" Gyro asked in alarm.

"No, no. Bad for planet. Nothing eat. They grow. Eat everything. Bad."

"Are you sure?" Pell asked.

"Truth. None in hair." He held out his hair on both sides with his fingertips. "No Bbydjrygurr here."

"Where are they from?"

"No tell."

"You will tell," Gyro said, raising his cane in anger.

Umber jumped up, spread his arms, and yelled, "*Waaarrrrgh.*"

Gyro stepped back, stunned.

"You hurt him and I'll hit this button," Pell shouted, waving the kill control.

Umber held out his hands. "No need. No hit. You want press button? Press button. I die then. No one save. Droc plague come. All die."

Pell fell silent, not knowing how to reply. Gyro held his chest. "You take old man back," Umber said. "Cold here." Gyro abruptly sat down. Pell tugged at him, but he sank into lethargy. Pell noticed they were on the edge of the kill line, and a gust of fear blew through him.

"No worry, Pell Penne," Umber said. "You shut kill, I carry back."

"No. Stay back. I warn you," Pell said, waving the kill control. Umber sat down. Pell turned and ran for the manor house, breathing hard. When he returned with his grandmother and Uji in the smallroller, they found Gyro sitting on Umber's platform with the alien's quilt over his coat. Umber's arm was around him.

"You. Here. What're you doing?" Uji yelled.

"He cold. Keep warm," Umber said. He jumped down and, lifting the old man, handed him to Uji, who sagged under the weight, hefted him, and carried him to the smallroller.

"You, Gorbie," Dyann Penne said. "Was all that true about the budgerigger?"

Umber stifled his laughter. "True," he said.

Very late that night Casio Polon kept three staff members scanning files for either a Bbydjrygurr or a Rrysarr. "They must be Gorbie words, sir," one young man said.

Eventually another spoke up. "There is a bidejuror here, sir. In Uuvian. Lancine sector. Long way from here."

"Plot it on the system chart," Polon said. As it came up, he stared at it narrowly. "Now back it up our orbit to the days of the encounter." They did.

"That may be it, sir," the young man said.

Casio Polon drummed his fingers. "You may go now," he said.

"Thank you, sir," both men said, rising.

Polon did not answer. He was already searching the files for information on the bidejuror, a creature the size of a large little finger. It made nests of the wiry tendrils of the Uuvian beach creeper. It fed on the sea cakes that washed up on shore but would eat other vegetation. Then Polon noticed something else. It had a central nerve trunk running the length of its small body. He knew little of such things, but he had never heard of such a similarity to humans, let alone in such a strange and distant creature. He pondered that problem, aiming his stylus at the wall.

At that time Umber, unable to sleep after the visit of Gyro and Pell, huddled under the worn quilt, staring at the stars. What was left of honor for him? he wondered. Nothing. Perhaps something more important than honor. How ignorant the Landsdrum people were, largely confined to their own planet. Yet there was something comforting and human-sized about such a limitation. But this planet! With no flying creatures, nothing singing at night, so few species, it seemed sunk in biological poverty. Yet the people were not fierce or hostile, and their cruelty seemed indifference as much as anything. Well, for now the numbers seemed safe. That was the important thing. Even as he felt reassured, a wave of regret, of grief for Atel and Alayynr, of loneliness washed up on him. He would be a rock, though, and force it to drain away, leaving him hard and insoluble.

☐ VII The Coward

THREE eightdays later Casio Polon appeared in his liaison ship at Potsherd Sump, setting it down in the landing dish in front of the manor house. Dyann Penne was in her potshop, deep in another slab project, when Phant notified her. "Droc druck," she muttered, then, with a glance at the monitor, said, "Send him out here, please, Phant. I can't leave this. He has come unannounced."

She made sure she had her back to the door when he arrived. He did not satisfy her by coughing or begging her pardon but took finished pieces one by one off a shelf to examine. Eventually he set one down especially hard.

She turned and said, "Oh. Dal Polon. I'm afraid you have caught me in dishabille again. One moment while I cover this, please."

"No need, Dame Penne," he replied. "I need to talk to the Gorbie."

"He is at Cluttered Rock with Uji and some others. Gathering droc seeds. If you will amuse yourself at the house, I'll have him sent for."

"You haven't reported lately."

"Nothing to report. Everything you know. He's grown more silent. Oh, yes. He asked permission to visit the landing site to pray."

"And you . . ."

"Refused him, of course."

"Yes. He wants something, no doubt. I wonder . . ." Dal Polon let the thought lapse.

"You will have to meet him at the droc sheds, I think. He's much too dirty to have in the manor."

"I hear you haven't let him wash."

"I want him to ask. He won't ask. He asks for nothing."

"That may kill him with winter coming. You ought to take care."

"He needs to learn to ask, Dal Polon. It's his way of saying we're abusing him. I want him to become a servant. Then I can lead him to a sense—"

"Of the wrongness, the guilt, of having killed your son-in-law? We don't even know he did it. It seems to have been automatic, a weapon on a piece of junk."

Dyann Penne's hands trembled. "The deep wrongness of the entire Gorboduc way," she said lamely.

Casio Polon rose. "I will await his arrival at the manor. You might have him cleaned up, please, even if in the droc shed. Have him hosed as you might a droc ready to slaughter if it makes you happier. And I will see him there."

Dame Penne clenched her jaw. Her hand trembled so that she put her scriber down.

* * *

Dame Penne did not permit Umber to bathe, and at last Casio Polon met the Gorboduc at a table in the droc shed, with Uji, who had just hosed him down, hovering in the background.

"You still stink," Polon said.

Umber looked at him and laughed. "Cold, too," he said. "You want know Bbydjrygurr."

"The Uuvian bidejuror, to be exact. Where did you get it?"

"Interesting animal. Twenty-five legs. Odd."

"Where did you get it?"

"Don't know. It on ship. Ourrnyl get. You kill. You ask Ourrnyl."

Casio Polon sighed. "What else is interesting about it?"

"You know. You study, then come. It have, how you say it? One end then other nerve. Like us."

"You knew that, then."

"Uh. Only animal this zykkor have that. But us. Shows."

"Shows what?"

"It . . . don't have words. Droc not teach many words."

"What of the herders?"

"Most curse. Many curse."

"What you are trying to say is that it contravenes Landsdrum religion by being a creature the slight resemblance of which to humans would indicate a natural tendency, an evolutionary pattern, a desire of organic materials to organize themselves in lines which are predictable because, narrowing the possibilities to a few, they include humans."

"What that?" Umber said.

"You understood."

Umber grinned broadly. "Some," he said. "No harm little creatures. You kill all."

"If you like them, why didn't you bring some here?"

"Bad. No control. Spread. Eat everything."

"So you cared for us enough so you wouldn't wish that on us?"

"Not you. Planet. Bad for planet, for species here. You in . . . in . . ."

"Incidental? You mean we are an incidental presence on the planet. You knew the word. You didn't want to use it for fear of appearing vaguely intelligent. Well, let me tell you, Umber —the nationals are interested in you. They say we've had enough time to learn about you. They will be rough. They will torture. They will not hesitate to torture you to death."

"Better hurry. I die cold first," Umber said, laughing.

"I really don't understand you. You went to great trouble to stay alive when you landed, and now you seem careless about your life."

"Not. Do care. Limits, though. Go farther, me die. If me die, you die. You all die."

Casio Polon was silent a long time, twirling his stylus. "If you mean an attack, that wouldn't be on your account. And we could sustain it." Umber merely smiled slightly.

"If you mean droc plague," Casio continued, "well, we know that superstition. We've been here hundreds of years without it. There were wild drocs when we arrived, and they were all right."

"Your droc put there by Being for you?"

"By God. Yes. Without human intervention. Drocs are not space travelers. They couldn't come by themselves. Obviously a divine hand intervened."

Umber sat still, staring. Then he looked up and threw up his hands. "So dangerous," he said. "For drocs, for gluusares, for dreecons. Even for you. Think." Umber stood and jabbed his forefinger at Polon. "Think. God bring *Drusculla metoxens* from Fantine System? Why God do that?"

Casio frowned, stood, paced the room. "You are saying the drocs came from the Fantine System and the mud pests with them? Who brought them?"

"Say no more. Too much now. You big stuff. You think. Now. Me tell you that, you owe me."

"I owe you nothing. You agreed to trade your freedom for your life, remember? Slaves are not owed."

"True," Umber replied, then would say no more. With Uji there, Casio Polon did not question him more than his dignity would permit. Then he turned and left, his narrow back straight, the comb of his helmet gleaming red in the sun.

☐ VIII Fights and Fences

DAME Penne looked up from her examination of a deep blue glaze flecked with red as Uji's face grew sharp on the screen. "Yes?" she asked, her eyes swimming up from their concentration.

"Begging your pardon, Dame Penne. About the new droc berms."

"Yes? Have you not begun?"

"Umber says we don't need them. He says we can get the same effect by water fences and have them ready tomorrow."

"Crimecrutches. Umber. Water fences. What are you talking about?"

"Uh, yes," Uji returned, embarrassed by her language. "He explains they use them on several Lancine worlds. Drocs will not cross columns of fast-falling water willingly. You arrange pressured pipes with holes, and they act like fences or berms. You use upper stream water by gravity or recirculate the swamp water. The leaf plates like the water, he says, and you can add nutrients for the vines."

"Umber says all that?" Dame Penne said, frowning.

"Yes. You asked me to report on him. I thought . . ."

Dame Penne tapped the ceramic sample in her hand. "What do you think?"

"Well, I thought . . . Why not try it? It might save us in moving the earth and disrupting the pans now the drocs are multiplying."

"Make a test, then. Try it out. I'll have the Lancine data checked if we can. Don't waste time on it, though, if you think it isn't going to work. Winter's coming, and we can't play games to please the Gorbie."

"Yes, ma'am. Thank you," Uji muttered, blanking the screen.

Dyann Penne turned, hearing Phant's heavy step in the passage. "Yes, what is it now?" she asked, sighing.

Her old servant looked grave, his hands clasped in front of his robe. "Pell, Dame Penne, has been in a fight."

"A what?"

"He has been beaten by other boys. From Matted Plain, madam. He is, well, bruised and . . . bloody, some."

"Beaten? I—what is this? A primitive place? An unruly— are we Gorbies? What did—" She subsided a moment, then added, "Is he all right?"

"He is . . . shaken, madam. Ello is with him. He will be intact, of course." He raised his hands and let them fall. "It was the Raider, madam. Like everything else around here lately, it was the Gorbie."

"I don't understand," Dame Penne said evenly. "Please explain yourself."

Phant hesitated a moment. "Some boys teased him and attacked him, he says, on account of the captive."

"Yes?"

"They . . . don't like the Gorbie in town, madam. Say he should have died with the others. Pell apparently defended his being here . . . because of you. You wanting it, madam. He doesn't like the Gorbie, either."

"Nor do you, is that it, Phant?"

"I? My wishes matter not at all, madam."

Dame Penne pursed her lips. "Of course they do, Phant. You are our old friend." She flashed him a quick smile. "Bring the boy to me, then, when he's cleaned up." As the old servant turned, she said, "Oh, Phant?"

"Yes, madam."

"Are you aware that many feel just the opposite about the alien—that he affords us a chance to observe and learn?"

"I—I had not heard that, madam."

"I thought not. Well, get the boy, then, please."

"Yes, madam."

Dame Penne turned, rose, wiped her hands, and stared out the window, then touched up the code that let her watch the droc workers. Umber was stooping over a pipe length, measuring and lasering holes in it as a young man slid the dissipator inside on a rod. She could see the Gorboduc gesticulating as Uji stood, watching. The alien wore a small droc over his shoulders like a cloak. It had curled its forelimbs in under his arms and was clinging to him for the heat he emitted. She shook her head in disgust. Then she laughed. The effect was comic.

When Pell was brought in, Dame Penne saw that one side of his face was bruised and his left eye was slightly puffed and blackening. His head was lowered slightly in embarrassment, his red hair gleaming. She looked at his hands and saw that his left knuckles were skinned. He held his shoulders up and squared.

"So it was the Gorbie," she said.

"Yes, Grayma."

"Who did it."

"Just . . . some boys. Some swampedge boys."

"What did you do?"

"I tried to stop it. There were too many."

"What did they say?"

"That we all ate raw droc like the Gorbie. That we were Gorbie lovers and cowards like him."

"How many were there?"

"Six. No. More. It doesn't matter, Grayma."

"Six? Who were the cowards, then?"

"We . . . all did wrong, didn't we?"

"Wrong? Yes, of course. Crime. None of it should have happened. But it did."

"Can't we get rid of him?"

"The Gorbie, you mean? Why?"

"Nothing's the same since he got here. And . . . my father. My father."

"Do you really think he killed your father?"

The boy said nothing for a long time. Then he said, "Yes."

"Would you have us kill him, then?"

Again Pell was silent, his face tight. "No," he finally said. "Just get rid of him."

"Why don't you want him killed like the others?"

"He . . . he didn't hurt Graypa when he could have. He

doesn't hurt like Gorbies. He—we've hurt him with cold and
. . . no care. I am ashamed. I am too curious about him. I
don't want to be. I don't want to worry about him out there in
the cold. I don't want to feel his pain. We have pain from him,
Grayma. It's too confusing." The last came out in a rush.

Dame Penne touched up the picture again. The first of the
water fences was in place, with the pipe rod mounted across
the grazed end of a droc pan, its holes pouring water down
like thin, clear rods into the pan. Four drocherders were moving the water fence very slowly toward the center of the pan,
and the drocs were moving ahead of it. "Umber's idea," Dame
Penne said. "He said they did that on the Lancine worlds."

"That's just it."

"What?"

"Nothing's the same with him."

The old woman laughed. "We'll send you with Phant," she
said. "To Matted Plain Infirm. To draw out the discoloration."

"Oh, Grayma," Pell whined in disgust. "It isn't that much.
It's just . . ."

"That you expect them to do it again."

"Well, they might try it, you know."

"Yes," she said, unconsciously holding his hand, thinking.
At last she sighed and said, "We'll think of something, young
one. Something."

Another signal from Uji drew Dame Penne's look to the
screen. "Yes, Uji?"

"Umber says he can build a filter that will take out mud
pests as we recirculate the water."

"Umber says . . . Forget it for now. Crime. Umber says.
You can tell Umber his job is to shovel and carry. Tomorrow,
in fact, I'll use him in the clay pits. Have him ready by nine
measures. And get him to bathe. I don't want to smell droc all
the way to the pits and back." She saw Uji staring and realized
that Pell was still there.

"Yes, Uji. He's hurt. In a fight. A fight. Over the Gorbie.
Can you believe that?"

Unaccountably, Umber's face, bearded and shaggy, appeared for a moment behind Uji's. "You tell me teach him
fight," Dame Penne heard him say before Uji pushed him
away.

Dame Penne cut the screen and pounded the table, her fist raising a small drift of clay powder. Pell looked at her solemnly. "He gets in everything," the boy whispered.

"Yes, my dear. He certainly does. But one good thing I forgot to tell you. Your mother is coming home."

"Mother? When?"

"It's a long journey in a loaded freighter, but she's coming."

"Why? Will she stay?"

"I don't know. It's . . . the Gorbie again, as well as you, of course."

"The Gorbie?"

"Yes. She's furious we have him here, especially after your father's death."

"Oh, Grayma. You know they didn't . . . get along."

"Of course they did, silly boy. Oh, they argued, but that was their way. She's still furious over his death. And she wants to see her boy. I don't know. I promised Dal Polon, but this may be getting out of hand."

"She can't blame the Gorbie."

"Yes, she can. Now you go with Phant and get your face taken care of."

"Are you going to let the Gorbie teach me to fight?"

"Cr— No, of course not."

"I wish somebody would," Pell said over his shoulder as he walked to the entrance already sliding open for him.

That night, in response to a call from Dame Penne, Dal Polon came to Potsherd Sump. They took a smallroller out to the droc pans, and he stood there watching the dimly seen line of falling fountains from the newly installed water fences. Dame Penne was irritated. He seemed not to have heard her complaints, her concerns. Nearby, Umber, hunched on his platform and clearly cold under his old sleepcover, loomed like an accusation.

"Huh," Casio Polon said, taking Dame Penne's hand and guiding her toward the smallroller.

"Is that all you have to say?" she hissed at him.

"He's made you wealthy. I'll begin the work for you tonight."

"What work?"

"Your exclusive right to license the water fences."

She stopped and faced him. "I—"

"You can call it the Gorbie water fence, or some such thing."

"Never."

"Well, then, the Potsherd Sump water fence. The point will be made. You'll be rich, and a certain aura of approval will descend on our . . . subject there on the platform."

"Did you see? He's got a small droc up there with him."

"Trying to keep warm, I would judge. Can you blame him?"

"He'd better not stink tomorrow when I take him to the pits for clay."

"Then you'd better give him the means to clean himself."

"I . . ." Dame Penne sighed to herself. Somehow it all seemed wrong.

"One thing we know," Polon remarked. "He's been to the Lancine System. Why I can't imagine. The only inhabitable planet is a fetid jungle. They haven't a thing worth raiding for."

"When did that ever stop a Gorbie?" Dame Penne spit out.

Polon smiled slightly. "I hear Leda's coming home," he said.

"Oh. Yes. Angry, I suspect. Don't push her with your proposals again, please."

"It seems logical. But I won't. Time must pass."

"She's very independent, Casio. I'm not sure . . ."

"For all of me she can be, Dame Penne. But I'll eventually try again."

On his platform Umber stirred slightly, readjusting the droc and slowly massaging its core knobs. He smiled to himself, receiving comfort from the alien beast. The creature touched his forearms with light taps. In return, Umber touched its underplates in a pattern, smiling slightly.

Overhead the starswarm gleamed and winked, but nowhere could Umber be sure from that vantage that he was looking at a star he had been near. He thought of Sound of Water, in Far Cloud Province at home, then shuddered slightly as an evil bloom of red flame burst up in his memory. The droc seemed to sense his trouble and clung to him a little tighter. He rubbed its core knobs, singing the numbers again to himself, cold and heavy with sleep.

☐ IX   The Telltale Strata

MORNING dawned crisp and foggy, a typical Landsdrum fall day in the alluvial lands. Dame Penne embraced her husband early and strolled out to the heavy land-transporter for a trip to the clay pits. Uji waited for her by the vehicle, Umber behind him in a clean worksuit, much heavier than the summer labor longblouse he had worn.

At first Dame Penne did not look at him. She had her mind on clay and the trace analyzer Phant and Wahn were loading carefully in under the front seats of the transporter. Then she turned and was washed with a moment of strangeness. For the first time since she had seen him, he was freshly shaved, and his dark hair had been sheared back and knotted behind his head in a short braid. His gaunt cheeks and their wide cheekbones, his penetrating eyes and still tangled brows, seemed oddly commanding. Still, he had the small, tense mouth of a schoolgirl, she thought, set strangely in a wide jaw. She jerked a thumb. "Put him in back," she said to Uji. "In the claybin."

The Gorboduc nodded and vaulted lightly over the side of the bin, nearly disappearing into its belly. Dame Penne gave him one more glance and found him staring at the sky.

Uji handed Dame Penne into the front left passenger seat as Pell ran from the house and piled in beside her. She looked at him. His face was only slightly tinged with red, the bruises drawn out. "You—" she began. "All right. You come. But try to stay cleaner than usual."

Wahn put the vehicle in motion and steered it down the long drive toward the ford over the River of Good Intent, where the flow spread and trickled over a wide gravel bar. Then they arced north, following a broad meander of the river, and took a rough road along one of its sluggish, marshy tributaries. They passed below the low bluffs of a wide sweep of the stream, where it rolled against the first of the clay hills, bit into it, and turned aside. Only after the winter rains was the stream high enough to cross that bluff and take a shorter route to Purple Lake, then through the islands beyond and out into the broader reach of the Sea of Cruel Mouths. It was a complex, changing area of erosion and deposition, always different after a hard season, sometimes offering Dame Penne new clay, sometimes covering established pits deep in new gravel and sand. But the bank was an ancient one, newly exposed by last year's freshets.

Pell glanced back and saw Umber staring intently at the high-cut bank, shading his eyes. Then the boy looked ahead again, but as they lurched over a hump several hundred measures beyond, he turned again and saw Umber was gone.

"*Ahhhh*," he called out. "Stop, stop. The Gorbie's gone."

"Crime," Dame Penne said. "Give me the box."

"Don't kill him," Pell yelled. "I think he's back at the high bank."

"Back up, Wahn. Why? Why do you think that?"

"The way he was looking at it. As though . . ."

"Well?"

"Afraid."

By then the big vehicle, touched into automatic, had followed its own recorded track backward, and as they approached the wide stream curve, Pell, standing up, could see the Gorboduc up on the bank, clinging to its loose surface, furiously digging into it underneath one of the dark bands near the crown of the loose exposure.

Dame Penne touched the discipline command, and they watched Umber's head jerk up and back. Then he returned to his work in a flurry. She hit the button again, holding it down several moments. Umber jerked again, fought with his head, and tumbled down the bank to the brown water of the stream.

"Don't. Don't hurt him again," Pell cried out, jumping from the transporter and running down the bank. "You," he shouted. "Gorbie. Come now and she won't hurt you anymore."

Umber lifted his head and shook it again, then looked at his hands and rose slowly. He looked up again, then waded the stream to where Pell waited. "Up the bank. Now," the boy commanded, waving his arm.

Umber came up to him, a strange, taut look on his face. He turned and pointed. "Look. Look, young one. There. See dark lines? Plague lines. Plague lines. You look at own death there."

"What?" Pell said, feeling oddly helpless.

Umber held out his hand. "Here. You take."

"Take what?"

"Droc beak. Old. Under dark stain. You look. You take."

Pell took the old, fragile bony bills for a few moments, then cast them down and wiped his hand. Instantly the Gorboduc picked up the boy and held his face at eye level. "You, Pell. Old woman not listen. You listen. It you life, all life. Important."

"Put him down!" Dame Penne shrilled from the transporter. She touched the discipline button repeatedly. Umber shook his head and set the boy gently down.

Pell stared at him. "I don't understand," he said, strangely unafraid. Umber stooped and gathered up the crumbly droc bills.

"You get me big one—Casio? Me tell him," Umber said. "Come. We go your grayma."

At the vehicle, Umber lifted Pell across Dame Penne as though he were weightless. Then he vaulted into the clay bin and sat down, arms folded. Dame Penne glared at him and said, "Go on now, Wahn."

At the clay pits Umber worked steadily, furiously, without a word, seeming almost instinctively to know precisely the lens of clay Dame Penne directed him to. Through Wahn he passed up samples to her for quick analysis. To Pell his eyes seemed to flash everywhere, taking in everything. The boy still seemed to feel the grip of Umber's hands as the big Gorbie had swept him up and talked directly at him, earnestly, intently, close in, with his purring depth of tone and no feeling of hostility at all.

"Are you all right, Pell?" his grandmother asked him at one point.

"Yes. All right," he said. "What's a plague line?"

"Plague line? I don't know. Why?"

"Umber said the lines in the bank were plague lines. He seemed afraid."

"Don't you pay any attention to the Gorbie. He didn't hurt you, did he?"

"No. He was afraid."

"The discipline button has its uses."

"No. Not of that. Of the plague lines. He gave me these," he said, holding out the old droc beaks.

"What are they?"

"Old droc beaks, he said."

She glanced at them. "Throw them out," she said. "You find them all over."

Pell threw them down and dusted his hands. He saw the Gorbie look at him, then turn back to the clay. The big man paused, rested his hand against the gray bank, seemed to waver, then looked up to Wahn for directions, his mouth straight.

When Dame Penne directed him to fill the extended load arm with clay from one lens, he did it rapidly, almost wildly, breathing hard. Wahn had to stop him before he overloaded the scoop. With Umber's mood as it was, they loaded the clay bin almost in a frenzy, Wahn strangely picking up his urgency.

On the way back, Umber sat on the clay. As they neared the cut bank, Dame Penne turned and said, "You're not going to jump out again, are you? I still have the discipline button."

"No need. Know answer," the Gorboduc replied. "Like tell you, you stop. Me tell."

"No. We need to get back. You have droc work, no doubt."

Umber threw up his hands. "Even Tistan worry. You not worry. Who smarter?"

Dame Penne turned around again, her mouth tight. Umber seemed to turn everything into an insult. Why did he make her so uneasy?

Pell turned and asked, "Who is Tistan?"

"Big droc, pan eighteen. Oldest one."

Pell laughed. "The droc told you? With which mouth?"

"Signed. Not told. You come. Me show you sign Tistan."

Wahn looked at Dame Penne and rolled his eyes. "Just drive us home," she said to him in a low voice. Behind her, Umber let out a long, wild laugh.

That evening Wahn came to her as she continued to test the new clay and said, "I've been thinking. He does communicate somehow with the drocs."

"Wahn, please. This is all going too far."

"No. He squats by the pan. They come up to him, hold out an arm. He spends long periods touching their arms, and they touch his. It is very strange to watch. The big ones especially. He does things with the drocs I've never seen anyone else do. Like wearing them for coats. Moving them at will. Healing sores. He knows more about droc anatomy than any droc raiser—as much as a biologist."

"So you think he's a biologist?"

"Yes. I wish I knew what he was worried about out there. He seemed so worried. He's not stupid. He knows something."

"Perhaps you should let me concern myself with that, Wahn," Dame Penne said mildly, continuing to adjust the dial on her analyzer.

"I certainly wish you would," Wahn said, his mouth straight and serious.

Dame Penne stared up, astonished at his rudeness. "You may go," was all she replied. He left, shaking his head.

Late that night at MHQ, a communications monitor began to blink and sound. The attendant's wrist tickler called her over and caused her to replay a routine commercial message broadcast out across the freight lanes. The message was slightly broken up, and the monitor had picked up the anomaly. She called her superior. "I don't understand," she said. "Why this was noted, I mean."

"Something the monitor has detected. Ask it."

In reply to her coded inquiry, the listening monitor intoned, "Omission message on standard message. Cannot read."

"Replay and record," the monitor officer said. "Thank you, Kai. I'll send this to LSHQ Cipher Office." She also thanked the monitor, which intoned a slow "You're welcome."

At the cipher office the piggybacked message was examined and found to be coherent, not the result of any electrical fault. But no one could determine what the patterned signals meant. "Send it to the academy," the OIC said. "High priority. The linguists might tell us something. We can only wait. Some agent. Are we aware of any agents here currently."

"No. There's the Gorbie," the secretary remarked with a smile.

The OIC laughed. "He's out there wallowing with the drocs, I hear. Grunting. Nowhere near the Spacecom Link System. I wonder when they're going to get sick of him. I wish we were rid of him. He's a pretext for Gorbie attack if there ever was one."

The next morning Wahn came up to Umber as the Gorboduc was swabbing the droc station after a routine shipping of young adults to processing. "Show me how to talk to the drocs," he said. "I'll do what I can to help you—at least to get a roof during the heavy rains."

"Only know a hundred eighty-two unit signs," Umber replied. "Will teach. When we time. Now have clean pan eleven. Maybe you help me go pray. At wreck place."

☐ X Conversation with a Droc

LATE that afternoon Wahn and Umber squatted together at the edge of pan eighteen. Umber patted the water surface with his palm lightly, as all drocherders had seen the drocs do occasionally. Most assumed they were washing something out of their beaks. "Tistan come," Umber said at last, as right before them a large droc rose through the water surface, pouring brown liquid from its whole knobby surface.

Umber began to stroke the ridges on its legs rhythmically, toward the core. "They like," he said. "Relax. Make friend." The process took a long time, but Umber made no attempt to hurry it. Even before it was over, Wahn was losing the circulation in his feet. He could see Uji watching them from across the pans.

Eventually the big droc raised an arm and extended it, beaks closed. Umber touched it lightly. "You see plate? Greeting is touch five down with side stroke. Like that. You see? Me tell Tistan you want talk. We see what it say." Wahn was unnerved as the large droc arm eventually was extended toward him, but he counted the plates and stroked the right one sideways lightly. The big arm lifted and waved briefly, then turned back to Umber.

"It pleased. Think funny way you talk." Umber made a few quick strokes with his thumb and palm across the plates of the upraised droc arm. The creature responded by touching his palm with its bony arm tip several times.

"This part game. It want play. Take long time. Think move all day. Not fast to think. Me play my side easy."

"Where'd you learn this?"

"All droc play. Many know other place. In space many play. Keep droc happy. Tistan just make bad move. Me counter only . . . sideways. Not want win just now."

Tistan lowered its arm and raised the other toward Wahn. "Hold up hand, palm up—both," Umber said gently. As Wahn complied, the droc tapped his clawed leg tip gently on various parts of the forearm. "It want know you play. Now you tap twice on plate three, outside, go down plates on inside from one to four, then tap nine, inside, and stroke it. Say you don't know how."

Wahn complied, with coaching from Umber, and the big droc turned once again to the Gorboduc and signed to him. "It want me teach you. Me said would teach. It want play you. Think it can win."

"Win. A droc?"

"Oh, it win first times. Then sometimes. Then maybe mostly you win. Now it want talk me again."

Wahn squatted by Umber as he and Tistan signaled, sometimes quite rapidly. "Me tell find big danger for both droc and people. It right to worry. Me say not know if can fix. If not all die."

"Crime. You said that? What did it say?"

"It urge me try. Me say will. Now say good-bye, Tistan. Like this. One, three, stroke, stroke, run finger down center."

Tistan held up its other arm, and with Umber's coaching, Wahn said good-bye, then held his forearms up so the droc could signal its reply. It felt extremely strange. Tistan then slowly subsided back under the roily water surface, backing up. Umber rose stiffly and helped Wahn up. "That talk to droc. Learned by Onic people long time. Taught to many. Not Westsector, look like."

"Do the Gorboducs talk to their drocs?"

Umber's eyes narrowed. "Many kind Gorboduc," he said. "Not one. Many world. Some talk, some raid, some stay home and grow fat. Mine talk droc." Then he stretched and yawned noisily and added, "Time wash off droc."

Across the pans, Uji turned off the recorder, covered it in his sweep cart, and guided the cart slowly toward the outsheds. In his office, Casio Polon, who had watched the whole interlude, tapped his stylus. "What do you think?" he asked Matted Plain Security Chief Doles.

"Don't know. Have to analyze it. We may have learned something. There are many kinds of Gorbies, he said. Could be a lie. We know nothing of them, though. He said only some raid. That was a deception, I suspect. About the danger he sees? That may be a deception, too. We have to find out what it is if it's anything."

"Do you think he talks to the drocs?"

"Looks that way. Or else it's very mysterious. Dame Penne has to get him to teach Uji or Wahn the system. Then we'll know."

Uji's face blinked on the redcode scanner. "Yes?" Casio Polon asked.

"Umber just told Wahn that what has the drocs worried is the high rate of reproduction seeding at this season. It isn't normal. At Potsherd Sump that's true. Seeding is high. Umber makes no secret of that being a sign of impending droc plague and wants to give you the evidence."

"Thank you, Uji."

"Oh. He also wants time to go to the crash site to pray. Says that will be a help."

"Does he ever pray?"

"I don't see it, sir. He does chant or sing some when Dal Penne isn't around to scold him for it. But he may pray at night when he's alone."

"Thank you, Uji. That will be all."

The screen winked out. "Pray? A Gorbie pray? Some trick," Doles mused. "He left something at the crash site. We've been over the whole ground, but the flashing of the craft consumed most of it. Only shapeless metallic lumps. No information."

"I think we should let him go, Commander. Let the boy take him. He seems to like the boy. You'll have your men around, of course. I think I can convince Dame Penne." Dal Polon tapped his stylus on the desk again. "What do you think?" he asked.

"We'll try it, Dal," Doles replied. "Droc plague. A myth. But who knows? Maybe it's nothing. Maybe there's something to it."

About that time, at Cipher HQ a message came from the academy about the piggybacked message.

INQUIRY 87BXX29
FROM: Cipher HQ, LSS
RE: Negative message on commercial broadcast

Still working on message. So far we have this in Onic, interspersed with what looks like garbage:

Landsdrum 3238. drocyc. unknown but very late. type 328, vector 6, probl 6.35. usual accomp., incl. *Magnalla trescens*; *Trifol. vakuus vakuus*; *Platus platinus* (fan.); *Fantus mariana* (fan.); *Drusculla metoxeins* (fan.); *Pinnus arrayarc* (oryx.); *Hostilus minifol.* (source?); *Salbus victimini*, *Miniflora atel umb.* (transfer.?) Native life mostly marine, unknown. Land.

thinks drocyc. myth. Released *Grandaradix gentila*; *Bucklow daktiloid*; *Sekale sereal*; *Axonopus affinis dura*; *Marmota flaviventris* ter. *Encaps. unipurp. quatrilob.* danger.

Suggest most names in early stage biology tapes, and Onic is widely used in early encoding classes as a language wholly unlike Westsector. Probably the rest is made up, including the garbage, by some bright child who wanted to test her ability to penetrate a common communications broadcast. Perhaps she wanted to make the news and provoke a stir. The Onic section of the message seems clear enough, though some is nonsense. I believe we have been victimized by a child. Do you want me to pursue this any further? If so, budget charges will be necessary.

> Professor Vadid Nocrel, Cryptographer
> NorthLandsdrum Colonial Academy

"Budget charges," the OIC muttered. "Aren't they paid enough?"

"What should we do, sir?" his aide asked, hesitating.

The OIC drummed his fingers. "You work on it. In your spare time. We don't want to let it rest. Nocrel may be right. It may be a child's game. But I don't know. I doubt the message was interspersed with garbage. That merely means she was unable to understand something. We let this go and we could be out on our crimefilthy ears. No hurry. Just keep at it."

"I promise, sir," the aide said, privately rolling his eyes.

That evening, in a strange surge of clarity, Gyro Penne strode limping out to the droc pens, picking out Umber's platform with his hand light. Again, urged by Dame Penne, Pell followed. As Gyro approached, he could hear the soft chanting of the Gorboduc. "You," he began. "I told you never to sing. I meant it. Never sing."

"Uhh," Umber said. "Never sing."

"Never sing. Now what is this swamprot about a plague line?"

"Three plague line. Saw three on dirt slope. Mark when all droc die. Leave seeds to renew. All big ones dead."

Gyro hesitated. "You'd better explain yourself. It better be good."

"Glad. We not know sure all reason, but droc all die together now and again. Regular time. In droc plague. Seed heavy first. Droc plague kill many people. Ruin droc planet. Not know words to tell Westsector. If come soon, all here die."

"Crimerot!" Gyro said, then with a sudden irrelevancy, "What did you just say?"

"Me say droc all die. Take people."

"If God gave us the drocs in the first place, God will certainly be sure they are safe, you deceiving Gorboduc," the old man said fiercely.

"Droc come on early migration. Come here from Fantine System. Get there from Oryxx, think. Behind that from Kkoterr, we think. From Kkoterr, nine vectors. From here go to Urrget, Onic, then Klluum, Fortoff, Rrissr. Think."

Gyro pondered a few moments, then sat down. Pell came up behind him and took his shoulders. "What do you mean?" he asked. "We all know we found them here when we came."

"Not you, Pell. Migration before."

"Then why didn't we find any remains? All this is well known and taught by the ministers. I learned it last season."

"Long time ago. At least three thousand Landsdrum revolutions, some more maybe."

The boy hesitated. "Don't listen. It's heresy," Gyro mumbled, then looked up and shouted, "What do you say to that, Gorbie?"

"Three plague lines give date, old man. Send rock scholar from university. Me explain."

Gyro laughed. "Me explain," he repeated, then laughed again.

Umber replied in a bitter tone with a long tirade in Gorboduc.

"What was that?" Pell asked.

"Me know some your tongue. You none of my. Who stupid?"

"Silence!" the old man shouted, rising.

"Pell, me help take Graypa to manor," Umber said.

"I said silence!" Gyro shouted as Pell took his arm.

The boy glanced up at the platform. Umber sat unmoving. Pell shined the hand light at him and saw lines of tears on his cheeks. "What?" he exclaimed. "Why are you crying?"

Umber shut his eyes against the light and said nothing.

☐ XI   Fast Praying

THE next morning Dame Penne was feeding Gyro, who had had a bad night, when the visiphone announced Casio Polon. "Are you up to another expedition with the Gorbie?" he said abruptly.

"After the last one I'm not sure," she replied evenly. "And he's now supposedly teaching Wahn to talk to the drocs. He even seems to be doing it."

"Yes, I heard about that. The academy has been making some experiments with that."

"But they are nowhere near so far along with it as my drooling Gorbie."

"That's true, too," Polon said, tapping his stylus. "When the time is right, we'll have to get him to teach us about it."

"What time?"

"There are more important things. We'd like him to be allowed to pray as he desires. At the crash site."

"Because you expect some deviousness of him and want to catch him at it."

"Obviously. We'll have the place well managed, shall we say?"

"When?"

Polon drew up slightly. "Tomorrow? Is that satisfactory?"

"In the morning," she said. "As you see—"

"How is Gyro? I understand he had another visit with the Gorbie last night."

"Yes. It upset him. Full of heresies."

"But also an incredible amount of information. The Umber project is really beginning to pay off."

"Not for my poor husband. Now. We'll have him go tomorrow. All of this is . . . wholly upsetting."

"Yes. We understand. And Matted Plain is extremely grateful for your foresightedness in saving the Gorbie's life. By the way, I've arranged for a lump payment for the idea of the water fences, subject to your approval."

"Not now, Casio, please. Later."

Later in the morning Dame Penne summoned Umber to her potshop, and when he came, she said abruptly, "I am letting you go to the crash site to pray, as you requested. I am asking of you not to try to escape." She looked hard at him. "Do you understand?"

"Me understand."

"Me understand," she mimicked. "Why not say 'I understand'? You've heard us talk enough to master that, anyhow."

"I understand," he said.

"Do you agree?"

"Me . . . I promise be back here to work."

"When?"

"Soon possible."

"Say, 'As soon as possible.' "

"As soon as possible."

"You haven't promised not to escape. If you don't promise, I can't let you go."

Umber looked down. "Me come back," he said.

"Look at me," she commanded. He did. "You must promise not to try to escape."

Umber sighed, then unaccountably, suddenly, knelt by her and put his forehead against her knee. "Please," he murmured. "I do what need do. Helping. You let. Not wrong. I come back soon possible. You trust. All for good."

Dame Penne drew back. "You will not promise, then."

"Not want lie. Important. You let."

She took the front of his hair and drew his face up to look

at hers, glaring at him fiercely. She saw tears in the corners of his eyes. "You will not promise, then."

"No. But I come back. Promise that."

She let go of his hair and put her hands in her lap.

"Pell. He's going with you. You—"

"No hurt boy. You no tell Casio Polon?"

"He knows."

"Yes, but of what we say here."

She stared at him. "No," she said. "As you put it, 'No tell.' Why am I trusting you? Why do I need to?"

"You need. Not disappoint."

She brushed the clay powder from his hair and said, "Get up. Go back to work. You'll go with Pell tomorrow. Go now." After he left, she found her hands trembling. All this was so strange. But he would not lie to her. She saw that. She felt absolutely that no deeper deception was implied by the conversation. She was amused at his "yes, but" when she had said that Casio knew. So he knew of Casio's monitoring. Well, she supposed it was obvious.

The next morning Uji drove the landroller with Umber, who had been permitted to bathe thoroughly and put on a clean worksuit, and Pell, who held the control box for Umber's kill collar. The keying had again been switched over to him. Casio's men were in place and monitoring the progress of the low, blue vehicle. Umber insisted on being barefoot, and since the sharpweed was at its autumn height in the area, the Groundarmy intelligence operatives felt confident about his security.

Umber sat bolt upright and very still during the whole trip, and when they arrived at the plain shore area, near the Crescent Vine Tangles, where the Gorboduc escape pod had crashlanded, he eased up out of the vehicle very slowly, walked forward to the bright green disk where the vessel had flashed and burned, and stood with his eyes closed, his hands up, a long time.

Eventually he stripped off his worksuit and, standing naked, unmindful of the cold, began to chant and recite words, none of them intelligible to the monitors. His chanting went on a long time. It seemed to Pell it was endless. Every so often Umber would abruptly fall silent for a time and lower his arms.

A full tenthday passed and the boy was growing supremely bored by it all. It all seemed so foolish. He wondered how Umber endured the cold. Pell lounged in the landroller. Fortunately, he had brought along an edviewer, and as the procedure went on, he turned to it and began to work on the mathematical explanations of his current level.

The chanting paused. He glanced up and saw Umber motionless, then returned to his calculations. Then, in a few moments, he heard a shout and a whooping alarm and jerked his head up to see Umber streaking for the vine tangle. Pell reached for the control box, hesitated, transfixed, and set it aside. He saw two uniformed men rise up in Umber's path, saw the Gorboduc knock them aside with scarcely a pause and leap into the tangle, followed by a skein of uniformed men yelling.

"You stay here, Pell. It won't take long," Uji said. "They'll have him."

Umber, gritting his teeth against the pain of the sharpweed, raced along his path of the previous year. He splashed through the muck and water of the stream he remembered, noting with a fleeting glance the spreading stand of grasses there, then dived for the slight rise and the huge corkscrew vine he remembered. He dug furiously at the mud at its root and pulled out a small ceramic egg, twisting it open with the same motion. Reaching in, he separated its contents with a forefinger, dabbed some on his tongue, chewed briefly, and swallowed. Then, as the shouts behind him closed in, he carefully put the rest under his tongue, flung the egg into the tangle, and waded back out into the stream to resume his chanting, arms up, as the Groundarmy men ran skittering onto the bank.

Umber held up his hands, chanting skyward, as they surrounded him. Then he held his hands by his sides in silence as the men, chests heaving, stood around him, stunners at the ready. Then he looked at them and said, "Me thank. Go back now?"

"Some answers first. You broke your word. You ran. What were you doing?"

Umber looked surprised. "Only to follow last path. Part of

prayer. Ask forgiveness where captured. Like last time, you catch. Now me understand. This right. We go back now? Me no trouble anymore. Work for Dal Penne. All good."

The officer looked doubtful but then jerked his head at the nearer men, who led Umber back through the sharpweed. He walked gingerly, his feet bleeding, grimacing in pain.

Pell ran forward, holding the box. "No hurt, Pell Penne," Umber said. "I good. Men no understand prayer. Think I run away."

"You did. You broke your word. You did run away," the boy shrilled.

Umber knelt in front of him. "No, little one. No run. Only pray for our good. Now go home?"

"Not so fast," the Groundarmy officer said. "We're going to examine you first." He motioned to a brown vehicle whining across the marshy ground. "In there, Gorbie. You, Uji. We'll bring him back when we're done."

"Back soon," Umber called to Uji with a wild laugh. "See? Nothing to hide." He was still naked, shivering a little, his body drawing up tight against the cold.

"Here, you. Put this on," an officer said, handing him his worksuit.

"Yes. Yes, ma'am," Umber said with another laugh.

☐ XII   Feeling the Heat

DAL Casio Polon sat with the Groundarmy intelligence commander reviewing the latest interlude with Umber, who, against his murmured objections, had not been allowed to go back to Potsherd Sump. "What he was up to we're not yet sure," the woman said. "We're reviewing the whole set of events again. What passed for praying was only repetition, the same long passage said again and again."

"Much praying is like that," Polon said, amused.

"True. But we are convinced the whole point was to get into the vine tangle. It was a sustained deception to get the surveillance to relax."

"Seems to have worked."

"Only briefly. When he saw he would be caught, he gave up and resumed his pose of praying."

"Hmm," Polon said. "He was captured at the stream?"

"Yes."

"And said he wanted to relive his former capture?"

"Yes."

"But he went past there before, far down into the garbush toward the shore."

"True. It must have been something about this area."

"Put up the picture again."

The two watched again as the hovering camera came with its operators in a rush through the tangle to where Umber stood naked in the stream. They ran through the sequence twice more. Polon asked, "And the whole area has been examined?"

"Yes. He ran beyond the stream only a short way, then came back, but the surveillance force surrounded him and befouled the prints so badly, it was impossible to make anything out."

"And the whole area has been gone over?"

"Yes. Nothing was found but a few picnickers' booze flasks, discarded amusement tapes, metal fasteners, a ceramic pocketbox, several old strollboots, some energy cartridges, parts of a junked landroller, and the like."

"If he had found anything alien, it would have stood out in all that?"

"Certainly. Everything is recognizable."

"Let's run through the sequence again at quarter speed."

The two did, seeing nothing. "There is something there," the GIC hissed, pounding her knee.

"Let's go out there, then," Polon said.

"Oh, Dal Polon, you needn't trouble yourself. I'm sure if there is anything, we will—"

The legislator had risen and started for the entrance. The GIC followed, arms still in midprotest.

It was late afternoon, after the determined Casio Polon—with the hapless officer following—had walked over the whole area several times, his mouth growing more and more grim, when they stood once more on the shore of the small stream in the tangle. At last Polon groaned and hit his forehead with the heel of his hand. "Oh," he said. "Oh, no."

"You found it, then?"

"Look. What do you see?"

"Dal, we have been looking all day and I have seen nothing at all."

"That, Commander. That green. I have never seen it before. Anywhere. Nor anything like it. Certainly never here. He came to see it. To see if it had taken hold."

"You mean . . . an alien plant? Stand back, sir. We'll cordon off the area."

"No. Umber wouldn't have come back if it were dangerous to man. He values his life, eh? No. Gather some. Where is he? Still in the hospital? We'll confront him with it. Meantime, keep it wholly quiet. All right? Only your chief officers can know." Casio Polon strolled over to the spreading grass, bent down, and plucked some up, scrutinizing it. The intelligence officer backed up in front of it. Casio laughed lightly. "Come. To the hospital."

When Casio and the GIC strode into the hospital room, they found Umber strapped to a bed, his bandaged feet toward the door. He was surrounded by blue-clad Groundarmy people plying him with questions. The Gorboduc looked up at Dal Polon, who smiled and said, "We know. Now, if you all might excuse us, we wish a word with our subject. Please silence your listeners for the moment."

The interrogators looked at him with a mixture of resentment and apprehension, then silently took their equipment and withdrew. Umber regarded the two with a mild listlessness.

Polon sat down, drew from his pouch the grass stem he had broken, and held it up. "*Bukloe daktyloid*," the Gorboduc murmured.

"From where?"

"Very far off."

"How will it harm us?" the GIC asked.

"Not harm. Good. Brought three species. Couldn't stand to destroy."

"We'll certainly have to now, though, won't we?" Polon said. "We can't have careless introductions of species in our world."

"Not careless. Had many species on board, from many place. Kept the three. Look your hill and mountain. Nothing hold soil. This hold soil, stop wash."

"The others. What are they?" the GIC asked hastily.

"All three called grrrazz. All different. All good. Your biologist will say. Might try *Sekale* on droc. Also people can eat seed. Do eat seed many place."

"Grass," Polon said.

"Grrrazz. I tell you something, you not tell all yet?"

"Agreed," Polon said.

Umber looked at the GIC. She dropped her eyes. "Agreed," she said.

"It from home planet."

"What?"

"All from home planet all people. Far across galaxy. Came all way with people."

Umber saw the GIC's mouth tighten. "Know you think that heresy," he added, "that we devil imitations, you people. Not so. This come all way with us. This here only left now in this part stars. Very important."

"How can we know this?" Polon asked.

"General encyclopedia have," Umber said.

"That's heresy, too," the GIC hissed.

"It common even in some Westsector. Me know," Umber insisted. "Somewhere on planet must be record. You get code, touch up. You see. That all reason me go pray. Must check. Now, you, Casio. Take me back. Promise old woman. You help."

"We're not through with you yet," the GIC said.

"It important I go," Umber insisted. "Me there. Not go anywhere. You come grab me anytime."

Polon put his hand on the GIC's arm. "Let me send him

home for the present. We need to keep this grass thing quiet until we can examine it and then check it all with him. Understood?"

"You take me back?" Umber asked, looking at Polon. The lawmaker shot a quick glance at the intelligence officer and then dropped his eyes.

"I'll take you back myself," he said mildly. "I need to confer with Dame Penne about the water fences. I assure you, Commander, he will be at your disposal when you need him." The GIC looked doubtful, but she had no family connections, and it never was wise to run afoul of a Dal unnecessarily. Besides, she was chagrined that Dal Polon had been the one to discover what the Gorbie was after.

On the way back Umber limped directly to the passenger compartment of the landroller, not getting into the servant's bucket, where he belonged. The driver ordered him out. Umber sat still but shot a glance at Dal Polon.

"He's been through a lot. Let him be," Polon said quietly. "Besides, I need to interrogate him further." The driver's mouth dropped. "I'll be safe," Polon said, smiling and pulling out a small silver box. "I have an alternate kill switch." He saw the driver relax slightly as he handed Polon in.

As soon as they started, Polon said, "You are much out of place. What is it you want?"

"More trouble with grrrazz," Umber said. "They from planet of origin, but also sexual."

Dal Polon jerked back as though slapped. "What?" he whispered.

"Not like people. But have male and female part. Must merge self or other to seed. Wind do work. Not know Landsdrum belief that people alone that way when I brought."

Dal Polon, flushed with anger, pointed a finger at Umber and said, "Deity made man alone to reproduce in pairs. That is a basic tenet of the true philosophy I and all on Landsdrum support. Is this your devious Gorboduc means of wrecking us? I could have you executed now."

"Against reason. This sector you right. I biologist. Know this. Some places four sexes needed for reproduce. Grrrazz come from far off, like us. When grrrazz studied, they learn it sexual. Take a while, but they learn. Make trouble, I see."

"It must all be destroyed."

Umber laughed brutally. "I bring you great gift. You destroy against all reason. Remember, though. Other planet have use for grrrazz. We need. You hurt many, even more than already."

"We never hurt anyone. We have a right to defend ourselves," Dal Polon said, still dizzy with all he had just heard.

"Do, though. Much destroyed with our vessel. Many lives blighted, lifeworks lost. But to question now. I beg. You can get to encyclopedia? You ask it about grrrazz. If you no believe, then you destroy. It only hurt Landsdrum now. But if you keep, get out of droc culture some. Other food. Trade. One grrrazz, *Sekale sereal*, make Landsdrum rich."

Dal Polon was silent, bouncing with the slight motion of the landroller. As they approached Potsherd Sump, he asked, "Any more surprises?"

"One," Umber said. Polon rolled his eyes. "One more species. No worry. Not sexual. Called *Grandaradix gentila*. From Archoxun System. Called by Ettux people 'earthbeast.' I throw just beyond stream. Big leaves in five lobes. Huge root. Delicious. Can sustain many people. Not from home planet. Not sexual. Nobody object. It make Landsdrum rich, too. Give stylus. I draw," Umber said, reaching out.

Astonished at his boldness, Polon nonetheless handed over his platinum-clad stylus. Umber pulled the light board to him and rapidly sketched the earthbeast, finishing after the landroller had stopped and the driver had slid up the door.

"A moment, Enbot," Polon said, waving his hand.

Nonplussed and offended, the man stood back, hands behind him. "This my gift to you, Casio Polon," Umber said. "Only one on planet. Soon to dip vine tips and start next ones. Yours only. You very rich with this."

Polon saw Enbot's eyes shift, and when Umber handed back the stylus and surged out of the landroller, Polon beckoned to his man and said, "I expect full discretion, Enbot. And, oh, yes, you may expect a doubled salary this year."

"Of course, Dal Polon," Enbot said, his head swimming. Dal Polon, too, felt strange, having just committed so much funding to something he knew nothing about. But in that, anyway, he trusted the Gorbie. The grass, though, might have to be sacrificed. The idea cut at the vitals of all his beliefs. It had to be unacceptable heresy, some Gorbie trick.

"I will be a tenthday or so," Polon said, smiling, as he left the driver, watching Umber far ahead of him, hobbling rapidly toward the droc pans. He frowned. Something still was odd about all this.

☐ XIII   The Heat On

DAL Polon spent much of the night trying to access the general encyclopedia Umber had mentioned. The Landsdrum religionists had produced an excised copy, the labor of many years of editing the original to suit the beliefs of their fraction of the Westsector. The lawmaker found himself more and more astounded at their immense efforts, their thoroughness. But he was persistent, and he remembered the deviousness of his youth in finding sources. He finally penetrated the electronic echoes of the Godworship working copy. It was simple then, to find what Umber had called *Bukloe daktyloid*.

As the Gorboduc had said, it reproduced by seeds. He could not understand the anatomic discussion, hard as he stared at the diagrams. As to its origin, the text simply indicated it was ancient and unknown. He also noted the sentence "The seeds are edible, but far more labor is involved in producing them than seems warranted, given the availability of *Whantaca cyrus* and other such crops." Polon tapped his stylus. He knew his planet was species-poor, though they had a workable environment. He knew Landsdrum was not extremely interested in its natural habitat—perhaps, he mused, because it seemed so drab.

He wondered what had been destroyed with the Gorboduc ship and why the Raiders had been carrying it. All of it seemed so irregular. Late as it was, he determined to return to the crash scene again, with Umber's sketch, to find the earth-beast and have it brought to his estate. He would alert his people and be there before sunrise. He well knew that Groundarmy intelligence would be there soon enough with their own botanists.

Before he retired, he went through his messages. Most were routine, but when Uji's face appeared, he stirred himself. Frowning, the drocherder said, "Dal, I wanted to report to you that when Umber came back, he went right off to the droc pans. He patted the water for the one he calls Tistan and had a long, uh, interchange with him lasting until well after dark. He never even bothered to eat. I called him twice, too. This is very odd for him. He generally eats anything we give him. He looked very serious, too. No jokes. No wild laughing. That is all."

Dal Polon mused about that for a while, then, his weari-ness overtaking him, sank into bed. His last thought was that somehow the Gorboduc had tricked him. But he also found himself trusting Umber's motives. He only hoped that they were intelligent enough, that furor could be kept to a mini-mum.

In the morning Dame Penne summoned Umber to her pot-shop. The big Gorboduc looked subdued as she continued with her work, paying no attention to him. She eventually turned to where he stood, hands clasped behind him, waiting. He was staring at a hologram of Leda, Pell's mother. "You," Dame Penne hissed. "Pay attention. You have no right."

Umber dropped his eyes. "She look Uuvian. Very beauti-ful."

Dame Penne seized the kill box and pressed hard on the discipline coder until Umber reeled and gasped. "You. None of this is any of your business. When will you learn your place? She is too . . ." Then she simply stopped. "Oh, what's the use?" she said.

"Me try do what you say," Umber murmured, looking at the floor.

Dame Penne stood and walked up to him, glaring. "So," she began. "I made a concession to you, because you said you needed to pray, and you played me for a fool. You've forgotten that I saved your life. I have put up with you. I have harbored you. My grandson has been mocked and beaten because we have had you here. So all you wished to do was check your alien plants. Why should I not have you executed now?"

Umber looked slightly listless. "Can if you want. Let see Pell first? Apologize to him?"

"You surmised he would not press the kill button, didn't you? You presumed. You took advantage of his . . . natural affection, didn't you?"

Umber laughed, but only slightly. "No. Nullified kill part of collar beforehand."

Dame Penne felt a fury rise in her. Then she sank back. It seemed not worth it. "How can you be sure? Are you that much an expert?"

"Not sure. Think so, though. Dame Penne, all I do necessary. How you say it? Must do. Must. For plant. For droc. For you."

Dame Penne laughed ironically. "Yes. Surely for us."

"Is for you. You will see. Me . . . I hope." The big Gorboduc seemed to wilt slightly.

"You picked a wonderful time to do this. My daughter is almost home. She is sometimes not a nice person. She is still angry about losing her husband. She—"

"Pell's father," Umber said, interrupting.

Dame Penne's mouth tightened. She determined not to be angry. "Yes. Pell's father. She will likely make your life miserable."

"Life miserable long time. Nothing new."

Dame Penne raised her eyebrows. "Yes. I know. We have been beastly. You haven't deserved any of it. The Gorbies have always been wonderful to us. Rad died in an accident."

Umber raised his hand slightly, then dropped it. "Did Dal Polon tell you about the earthbeast?" he asked.

"Earthbeast? No. What's that?" Dame Penne asked.

"I cannot tell, then. He mad, too."

"I command you to."

Umber smiled wanly, then briefly recounted the whole incident involving the earthbeast and his gift of it to Dal Polon.

"Haven't we done enough for you? Why didn't you give it

to us? Even Leda might have appreciated that."

"He might save my life. I coward."

Pell burst into the room at that point. "Mother," he shrilled. "Mother will be here in two or three days. I just heard." He looked accusingly at Umber, who unaccountably touched the boy's forehead with the back of his hand, frowning slightly.

"You feel good?" the Gorboduc asked.

Pell rubbed his forehead, drawing back. "You," he began. "You knew I wouldn't kill you. You betrayed me."

"No. He says he disabled the kill collar," Dame Penne said mildly.

"Do you believe that?" the boy said, gasping.

"I'm inclined to. We will check it," she replied.

Umber touched Dame Penne's arm. She drew back, offended. "I see slippery shale at stream you might try for glaze," he said.

"You are growing too presumptuous," she said.

"No. Not. You send Dal Penne away? Please?"

"What are you talking about?" she yelled, standing.

"Important. He old, not strong. Bad time coming. Know I ask for too much trust. Must."

"Explain yourself!" she yelled.

"Soon drocs not well. Have long talk with Tistan. Talk over."

"Ah, your tiresome droc plague. It is time you were wholly explicit. Remember, you are our prisoner."

"I Dal Penne's slave. Want good for him. Will be explicit. Promise. Must see Dal Polon soon. Must. Must."

"You have gone too far with your musts," Dame Penne spit out, picking up her control box and pressing the discipline button repeatedly.

"Not fixed yet," Umber said, shrugging. "Pretended before. May I sit? Very tired."

Dame Penne had turned her back. She only said, "Pell, get Uji. Immediately."

The boy looked at Umber, who shrugged lightly. His face was strangely flushed. "No need to get Uji, Pell Penne. I go to him. Got worse worries than all this. Worse."

Dame Penne whirled on him and hissed. "What worries? What mysterious worries?"

"Might die soon," Umber replied softly. "Then all go wrong." He turned on his heel and walked out as Dame Penne and her grandson stared at each other.

"Madness," Dame Penne hissed. "He's slipped something. We must keep your mother from him until he calms. She will slice him up with droc cords."

"Grayma, I . . ."

"Yes?"

"I think we should let him go. Until she goes. He acts crazy, but he . . ."

"You like him, then. Well, young one, we can't do that. Perhaps she has grown milder."

Pell shuddered and turned away. "I think it was my father made her that way," he said, almost in a whisper.

Dame Penne rose and came up behind him, putting her hands on his shoulders. "We have to see. We have to be strong. Now we have to prepare Gyro to go to the infirm for a time."

Pell whirled. "What for? Is he . . ."

"He's the same. I'm doing it because the Gorbie said to. I don't know what it's about, but this once I'm going to accept what he said. Besides, your graypa tends to infuriate your mother." She felt Pell shudder again.

That evening Dal Polon, reviewing the news highlights, picked up a report of a strange reddening of all the drocs on Windlash Island, far to the south in the volcanic archipelago. He was bemused and somewhat chagrined to see a report on the alien species found near the crash site, and he was relieved to see that the earthbeast, now in his own laboratories, was omitted.

He hesitated, held his stylus between his forefinger ends, then sighed and coded the Potsherd Sump visiphone of Dame Penne. She came on, looking weary. "I know this is irregular, Dame Penne, but I need to speak with the Gorbie. I would like your presence at the time. Please bring him if it isn't too much trouble." She nodded, serious and curiously compliant.

When Umber appeared, Dal Polon said without preliminaries, "I have heard that some drocs have been reported to have reddened limbs. I—"

Umber interrupted with a long wail. "Start of plague. Too late. Too late. Where?"

Dal Polon recovered his composure, then said, "At Windlash Island, far to the south."

"Volcanoes there or much cloud?"

Polon was taken aback by Umber's divination, for it had been an active volcanic year.

"Yes, I believe so."

"Quarantine all people. Remove from place to isolated area. Island best. Kill all droc. From air. Must do now. Maybe save people yet. Not much time for rest of planet."

"That is probably fifty thousand beasts you are talking about killing, Umber."

"They die anyway. If kill, help save people."

"You'd better explain yourself clearly."

Umber dropped his head. "Can't. Soon can. Not yet."

Polon sighed. "How soon?" he asked.

"Give two day. Must secure health of Penne drocs."

"How?"

"Give two day. Then I in place . . . position . . . to tell all."

"Umber, this is hardly the time, if it is such an emergency, to worry about one droc herd if they are all in danger. I beg your pardon, Dame Penne, but is that not so?"

Umber laughed, but somewhat faintly. "Dal Polon, this herd become basis for health of all. You see. Dal Penne become fabulously wealthy—almost like you with earthbeast. Give two day, please."

"You can have one."

Umber stared at his hands and sighed. "Don't know if I can . . . well, yes. One day if . . ."

"If what?"

"You let me talk to all planet at once. From academy. Get me Onic translator so I can talk plain. Not good in Westsector. It all complex."

"You ask too much."

Umber grinned boyishly. "I give you credit. If all planet saved, then you get rid of Dal Baats."

Dal Polon jerked his head slightly, then ran his fingers through his hair. "I suppose," he said, sighing, "it's too much to ask a Gorbie to have discretion."

"I have perfect dis . . . discretion in Onic, Dal Polon. You see. Not bring up *Bukloe* problem."

"I should hope not." Dal Polon paused a long time, musing. At last he said, "What proof can you give me that you are being sincere, that all this isn't nonsense you are devising to avenge the loss of your vessel?"

"Not happy vessel lost, nor son, nor wife, nor others. Owe it to droc, and for my life to Pennes. You see some proof in two day or so. Promise. I think plague lines on bank good proof. When droc die back, corkscrew vine and even more *Platus platinus* flourish. Where mud laid down, like bank, it leave sudden dark line from too much dead plant. After time, droc recover, eat, bring back light color. Can figure how long between plague if you know how fast mud soil laid down. Make sense? And soil under dark line full of droc beak. Can test. All record in mud soil, some places."

"Casio," Dame Penne broke in, "I know he's asking a lot, but if it can be arranged that I take the sponsorship, I take the chance, I think we should go ahead with this. I don't mind public anger. I am more or less isolated from it."

"No," Dal Polon returned. "I can't let you do that. All right, Umber, you'll have your forum and your translator, but you must promise me not to make a fool of all of us. I guarantee you that if you do, that hide of yours you take such care of will be a bad one to be in."

"I tell all I know. That much," Umber said.

Polon darkened his transmission, and Umber turned to Dame Penne for permission to go, wavered a little, and almost fell.

"What is it?" she said.

Umber's eyes swam back into focus. "I . . . nothing," he said. "It help I have time to get ready. That possible?"

Dame Penne looked hard at him. "You're not well," she said. "You have the plague somehow, don't you?"

"Not plague, I hope. Only substitute. I explain tomorrow. Please." He bowed very low to her, backing up. She frowned, hesitated, shut her eyes, and turned away, wondering why she trusted him and who, indeed, was the master there.

☐ XIV   Umber Articulate

WHEN Dal Polon awoke the next morning, he found a message from Uji. The solemn-faced drocherder said, "Umber has asked me to tell you he is ready to make his talk this noon. I ought to tell you that late last night he spent much time talking with the drocs. In fact, I think he touched drocs in all the pans. It took him a long time. He is now cleaning up for the talk and hopes you're able to put it all together."

Dal Polon had put his people on the question the previous night and had found that the North Colonial Academy at Matted Plain was eager to host such a presentation, donating a large lecture hall for the purpose and providing an elderly professor who spoke fluent Onic to translate. They also stipulated that they wished a question period. Polon was unable to dissuade them from that, but he managed to limit the questioners to fifteen. He himself was to have the opportunity to ask the first questions if that was necessary.

As noon approached and Umber prepared to leave Potsherd Sump, Dame Penne confronted him. "You aren't going to shame me, are you?" she queried.

Umber seemed very subdued. "No," he said. "No shame. Promise."

"You don't look well," she ventured.

"Not well. But well enough. You want fix kill collar?"

"No. For now, if you agree, we will maintain a pretense regarding the kill collar."

"All right. I not take advantage."

She found herself smoothing his shirt before he went out to the landroller. "Good-bye, Dame Penne," Umber said. "Hope you proud." She did not reply.

As the time for the broadcast approached, it was announced by the communications staff deprecatingly, and then the introduction was turned over to Dal Polon.

Polon, with Umber seated in a white worksuit behind him, put his hands behind him and said, "I wish to thank the academy for its indulgence in this matter. The Gorbie has assured us he knows materials relevant to the present illness among the drocs of Windlash Island. I am inclined to discount his claims but nonetheless feel that the crisis is sufficient enough to warrant investigating it.

"The Gorbie has insisted he will divulge his information only in a context like this one. He also insists on speaking in Onic, with a translator, and since we all know the severe limitations of his communications in Westsector, we agreed to that. Perhaps we could put this down as an academic exercise. Perhaps it may have more significance. It will certainly be the first time, if all works out as promised, that we will hear articulateness from a Gorbie. I am inclined to doubt it all. However, I wish to thank you for your indulgence. And now, with no further remarks, I wish to turn the meeting over to the Gorbie."

Umber stood up, his hands on the table in front of him, looking flushed and a little unsteady. He spoke several sentences of rapid Onic. His translator stared at him a moment and then said, "My name is Umber Trreggevthann. I am a botanist from the planet of Essttrremadrr, a Gorboduc-speaking planet some light-years from here. Although I am a botanist, my work has necessarily been also biological, because while I began my career as a botanical explorer, the necessities of space travel have meant that I have had to assume further roles."

A murmur passed through the room. Some academicians understood enough Onic to know that that statement, coming from the brute that had lived for much of a revolution at Potsherd Sump, spending his nights on a rough platform, his days working with the odorous creatures basic to their agricultural economy, was astonishing.

Umber passed a hand across his brow and continued. The translator intoned, "Like Landsdrum, Esstrremadrr is not a planet rich in its biological communities. At least I assume this is not, though I understand that the underwater creatures abound. For human purposes, both planets are in poverty, and Esstrremadrr has a much harsher climate. Furthermore, we are forced to pay tribute to the Dark Sector Raiders, the same Gorboduc culture, I assume, that has attacked you in the past. You call them Vandals, an ancient word not used now. One of our efforts at survival has been to send expeditions, like the one of which I was a part, to gather useful species, sort them out, and see if we could introduce them successfully on Esstrremadrr.

"As you might imagine, this is an onerous task, since the precautions we must take are extreme and the tests we must make are extensive. We have not the advantage of an evolution of a teeming community of species, botanical, zoological, or lithoformic, that so many planets enjoy. Our mutual planet of origin had a teeming community of many forms. We have had to guess. Fortunately, we have made no gross mistakes. Our efforts have been scattered so far. Had my vessel returned home, it would have brought with it over seven thousand new species for testing. Some were extremely precious. Others were marginal in apparent value. Still others were potentially dangerous."

Umber paused for a sip of water as the translator caught up. He seemed to waver slightly, but steadied himself and continued, "If any of the Gorboduc peoples sometime manages to monitor this presentation at any time in the future, I hereby apologize for my cowardice in remaining alive when I should have firmly grasped the honor of death. I did it for two reasons, as well as one strange inclination. The first reason was that I wanted to preserve several obviously valuable species and if possible introduce them to this fragment of West-sector for the benefit of the people, because they would so clearly be useful and instructive. The second is that I had inadvertently become a part of a huge, multi-culture study of the drocs, including their vectors, and especially their problems. I will get to that in time."

"What was the strange inclination you mentioned?" Dal Polon asked.

"Oh. I have been most recently on the planet of Klluum, at first as an agent, then, when it became obvious to all that I was an alien, as a fellow student of the local biosphere. They agreed that I should spread what I knew on my return, which I also agreed to and supported. Klluum is too far from any Gorboduc planet to have experienced any incursions, so they don't know to avoid us, as you have. They are a gentle people. Having spent several revolutions with them, I suppose I must have been infected with their gentleness, their open, willing, generous attitudes, their love of compromise and agreement—to the point that my own cultural purity softened, weakened, and I have become malleable." Umber smiled slightly, and the assembled academicians later argued at length about how ironic his statement was. As though to prove his malleability, he turned for more water and almost lost his balance.

"But what is extremely important to us here today is the question of droc plague, which has occurred three times before on this planet and which is apparently beginning again on Windlash Island. Much of what I have to say will not only be new to you but will seem like heresy according to what little I know of your Godworship. I sincerely hope you will listen to all I have to say with care, and if you feel you must reject it, do so. I would never inflict this information on you were it not absolutely necessary.

"The question is vital not only to you but to every droc planet you know of. Already one entire planetary colony, both drocs and humans, has completely perished from the plague."

"What planet?" Dal Polon asked.

"Its name is, or was, Muur. It was an Onic- and Molod-speaking colony, known by the Rrissrians, settled, historically, from Klluum, with Ghee as an intermediate stop."

"Why, according to your theories, was Muur so . . . decimated while the rest of us have survived?" The questioner was a local geographer, a heavy woman who always waved her hands in circles as she talked.

"We are not certain, of course," was Umber's reply. He paused, coughing, then added, "But we are reasonably so.

The problem is one of revolution period, of seasonal sequence. Of course the whole situation is affected by the length of time the drocs have spent in space during transit. Known human settlement is comparatively recent. We have carried our drocs, as you well know, but we have also found them on numerous planets already."

"God put them there for us," came a voice from the back of the hall.

"No doubt," Umber said. "But perhaps God did it through an agency, that is, a previous migration. The Klluumians feel this was the case. They, with work from investigators of Urrget, a place I believe you know, and Fortoff, of this vector, in conjunction with some information from Mattheo, of what appears the fifth vector, and some others, have made some mutual hypotheses, but the distances are so great that it has been extremely difficult to confirm much. However, the present theory is that the planet of origin of the drocs is one called Kkoterr and that all the droc planets are the result of nine vectors of migration from that planet, with subvectors, of course. I have placed Landsdrum in the sixth vector, in fact I believe it is six point three five.

"What is peculiar about Kkoterr is its solar system. It is the fourth planet out from its star; that is, it is some of the time. Its distance out is greater than is usual for planets suitable for human habitation, though it has been visited. One of the other bodies in the system is an erratic one with an almost cometary orbit. It is also huge. This not only produces significant perturbation in the orbit of Kkoterr, but on its rare visits, it shadows Kkoterr for a long part of that revolution, and in doing so, it completely modifies the environment, plunging the planet surface into intense cold. All this is in the encyclopedia, perhaps even in your expurgated version."

"We wish no derisive comments on our beliefs, Gorbie," Dal Polon said.

"I apologize," Umber returned. He paused again, unaccountably, seemed to forget for a moment what he was saying, then took a deep breath and began again. "I only wish to be checked if it is possible. To continue: the theory is that drocs were present on Kkoterr when the erratic planet was captured in passing through the system. Now it wholly disrupts Kkoterr every 753 revolutions. The drocs, as you know, are quick to adapt, as is every life-form that depends on seed variation, and their reaction was to seed heavily as the revolution drew upon them, then to self-destruct all the adults as the cold set in. After the cold, the still-fat bodies of the adults were there for the seed hatchlings to feed on until *Platus platinus* grew again."

"Why could they not merely let the cold kill them?" one thin professor asked.

Umber shook his head, as though to clear his mind. His eyes seemed unfocused. Then he said, flatly, "I don't know. Frankly, I have heard no wholly convincing theory about that. The assumption has been that the debilitation of the drocs by the cold would make them less satisfactory food for the young. But that remains unknown. At any rate, the mechanism of their death lies in the small thumb-shaped gland in the droc hub commonly called the paralysis sac, which is routinely removed with great care and burned in processing drocs. Anyone dissecting one of those sacs does so, as you know, at peril. At the onset of cold, the withdrawal of paralyzing poisons from the sac permits the movement of multiplication of a viruslike body, the origin of droc plague. Thus, while the drocs produce and maintain their own biocontrol normally, suspending the microorganisms in paralysis, periodically they withdraw it to produce their own deaths."

"You must admit, Professor Tregethan, that this is an extremely fanciful conclusion," one dignified academician said.

"It certainly is," Umber said with a wan grin. "However, you also well know it is no more strange than thousands of known biological processes that are now regarded as commonplace. I have not gotten to the complex part yet. I may not. But I beg your further indulgence. I might add that this is not my theory. Its author is a Klluumian scientist named Aspar Meric. He is well respected. I accept his theory. It certainly seems supported by the experience on Landsdrum, though I would love to spend the time to confirm it, especially using the alluvial bank of Darkeye Stream, which I momentarily examined while helping the Pennes gather clay. What I saw there is duplicated elsewhere—the dark stains of vigorous *platinus* production, uncropped by drocs. Under them is evidence of a huge droc kill.

"But rather than boring you with an extended explanation, I feel we need to get to the heart of the matter. When it was mentioned to me that the Windlash Island drocs were reddening, I knew that there must have been heavy cloud there or else volcanologically induced cooling from heavy airborne dust. It apparently was the latter. This triggers the mechanism early. It has been the experience of research on the unoccupied planet of Turr, according to subsequent investigation of the strata. Normally, some internal clock in the drocs counts the seasons. When the viruslike body is released, it goes through the whole population at once and kills not only them but the human populace as well. This was the experience on Muur. It is possible, given time, to devise an antitoxin. We do not have that time. Therefore, I have taken the liberty to introduce another solution. It will enrage you, but it will, I trust, also save you, as well as saving the drocs—except those on Windlash. Those ought to be being slaughtered from above right now."

"It is easy for you to say that, not being affected," an economics professor remarked.

"But to the point," Dal Polon said. "What have you done?"

"The planet called Dark Forest, fifth vector, is also a droc planet with a revolution period more rapid than that of Muur. It seemed important to the scientists of Fortoff to investigate the means of survival of their drocs."

"That is the origin planet of the droc worms," a biologist remarked.

"Exactly. The *Unipurp. quatrilobus.*"

"You didn't introduce them here, did you?" the biologist shrieked, standing.

"*Quatrilobus* was the subject of intense study, after Muur, by the scientists of both Fortoff and Dark Forest. They discovered that *quatrilobus* not only carried the death virus without harm, but that this microorganism had metamorphosed into two other strains within their bodies. Strain A, the deadly one, was now accompanied by B, which is comparatively benign, and C, which is the key to survival. The C strain incubates much more rapidly than either of the others. It produces a comparatively mild fever. Study shows absolutely that the drocs themselves, in plucking *quatrilobus* from their plate joints, and eating them, were immunizing themselves from the plague. Controlled introduction of *quatrilobus* has now occurred on Fortoff, Rrissr, Klluum, Ghee, and Onic, and it looks as though Urrget will accept it soon as well."

"Get to the point, Gorbie. Did you introduce droc worms here?"

"In a completely controlled and controllable way, yes."

Umber made the statement quietly, coughing again and reeling slightly. The translator stared at him and repeated his remarks in a tremulous voice, but already those who understood Onic had jumped to their feet and were shouting.

Umber raised his arms. Dal Polon's security men prevented the audience from storming the dais. Eventually the hubbub quieted enough for the Dal to restore order. He turned to Umber and said, "You'd better do some fast explaining, Gorbie."

Umber smiled. "I may die from it, if it's any consolation to you. Please let me explain completely. When we crashlanded, I ran into the vine tangle, as you know. I sowed the grasses and secreted a common ceramic pocketbox under a corkscrew vine. It contained five *quatrilobae*. My chief reason for gaining permission to pray at the crash site, other than praying, which I did, was to prevent the droc plague by using the *quatrilobae*. When I recovered the box, I quickly chewed up one *quatrilobus*, a ghastly thing to have to do. I put the other four under my tongue, hoping that way to get them to the drocs. That was worse, especially when the warmth woke them up."

"What did you do with them?" a fat woman in the back of the hall shouted.

"I kept them under my tongue during the whole interminable interrogation. Fortunately for you, the Groundarmy interrogators thought of me as a thick-tongued dolt, anyway, so they weren't puzzled by my curious speech. But in the long delay I accidentally swallowed another worm. I am in the middle of the fever from strain C now, but I fear I may have gotten so large a dose of strain A that the antitoxin will not develop in time to overcome it. So I may have executed myself."

"But what did you do with the droc worms?" the same woman shouted.

"A moment, please. I must apologize, but everyone I have touched at Potsherd Sump and here is going to get strain C. I have tried to touch as many people as possible."

Again the audience surged to its feet, and many headed for the exits. The security force moved away from Umber, as did the translator.

"Not worry so much! It save your life!" Umber shouted in Landsdrum.

The old translator regarded him from twenty submeasures away. Addressing him in Onic, Umber said, "You have been exposed already, old one, and if you value your family and friends, you will expose them as well. You might as well come back. We have some further explaining." He reeled as though drugged.

"You are an evil man," the translator said in a surprisingly mild voice.

"Maybe. But I have the worst dose. I will need to be quarantined soon, I fear. Let's get on with this." Again he held up his hands. Academic curiosity fought against fear in the remaining audience. They clustered at the back of the hall. "Tell us what you did with the droc pests," one man shouted.

"The remaining three are all in pan eighteen at Potsherd Sump on my friend, the old droc, Tistan, with its agreement. I have tried to infect all the rest of the Penne drocs with strain C, but if I get much worse than I feel now, I will know strain A is developing in me, and I will have to be isolated completely. Even the air will need sterilizing. Now, if you are so afraid of me, what are you going to do about Windlash Island?"

A murmur of voices rose to shouts as the academics discussed and argued the situation. They were frightened enough to want to leave but logical enough to see they probably could not fear Umber without also fearing the drocs of Windlash.

Again Umber held up his hands for silence. It did not come until Dal Polon's men began pounding the tables with the butts of their stunners.

"Only one more matter. The *quatrilobae* in pan eighteen are the property of the Pennes. They will not leave the pan but stay on the droc. They can be controlled even when they multiply. Some will want to purchase them to spread the immunity, but that will have to be arranged with the Pennes at their prices. It would not be helpful to let them loose, as they multiply fast and will disrupt droc growth."

"We know that much, you Gorbie lout," a man shouted from the back wall. But Umber was not listening. He had collapsed, and the translator in fleeing to the back of the hall, caused a wash of people to pull back from him, pressing rapidly out into the hallway.

Dal Polon walked up fairly close to Umber. "So you infected me, too," he said in disgust.

"Only strain C," Umber said, gasping. "Stay away. Feel this worse one. Stay away. Isolate me. Isolate me."

☐ XV   Enter Leda Angry

THE hall cleared rapidly, and Umber was lifted from the dais by an isolation-clad med team and rushed to the infirm on a motor cart. He had a high fever and was only semiconscious. The med techs thrust him into a quarantine chamber, then drenched their covers with disinfectant and emerged, slightly harried, to scrub down. His chest heaving, eyes unfocused, Umber refused to lie passively but seemed to fight with the fever as though it were a perceptible enemy as successive specialists suited up to examine him and perhaps raise the oxygen in his chamber a point or two. They really did not know what they were doing.

Those who had been in the lecture hall went home, scrubbed, checked their immunizations, needled and cajoled the medical people to give them anything else they could think of, and prepared for the worst.

At Potsherd Sump, both the Pennes and all the drocherders

sat listless—feverish and flushed. The drocs also seemed inactive, some floating on the muck of their pans, slightly pinkish.

Dal Polon also had a strong flush. With a secretary nearby, he reclined in a white lotion bath trying to feel useful, wondering what he had allowed, awaiting a condemnation from Dal Baats but too supine to worry as deeply as he felt somehow he ought to.

At one point an aide came in and said, "Dal, the Windlash Island drocherders are taking high fever. Two have already died. The others are being isolated. Groundarmy is quarantining the whole island."

Polon lifted a hand and let it splash back into the sudsy lotion. "Perhaps I should feel vindicated," he murmured. "But it's only sad. So Umber was right. I should rouse myself and touch everyone I can with this light rash." The aide retreated. The secretary looked at the Dal, wary and alarmed but unmoving. Then, with a set mouth, he rolled up the sleeve of his blouse and held out his forearm to Polon, who took it and deliberately moved his forehead across it. "That should do," he said. "It isn't so bad—if it doesn't get worse." The secretary laughed.

Polon looked up at the aide, who had set down his lightpad and was also rolling up a sleeve. "Might as well," the man said, sighing slightly. He, too, held out an arm toward Polon.

The whole colony, with its thirty-eight settlement centers, reviewed, discussed, and analyzed both Umber's speech and the subsequent events. Waveridge Mountain sent a special envoy to borrow a Potsherd Sump drocherder to infect the venturesome, and Wahn went with them, reclining on a gurney, gesturing at the others, smiling slightly as he left.

Into the middle of the colonywide disruption, a huge, paunch-bodied freighter settled onto the mesa of Truncated Mountain, bearing Leda Penne, who had been following transmissions of the barrage of recent events as the ship approached. She was frustrated by her duties in supervising molybdenum, platinum and study-specimen unloading and grew more angry as the time passed, until, in a burst of final energy, she finished her duties and caught a smallshuttle for Matted Plain.

As it skimmed the shore of the Sea of Cruel Mouths and approached the arc of sharp-toothed islands enclosing Purple Lake beyond, she continued to monitor events on the ship screen. Her mouth grew tighter. Somehow the Gorbie had managed to infect the drocs of Windlash. She knew it. Why could they not see it? The fingers of her left hand drummed her thigh.

At Matted Plain she touched the code for Potsherd Sump and saw Phant's face appear. "Ah. Mistress," he said without enthusiasm. "Where are you?"

"At the plain. Come and get me, please. And soon."

Phant's head drooped slightly. "I . . . seem to be indisposed at the moment. All of us are. Perhaps someone would bring you?"

"Where is my mother?" Leda asked through gritted teeth.

"She is—ah, she is coming. It is Leda, Dame Penne," Phant said, turning.

Dame Penne's face appeared, smiling slightly. "Dear. Where are you?"

"At Matted Plain. I take it the Gorbie has put all of you under, and you can't come for me. At that rate I'm about certain nobody from here will want to take me out."

"Some would. Some would be eager, especially since I am getting better now."

"Pell—is he . . ."

"He's better, too. Sleeping now, I think. You must prepare to be ill a little while, Leda. I'm afraid it is inescapable."

"You've all been hypnotized by the Gorbie. What a culm pile! He's got you believing all his hooey."

"Poor Umber. He's fighting for his life now."

"Hope he loses it after all this. The rahnsucker."

"Yes, dear. Still in form, I see. Try to find transportation if you will. Promise the driver she can touch a drocherder. Now that they are dying at Windlash, a lot of people are getting scared. The listeners in the lecture hall are suddenly popular, and everybody seems to be waiting to see if they'll break out."

"Wonderful. What if this is only a lull—if you get worse later?"

"I doubt it, dear. Med analysis has shown only one strain in my blood, three in Umber's, as he told us. Late word from Windlash says the fatalities have a different one from mine. You might consider that we've been told the truth."

"Huh. You've been taken in. He's a Gorbie, remember."

"Yes, of course, dear. As long as you are at Matted Plain, you might stop in to see Umber. I'd like an account of him other than the med reports."

Leda set her jaw. "I'll stop only if I can unhook him from his life supports." She was surprised when her mother killed the connection. Well, if she wants to play it that way, then so be it, Leda decided. She would book a room and rest. She needed it enough.

Later, in a spa, she began to repent her decision, wanting to see Pell. He had seemed to side with Rad, but after all, he was small, and he was her son. She sighed deeply, lifting a foot above the swirling water, regarding her toes. Three of them had black nails from a rock's having fallen on her boot. Lucky it had been reinforced. She raised the other foot. Those toes looked better. Still, feet were strange appendages.

The religionists said they were made the way they were to be neatly symmetrical with the hands. She wondered. There could have been so many other designs. The small toe seemed vestigial, its nail an afterthought. She wondered if God had envisioned people as always wearing shoes. They usually did. Of what use, then, was the symmetry? Psychologists seemed to explain some of the odd-protuberances of the anatomy, such as the largely unnecessary breasts, as being love objects. That made Leda chuckle to herself. So much for symmetry. So much for the glorification of the strange machinery that made up a body. Clearly her mind was drifting with fatigue. She realized she was too exhausted to be angry anymore and adjusted the head sling to sleep where she was.

She awoke later feeling waterlogged, rolled out of the spa, and crawled to the sleepmat. Again she fell into a deep slumber, the first complete relaxation she had had since hearing of Rad's death. But something nagged her even as she faded out again. What was it? She could not say.

She awoke much later, feeling renewed. Why had she delayed? She dressed quickly, slung her duffel, and called a landroller. She found the driver eager to take her to Potsherd Sump, wanting to talk about the fever all the way. Leda let her rattle on, saying she had been in space and knew nothing of what had happened. "I hope I'm there in time to be infected," the woman said. "I hear they're all getting better and some aren't infectious anymore."

"Wonderful," Leda said, regarding her rock-scarred hands.

"Not for me. I'd like to get it early and then charge people to touch me."

"Oh. Would you charge much?" Leda asked.

"No. Not much. Enough so that if I infected a couple of dozen, I could reupholster this landroller."

"It doesn't look so bad," Leda said, looking at the scarred, drochide seats. "I've seen much worse." On a mine car, she thought.

"They're terrible," the driver said. "I've been to Choicity. They use imported hydrocarbon weaves."

Leda made a face. "Well, they're snobbly-wobblies. We're close to the earth here at Matted Plain. My mother is so close she has her hands in it all the time. Tell you what. I'll get Phant to touch you if you let me be quiet. I have a lot to think about."

The driver never said another word. Leda almost began to doze until the landroller rose steeply up and over the hard-faced flood barrier around the Penne compound. She shook herself awake and murmured, "Looks the same." The driver didn't reply.

Phant was amused when the young woman bent down and pressed her cheek to his. He hoped his wife was watching, but she was still asleep, her fever breaking.

Leda found her mother in the potshop, her fingers poised on a tiny cup, drawing the sides up on the whirring wheel. "Never tire of that, I see," Leda said in greeting.

"Oh. Leda. No. This is a commemorative cup. I want to see how delicate I can make it. A reminder of the fragility of our health, even now."

"Yeah," Leda said. "Where is Pell? He wasn't in his chamber. Is he better?"

"Completely well. He's gone to the plain to see Umber. Worried, you know." Dame Penne never turned her head, though her shoulders drew up somewhat, awaiting Leda's out-burst.

It never came. Leda had turned and was striding out the door. She caught the now-infected driver before she left. The woman was bubbling over with her good fortune. Leda never answered her the whole way to town, and finally the woman fell silent.

As Leda got out at the infirm, the woman said, "No charge. Good-bye." The landroller door hushed down behind her as Leda turned away.

Inside the building she found Pell staring through a window. His mouth turned down. She heard him say into the speaker, "Don't suffer so, Umber."

She heard a voice come back in a ghostly whisper, "All right. I . . . won't. Don't . . . worry." She came up behind Pell, hands on her hips, and looked over his head. Inside, lightly covered, she saw a very large man, his chest heaving, his face gleaming with sweat, staring vacantly upward as he struggled to live.

His eyes rolled over toward the boy, then unfocused and fluttered back. "Your . . . mother," he whispered, closing his eyes. "Good . . . bye," he added as Pell whirled and stared up at Leda. He flinched back from her slightly, seeing her angry stare in the window. She reached across him and touched the command, darkening the window.

"Good-bye, Umber," Pell shrilled as his mother touched off the sound. Then she hesitated, brightened the window again, and looked at the Gorboduc. So that was what they looked like. "He wears his hair like a Klluumian," she observed absently.

"He's been there," Pell said, taking her hand. "He's been everywhere."

Strangely, Leda's anger had drained out of her. The man seemed so helpless. He lay trembling, his chest heaving. She could feel only pity, and disgust with herself for its irresistible upwelling. "Will he recover?" she asked.

"They don't know," her son said. "I think so."

"Why?"

"He can't die, mother. He can't. It's too wrong."

She thought of all kinds of arguments but let them go. She

had forgotten how red her son's hair was, she thought, smiling down at his combed, gleaming head.

Well, she would go make peace with her mother. Who knew what all this meant? She still felt a rumble of resentment, though, and still did not trust the Gorbie.

"I don't want to go, mother," Pell said, still clinging to her hand.

She heaved him up on her arm, big as he was. "You can come back," she said. "The readout shows a drop in his temperature. A quarter point in the last tenthday."

"Is that good?"

"Depends how you look at it." She gave Umber a last look. His eyes remained closed and his chest still heaved.

A technician came up behind them. She frowned. "I don't like that dehydration," she murmured.

"Give him water, then."

"Can't keep up with it," the tech said.

Umber's fingertips twitched on the sheet. "I will remember," he said suddenly, distinctly. "I will." He paused, eyes dilating, staring at the ceiling.

He jerked. "Watch out!" he croaked. "Watch its tentacle, Jonson. Keep back. That suit isn't thick enough. Think of it, Wyster. How far it has come, we have come. Look at the strange changes. How wonderful, its paws, its eyes—his, I should say."

"I think he's speaking Uuvian," Leda said.

"I can't believe how soft his hair is," Umber continued. "Touch it, Wyster. He doesn't seem to mind. Look, his nose." Umber laughed. "It's like seeing a brother left behind fifty thousand years ago. Yes, a very little brother. Let me sit him on my lap. He won't mind, do you think? But Atel, if you had seen how dawn was, rising on those hills, all green with an ancient community of things, all still, with flying creatures awakening and moving across the low sky, coming to stand on the uplifted arms of the plants—huge plants, jutting up, their many arms like prayers, like scribbles of joy, all divided and subdivided, their leaves in myriads, their fruits almost immeasurable, and the creatures that came out and fed on them, as though these plants poured out generosity on them for the love of it, retaining only enough fruits to reproduce themselves.

Vegetable generosity. Atel, Atel, what a bliss it was. I could
have stayed there forever, or at least for my allotted time. If
Alayynr could run through those fields, climb those plants,
stand on those hills. What we have given up! How stupid our
people were to choose Essttremadrr. I know. We couldn't help
it, given the necessities. Jonson, be careful of the tentacles.
Think of it, Wyster. Ah, to show him to Ourrnyl. Look out!
The bastards are firing on us. The specimens, the specimens.
Aaaaiiie, Alayynr. Will remember. Will. Two hundred sev-
enty-nine, eighty-one, thirty-six, three thousand four hundred
ninety-nine . . ."

Umber's croaking shout died away. Amber lights flashed,
and a swarm of bodycased technicians blocked the view. One
turned, looked, and touched a command. The window turned
opaque.

"If he's so infected, why don't they give him fresh blood?"
Leda asked.

"Can't."

"Why not? Is his a different type?"

"Godworship says we can't put people's blood into him.
Gorboducs are the devil's imitations."

Leda raised her arms and let them fall. "Come on, then."
She tugged at his hand. He stood, staring at the blank window.

☐ XVI   Convalescence
and Discovery

FOUR days later Casio Polon coded the physician in
charge of Umber again. The man was obviously weary. "How
is the Gorbie this evening, specialist?" was the Dal's greeting.

"Better. Again better. Still in isolation. Temperature normal. Much weight loss. Eating, though."

"So he will make it."

"I trust so, Dal."

"Good. Very good. What is it that let him survive? The antibodies from strain C, I hope."

"I'm sure they helped—in fact may have made the difference. He is very strong. We treated successive symptoms. We think that helped. He wants to live, too, very badly, for some reason. He wouldn't relax, wouldn't give up."

"Hmm," Polon said. "Well, thank you again, specialist."

"Don't mention it, Dal." As the screen went black, the physician rose and went once again to look at Umber through the window. Wahn was there, back from his journey, well again, talking to the Gorboduc.

"Tistan taps my forearms for the game, Umber," Wahn said. "But I can't play it without you."

"All right. Get lightpad," Umber said, sitting up.

"Have one."

"Draw X with right angles. Then draw in line through hub —make it three dimension. You see any two line of three make cross. Put numbers on line. Start at end of each with one, number to four near cross-point. Each line have four numbers end toward center. Straight line have name, using ends. One is nov-skek. One is dray-mag. Other is beess-wok. So if angle used, you can make nov-mag, nov-wok, nov-dray, nov-beess. Also others."

"I think I have it," Wahn said, holding up the board.

Umber squinted through the window. "Yes. Keep fours away from cross-point. All right. First a goal number decided on. More than eight, less than twenty. Thirteen common. First player chooses number—like nov-four. Other player then choose. Usually four. No one can use another four in game unless blocked. Blocking done by choosing number outside one already picked by other player. So if one choose nov-four, other nov-three, that arm blocked to first player. Object to make unblocked numbers on any two leg add up to number choice, like thirteen. Most game not won. Droc have to remember. Player can clear block by sacrificing move to do it. If all choices blocked, closest score wins. If play ends on first player turn, second get to add three for missed turn."

"It sounds complicated."

"Is. And boring. But drocs like. Based on droc body, you see, and group of plates. Makes decimal base. It hard for them. They not smart. Very slow. But don't forget. Remember all move. Not easy for them to know what to do. Hard to hold all in mind. Not much mind there.

"You play by mark on board. You never lose then, but you might not win. Not fair, though. They hold in mind. When you learn, do in head. Make fairer."

"You'd better rest now, Umber," the physician said.

"Seem rest forever. Like in space," Umber said, but he lay back and covered his torso. "Good-bye, Wahn. See later."

The physician smiled at the drocherder and darkened the window. "Specialist," Umber's voice said.

"Yes," the physician answered without touching the window command.

"Need talk Dal Polon with connection to Dame Penne. About droc worm and proper care. Very important. To control spread and administration to droc. Please."

The physician noted the tape segment for his intelligence report. "All right. You need to rest. But I'll arrange it."

"Thank you," Umber said. The physician touched off the sound.

The physician did arrange it, and the next day the connection was made. The Gorboduc explained that the worms should be ready to seed soon. They needed to be removed to an incubation bed or droc fluid–soaked matting to ensure preservation of all the young and proper placement for subsequent use. Umber's instructions were lengthy and specific. Dame Penne recorded them for Uji. Dal Polon put them in his files. And intelligence, tapping the communication, made their own copy.

At the end of the conversation Dal Polon said, "You were right about Windlash. All the drocherders there have perished, and two researchers. The drocs have been exterminated, and the island is now deserted. We are using the C strain on all the remaining drocs, by contact between the core ridge and an infected human. It seems to be working."

"Too bad. Too bad about Windlash," Umber murmured. "Not in time. Did my best. Must pray. Couldn't think of better way. Not believed, you see."

"You did your best, and we're extremely grateful. Oh, by the way," Polon added offhandedly. "I had a communication today from a cryptographer. Her name is, uh, let me see. I have it here. Yes, Professor Vadid Nocrel. She says she was asked by Cipher HQ to work on a message piggybacked onto a normal transmission. It was largely a species list in Onic. She assumes you sent it, says it has the normal form of a report. That's so, isn't it?"

"Yes. Felt had to report to them and my own Gorbies. Part of preventing planet death from plague. Need to confirm all vectors to help determine time before drocs' internal clock come full circle."

"Ah, yes. I don't understand all that, but you did send the message, I take it?"

Dame Penne broke in. "How on Landsdrum did you manage that? You patched into an off-world transmission?"

"Ah. From droc station. I show you. Not hard."

"Did you send any others?" Dame Penne asked, offended.

"None. Needed to send only that. Dangerous even to send that."

"The things you did seem dangerous enough."

"Not to me, Dame Penne. Bad to send Gorboduc from here. Attracts Dark Sector Gorbies, maybe. Think I masked it, though."

"Wonderful," Dal Polon said. "You can explain that to me sometime. But what the professor wanted to know was what *Marmota flaviventris ter.* meant. She said she had accounted for all the rest."

"Ah, well. Not see any. Assume did not survive."

"What is it?"

"Oh, very precious species."

"A food source?"

"Could be. Precious for itself, though. Tell you about it later."

"Sketch it for me on the lightpad."

"Hands too sore, Dal Polon. Still sore. Will explain."

"This smells bad," Dame Penne said. "What've you done now, Umber? Is this trouble?"

Umber raised his eyebrows. He tapped his finger on the edge of the bed.

Dal Polon made a face. "Oh. Well, then, we must have a talk, I see."

"Yes," Umber said.

"What is going on?" Dame Penne asked.

"I have a meeting," Dal Polon said. "End of transmission."

That afternoon Leda and Pell pulled a small landroller to a stop near the high bank on Darkeye Stream where Umber had seen the sedimentary bands that he had said meant droc plague. She scanned the area, shouldered her collecting vials, and set out her survey apparatus.

"Right up there," Pell said. "He climbed right up there."

"Yes, I see. Well, you amuse yourself while I prepare a study. I'd like to check out the timetable he proposed."

"Can you really do that?"

"Even the primitives did, Pell. You amuse yourself. Don't go far. Nobody comes out here, but somebody might—some antisociety type, maybe."

She watched him wander off up the stream as she set out her equipment, recorded a calibrated profile of the bank, and began collecting specimens. With the seasonal flush of the stream, she found it comparatively easy to determine the buildup of the sediment. Clearly the water had pooled there until some bar below had cut through and allowed the rapid water to slice down through the recently built up sediment. It was an ideal site. She wondered how the Gorbie could have seen it so quickly.

After over three measures of absorbed collecting, she heard some calls from upstream. Pell was excited about something. She spoke into her wristmitter. "What is it, Pell?"

She heard his faint voice reply, "Little handprints. A line of tiny handprints."

"Handprints? Where?"

"In the sand along the stream here."

"A baby?"

"No. Too small. Like my thumbnail. Well, some bigger."

"This isn't a trick?"

"No. Oh, no. Come and see."

"Too busy, Pell. I'll come later."

She heard a whine from her son and turned back to her work. Clearly there was a concentration of droc bills at the lower edge of the dark stain. She wondered why no studies had pointed that out already until she realized that Landsdrum researchers seldom pursued anything without an obvious economic reward. She snorted to herself, wondering what she was doing there.

She worked for a time in silence, concentrating hard until she heard a piercing shriek both from her wrist and from upstream. Instantly she set down her vial, her collecting spoon, and her recorder. She looked at her hands an instant and scrambled down from the bank. Children are a pain in the maximus, she thought as she raced, splashing, upstream toward the viny bend.

As she rounded the bend, she saw Pell, mucky hands drawn up in front of his face, staring across the stream at the tangled bank.

"What is it? What?" she gasped out.

He looked at her, pale and trembling. "A face," he said.

"A face? Where?" She dusted her hands and took a personal defense stunner from a side pocket.

"There," he said, pointing at the thick, curling corkscrew vines surmounting the bank. "A tiny face. It had hair all over it. Two black eyes. Its face stuck out like this." He gestured with his filthy hands.

Leda looked and saw nothing. "I don't have time for games, Pell," she said.

He began to cry. "I was bringing you a tiny hand," he said in a wire-thin voice. "In the mud. I looked up and saw it. Up there."

Leda was confused. "How big?" she asked. Pell held his hands, thumbs and middle fingers forming an arc, looking at her seriously, tears streaking his cheeks. She frowned. "I have to get back to the specimen column," she said. "You say there are more of these handprints?"

"Up there," he said, pointing and whirling. "Not far."

She stretched. "I don't have time for games. But it'll be a break. Come on, bagbutt, let's go."

Pell swished his hands in the stream, then trotted on ahead, looking back often. They rounded two more bends, and he stopped and pointed. She could see Pell's deep tracks milling around, then following some tiny marks. She could see where he had squatted down and scooped out some mud in the middle of the pattern. She walked on ahead and stooped down. In the mud she saw the print of a tiny foot—or something like one. It was different, but it reminded her strangely of her own foot as she had regarded it above the bathwater in Matted Plain. She saw the patterns shamble on ahead, away from any of Pell's tracks. She followed them for a while and saw where they crossed the stream and scrabbled up the bank to the tangle. "Holy hell on a handle," she said.

"What, mother?"

"Something. I don't know. Something that doesn't belong ... I'll bet the Gorbie is behind it. He brought living things. He's brought a creature from somewhere. Crimestuffers. What a mess. Who knows what the thing is? Mother did something when she brought that deep-rock shovel dancer here."

"He's all right. He just saved us is all."

"Huh. Not crimeating likely. Well, let's not get heated up. We'll take some specimens. I have to finish work. Remember. Not a word about this. We'd best find out what he's up to first, the hairy heretic."

"Mother, you call him all these names. He ..." Pell let the sentence die.

"I've learned not to trust, Pell. Too disappointing. You and mother have trusted him. Remember, I've seen people from a number of crimethick worlds. They don't have Godworship like we do. They're always after something. We just haven't found out what this worm-eating leatherarm is after yet."

"Mother, he has just saved all of us."

"I ... That's just too good to be so, boy. We killed his whole crew, remember? And his wife and son. And he turns around and saves us? Sure. Happens every day. He's a Gorbie, too, remember. Left a trap for your father. What trap is in this, I ask?"

"I ..." Pell began and let it drop, trotting along by his mother, holding in his hands a glob of mud on which rode the track of a creature from beyond the nearer stars.

Try as he might, Dal Polon was unable to break into the unexpurgated encyclopedia again. Another block lay across his inquiries. It must be a self-defending system, he thought.

When I have more time, I'll have to try some other way. Of course, I could ask Umber. It must be another problem. He didn't want intelligence tapping us. Would they dare tap a Dal? he mused. The obvious answer was, of course.

☐ XVII   Marmota

THAT evening Umber left Matted Plain Infirm in Dal Penne's landroller to return to Potsherd Sump. Opinion about him had shifted drastically. He found people lining the boulevard leading from the infirm to see him, waving at him, smiling and laughing. On some he could see the remaining flush of strain C droc plague. He waved back, smiling slightly, wary of it all and worried now about his other importation, *Marmota flaviventris ter.* Still weary from convalescence, he tightened his jaw and determined to see it through.

At Potsherd Sump he saw Dal Polon's landroller. A tingle ran down his back. Something was up. He knew Pell's mother was there, too. Phant let him out in front of the manor. "I walk back to droc," Umber said with a slight smile.

"They want to see you inside," Phant said with slight hauteur.

"Oh," Umber returned, making a mouth at the old servant. For the first time he entered the main slider leading to a large, formal hall. There he found Dame Penne conversing with Dal Polon over drinks and small sea wafers. Behind Dame Penne, Dal Penne sat enrobed, staring off at the play of lights in the sheet lamp on the wall. On one side of him Pell sat on a low rollchair, and on the other stood a tall, thin, dark-skinned blond woman, her hair cut in a severe line just above her shoulders, one arm on the back of her father's chair. She had a face like Pell's but thinner, held tightly, warily. She regarded

Umber with suspicion. He flicked a glance at her, recognizing her from her holo, and then looked back at Dame Penne, coming to stand in front of her, respectfully back.

She continued her conversation briefly, then looked at up him and said, "Please sit down, Umber. Over there behind the table. There is something on the table for you to look at."

Umber turned and moved to the bench she had indicated, glancing at the table as he did so. On it were two of Dame Penne's blue hand-thrown bowls. In each a hemisphere of drying mud carried a tiny track. Umber glanced down briefly. "*Marmota flaviventris* survive, then," he remarked with a wry grin. They all looked at him severely. "Where you find?" he asked.

"Umber," Dal Polon began. "We want some answers. What is this *Marmota*, and what will it do to our ecology? No evasions."

"Will not harm ecology. I think. With grass spread, will certainly not. May need control since no rahntroc, no lynx or other meat eater here. Happy in mountain rock. Nothing to eat there on Landsdrum. May adapt to vine tangle. Doubt will, though. No time."

"You are evading, Umber. What is it?"

Umber sighed. "Hard to describe well," he said.

"Speak in Onic. I will translate," Leda said flatly from behind her mother.

"You say straight? No changes?"

"Mother, does your servant often doubt your honesty openly?"

Dame Penne made a vague gesture. Umber shrugged and began. "Servant hear hostility. Very well. Talk Onic. One of our researchers found *Marmota* on the planet of Reemang, extremely far back on the path of general human migration. It took two generations of investigators to deliver *Marmota*, together with a lagomorph, *Sylvilagus floridanus*, and feline predator, from the . . . same planet of origin, to us at Klluum. *Marmota* is a small, warm-blooded, furred animal much like humankind."

In saying the last, Umber paused, glancing at Leda, who translated it faithfully but with obvious distaste.

"Without much intelligence, though," Umber continued.

"We intended to release *Marmota, Sylvilagus*, and their predators on an island habitat, along with the grasses, which came to us from Aban, through the same researchers, along the same path of emigration. *Marmota, Sylvilagus*, and the grasses were old acquaintances and got along well."

"What did you intend to use this creature, *Marmota*, for?" Dal Polon asked, frowning.

"It's small but potentially a source of food and hides. The main reason we wanted it, though, is for what it is—together with the others, perhaps the most precious things in all our cargo. They . . ."

"Yes?"

"They are from our planet of origin and are distant relatives, split in evolution from *Homo sapiens* when well along, very different, but very much the same, too—certainly almost twins when compared to anything in this sector. I couldn't bear to let *Marmota* die in the attack. It was hard enough to let the bay lynxes die. They also were from our planet of origin. They had preyed on such creatures as *Marmota* thousands of revolutions ago, and for tens of thousands of revolutions. Who knows at what cost it was brought this far? Someone had an idea, but at such distances, ideas die out. Information fades. Great hopes and great labor go for nothing. So with the bay lynxes and *Sylvilagus* I had to allow a strain of life that had come as far as we have to burst in the vacuum of space." Umber put his head in his palms and wept, his back heaving, as Leda Penne translated.

For a short time there was a silence. Then he wiped his hands on his worksuit, sighed, and continued. "I knew *Marmota* was a potential trouble to the environment, but I had to try with them. They are not predators. What they might harm is vegetative, by multiplying and eating too much. Some of its relatives—even if I had access to them—I would never have brought, especially *Mus musculus*, which managed to accompany us—humankind, I mean—quite far in the emigration and caused endless trouble."

"*Mus?*" Dame Penne asked.

"Yes. Smaller, furry creatures, relatives of *Marmota*, more adaptable and evasive. My introduction of *Marmota*, though, if it proves to be a mistake, is a correctable one."

Dal Polon held his stylus between the tips of his forefingers. "You are sure?"

"With methods we have. And there are suitable predators remaining on Klluum—examples of these same creatures."

"Predators," Dame Penne remarked. "Like our sea creatures."

"Yes, and ourselves. We are predators of the drocs."

Leda translated this and immediately added, "God placed them here for our use. It is the nature of things, God-established."

"It is in the nature of things for felines to prey on *Marmota* and *Sylvilagus*, too, and the result is the same, but I've never been sure of the God part."

At that point Leda ordered Pell to leave. She herself was used to parrying heretical views in the off-planet mines, but she was not going to have her son's mind further contaminated. Dame Penne fumbled idly with the edge of the table next to her, touching on a link so Pell could hear from his chamber. They had anticipated his mother's reaction and planned for it.

"And you did not bring this predator?" Polon asked.

"A pair of lynxes. It would have been impossible to bring them."

"Why not? They have the *Marmota*."

"They need to eat often. I brought only two pairs of *Marmota*. They have to multiply. The lynxes might have preyed on human children in their desperation. Or simply starved."

"Umber, you've been referring to pairs. What do you mean? Are they so inexorably social?"

"No. Well, *Marmota* is. Lynxes tend to be solitary when they can be. Or they have been at home. Who knows how they behave now? We've attempted to maintain their predation skills. But we know what the loss of a complex habitat means."

Umber stood and began to pace. "This planet may have a true interactive sea community, but the land life is a mess. Tag ends of migrations. Oversimplified. Unbalanced. You must know it. But perhaps not. You've never been on a planet with a full complement of evolved life. Oh, that may be messy enough in its way, with things preying on each other, competing for resources, occupying every feasible niche for a chance to live, even becoming parasites. Some of it is awful. But it is also so wonderful. You can't know it until you've seen. The ecological poverty of Landsdrum is worse even than Esstrremadrr. We have been buiding our biosphere, though humankind can never really do that effectively. It takes many millions of revolutions and the natural tendencies of more or less equal beings to develop on their own without a dominant species like us."

"Stop," Leda Penne ordered. "I have to catch up." She did her best, with obvious loathing for some of what Umber had said, to render it correctly.

"The beauty, the complexity, the incredible ingenuity and variety of life if allowed to go its own course is something no one on our occupied and modified planets can imagine. If I had a choice, I would have been a biologist on our planet of origin. I can't imagine a more fulfilling destiny. But Klluum has some of it. The natural intellect that a world not interfered with shows is . . . unutterable."

Leda finished the translation glowering, but she was faithful to it.

"Tell us further about this *Marmota*, please," Dal Polon requested. "It is our immediate problem. How can we hold it in check?"

At that point Phant appeared, bowing deeply. "A message for you, Dal Polon," he said, shooting a side glance at Umber. He handed the Dal a lightpad, at which he stared briefly.

Looking up, he said, "I'll read this here, because it concerns you, Umber. It says a repeated message has been received from far out. Our cryptographers believe it to be in Gorboduc, but they have no way of translating it. They wish a translation."

"What message?"

"It isn't here. I'll touch the code." His fingers ran across a board, and they all watched the visiphone monitor. A young orderly's face appeared, saying, "MHQ here. Oh, yes, Dal Polon. Is your Gorbie there? We have a message. It's short but was repeated numerous times. We'd like to inquire for a translation if that is possible."

"Repeat the message, please," the Dal said.

The orderly held down three controls, and they heard the guttural tones of Gorboduc growling out, *"Hrasssarr fodrr drruubitt. Hrasssarr fodrr drruubitt. Nazk'kahmm verrutt. Drruubitt impurr jahhnnrrrah. Fazrrry jahhnnrrrah."* The message repeated several times.

Dal Polon raised his eyebrows and looked at Umber, who raised his arms and let them fall. "The Dark Sector Gorboducs' demand for tribute. Have they done before?"

"What exactly did it say?" Dal Polon asked.

"It said, 'Prepare your tribute. Prepare your tribute. We will come for it. Tribute must be generous. Very generous.'"

"So that's what you came for," Leda said.

"My child, please be quiet," Dame Penne shot at her. "Umber, what does this mean? Please explain so MHQ can get it all."

Umber looked at Leda. "You translate?" he asked.

"It's expected," she replied, still angry at her mother's rebuke.

"Well," Umber began, "the Dark Sector Gorboducs are one group of seven Gorboduc-speaking cultures. They are the most powerful of us, chiefly because they started that way. They prey on the rest and keep us weaker. What you've received is their call for tribute. Surely you've heard it before if you've had previous trouble with them. What it means is that they say they are coming. They want a considerable part of the wealth of your planet and ships to carry it in. If you give it, they will take it. They will go with it and leave you alone —for a while. Then they'll come back for a new tribute. We spend much of our economy in preparing tributes for them. Too much."

"When will they be coming?" Dal Polon asked.

"They never say. This is an announcement. It simply says to be ready for them."

"What if we decide to fight?"

"They accept that. They're very good at it. And they risk much—though not everything. You might win. You might drive them off. You might lose. They aren't kind to losers."

"We know that," Dame Penne said. "What kind of tribute?"

"Products of the planet, especially anything precious—metals and the like. Some food. Spices. Women. Fine art—your finest. If they don't like it, they destroy it."

"We have our defenses, this time," Leda said.

"If you go that way, be sure they're very good," Umber said. "The best defense is early warning. They can be on you before you know it. If the tribute isn't ready, they destroy a great deal even if you don't resist."

"Do you resist?"

"On Esstrremadrr? No. We pay the tribute. We have so far, anyhow."

"I don't believe all this. It's lies. You're setting us up," Leda said.

"For what? Tribute? No. I was telling you your options. This far out you stand a much better chance of resisting. They don't mind a good fight, but like all predators, they won't fight if they aren't sure they'll win without disabling hurt. They accept some losses, but they don't like losses. They calculate—weigh them against gains. This far out, on whatever sweep they're on, they can't afford it. The entire trick of defense is early warning."

"You found we have early warning," Dal Polon said.

"We weren't really looking out as we should have been. Passing through. We came this way in our anxiety to pass on the information about the droc plague. Your warning system is not early enough, from what I've surmised. They would go through that like droc beaks through *platinus*. It would whet their appetite for destruction."

"So you are saying we should pay tribute."

"No. Improve your early warning. Urrget has, and they've been successful. They know when the Dark Sectors are coming and have a full array of ships up there for them—make them turn away. When they turn away, you have to follow until they have committed fuel for speed. Then you have to send drone monitors."

"Ruinously expensive," Dame Penne said.

"So is tribute. Tribute is one big reason for my expedition. We want more heavy, coarse, and intrinsic wealth—things they don't know about, aren't interested in, or can't take—for our own progress."

"Why don't you follow your own advice?"

"Too close. They can commit too much to us. We have no real allies. They have agents among the Gorboduc planets. They monitor defense material and get information out. Hard to stop. You have to choose."

"You Gorbies are nothing but trouble," Leda said after translating.

Umber laughed loudly and said to her in Onic, "You don't know the half of it."

Dal Polon looked at the monitor. "Do you have what you need, orderly?" he said stiffly.

"Yes, Dal, thank you very much," the orderly said, waiting for him to kill the transmission.

He sat still, head in his hands, for a few moments. "Trouble," he said. "More trouble. Umber, you said they won't take heavy wealth. What do you mean? Metal is heavy enough."

"But it can be put to use in space. If your wealth is stone or grass or crude biofuel, they aren't interested. They can't transport it. If it's knowledge, that is weightless but also usually uninteresting to them."

"I see. This gives us something to think about. When do you think they will come?"

"Perhaps in a revolution, perhaps in four revolutions, perhaps not in your time. You never know. They come to Esstrremadrr too often. I've been gone a long time, though. I don't know how things are at home." He paused, then added, "I know much about early warning and can help you."

"Why would you do that?" Leda asked.

"Cowardice," Umber said with a light laugh. "Want to live."

At that point the Dal killed the transmission. They all fell silent for a time. At last Dame Penne said, "Umber, if we can get back to our first subject at so dire a time, two things have continued to puzzle me. First you spoke of this *Syl* . . ."

"*Sylvilagus floridanus*. Brought only one. It will die without offspring. Did not report. Did not kill because not needed to. I threw it out of the vehicle when we landed and let it run."

"You brought an alien animal and didn't even report it?"

"Only one. Maybe dead now. Not have offspring. Only one."

"This is still a puzzle. You spoke of bringing a pair of the predators. And two pairs of *Marmota*. What do you mean by pairs? I fear . . ."

Umber hung his head. "More trouble," he said. "Didn't know any your belief when I came."

"Be specific," the Dal said.

"Simple. Need pairs. One male, one female."

Dame Penne looked at him in dismay and disbelief. "But . . ." she began.

"True," Umber said. "They relatives. From planet of origin, called Monde. In species names called *terra*. We sexual. They like us. They sexual. Sorry. Not know of belief of Godworship that it bad other beings be sexual. Unfortunately a fact. *Lynx rufus*, too, but they now dead."

They all stared at him. He raised his hands and dropped them. "Even grass species have male and female part," he said. "Standard way on Monde. Have studied places where three, even four sexes needed for reproduction. Sorry. It so. You in backwater out here. Not hear. Godworship shield you in idea we only one sexual."

"I regret to say I had no idea we would have to hear anything quite this filthy," Dal Polon said. "I will go now. We will have to deal with this soon enough. Leda, it's wonderful to see you again, but I deeply regret it had to be in such a scene. I'm sorry, Gorbie. It seems to me all the good you may have done with the droc plague is nullified. If you survive this when word gets out, it'll be a miracle."

"That bad?" Umber said with a slight, disbelieving smile.

"How dare you smile, you filth! Making us bestial, nullifying the distinction God gave us!" Leda shrieked out.

"Can't change way things are. They are that way," Umber said. "No Godworship can change it. I thought God made it this way."

"Umber," Dame Penne said. "Please don't push this. You have no idea how unutterably loathsome what you've just said is to us. How can we eat the flesh of drocs if we are like drocs?"

"Not like droc except in chemical structure. Like being from own planet."

"Uuuhhh," Leda moaned.

"I find this reaction very peculiar," Umber said in Onic.

Leda mumbled a translation of what he had said almost automatically, then, with a scream, leapt across the room at him and beat him with her fists. He threw his hands up to protect his face. She hit him in the stomach and groin, and with a groan, he collapsed.

"This not change fact," he said from the floor, curling up to protect himself as she kicked at him.

"Leda, you will stop this instant!" Dame Penne shouted. Her daughter ignored her, but crying in a high voice, Pell ran into the room and covered Umber with his small body.

"Get away!" Leda shrilled, kicking her son hard in the ribs. Pell shrieked in pain.

Umber rolled to his feet, nose bleeding, saying, "No hurt boy." He grabbed Leda's wrists and held them as she struggled to kick him.

"Umber! Let her go," Dame Penne yelled. He released her. They glared at each other a moment, and then she turned and ran from the room.

"Umber, she's going for a laser," Pell gasped from the floor.

He swept the room with his eyes. "I go so she cool down," he said to Dame Penne, and headed for the entrance as Uji stepped into it with a stunner. Umber rolled aside as Uji pointed it and in one motion came up under the drocherder, hefted him, and threw him into the wall, grunting out, "Here, you spy!"

Umber turned to see Leda race back into the room with a heavy laser pack. As he dodged for the entrance, she threw the beamer to her shoulder and touched off a slicing beam that left a flaming line across the wall and door slide.

Umber cried out, the beam searing his back as he leapt through the entrance and fled, still weak, toward the droc pans. As Leda ran across the room, Pell shoved the low table in front of her and she fell across it. She rolled to her feet, grimacing in pain, turned to hit him, and saw him looking at her from the floor with blood in his mouth. Suddenly her fury was flooded over with guilt and shame. She rubbed her shins, saying, "I . . . didn't . . ."

"You did, you unhappy woman," her mother said, rising to kneel over Pell. "Don't move now, little one," she said to him. "You'll be all right. Phant, douse the wall fire there, please," she called to the old servant. "You, Leda, call the infirm hoverskimmer. Uji—are you . . . do you want to go, too?"

The drocherder leaned against the wall. "I—no. I only need to rest, Dame Penne."

"Call the herders to bring Umber back, please," Dame Penne said. "He'll need to go to the infirm, too, with that burn."

"Pell, I . . ." Leda began.

"Get away from me!" the boy yelled.

"You'd better get away," Dame Penne said.

"Please, what is going on?" Dal Penne interjected.

"It's all right, dear Gyro," Dame Penne said. "It'll all be taken care of."

"One thing that will be taken care of will be that Gorbie," Leda said through gritted teeth, and grabbing her laser pack, she raced out the door, ignoring her mother's cries.

Leda ran heavily out the road to the droc pans. She passed Umber's platform, sweeping the area with her eyes. The drocherders had already lit the whole complex. Thinking she should get beyond the pans to the vine tangles along the river, Leda chose a berm and raced along it. Suddenly, ahead of her, a wall of drocs lifted their arms, beaks clashing. She heaved herself to a stop. Turning, she saw drocs beginning to climb the berm behind her. She raced back, at one point leaping over a waving droc arm. At the far end of the berm she met Wahn.

"No use, ma'am," he said. "They've blocked all the ways. I've never seen them angry like this." He paused. Behind them they could hear the clack and snap of droc beaks all over the pans.

☐ XVIII Umber Gone

EARLY the next morning Dame Penne's visiphone sounded as she was feeding Gyro. Dal Polon's face bloomed on the plate. "Please forgive me for calling so early, Dame Penne," he began. "LSHQ wants to talk to the Gorbie—about early warnings. They are alarmed."

"He's gone, Casio," she said simply. "Leda became infuriated, and he fled for his life. The drocs blocked pursuit. The herders are out looking for him now."

"What about his collar?"

"Every time we'd renew it, he'd nullify it. I don't know how he did it. But I came to trust him and left it on simply for appearance."

"You mean he . . ."

"True. He could have attacked and killed us at any time. He upended our chief herder in two moments on his way out the entrance. He didn't hurt us, though. He could be trusted, and he knew I came to know it. And Pell."

"I—I regret I left so quickly. It was the obscenity of what he said. So gross."

Dame Penne shrugged. "He didn't see it that way. Perhaps I'm less subject to revulsion. My hands are so often in the clay. I admit to shock, of course."

"To think that we are a part of the beast world, cannibalizing our brothers."

"We needn't rehearse it, Casio. To the point. Pell is in Matted Plain Infirm. Leda hurt him, almost by accident, as he protected Umber. She's there trying to make peace with him. It seems he began to confuse Umber with his father."

"But . . ."

"It happened. Leda learned her violence from Rad, most of

it in self-defense. Ironic, isn't it? In an odd way I almost think she associates Umber with Rad's unmanageability. We'll need intelligence help in recovering Umber. But perhaps we should let him stay in the tangles until the public gets over their fury at his importation of *Marmota*. And the other thing."

"I can't imagine it's true."

"It is. Umber is a trained biologist. I have no doubt of it. I spent much of the night trying to get used to the idea. Now I'm weary as winter, and once Gyro is fed, I'm going back to my chamber."

"Intelligence will be out to see you today, I'm sure. They want to know anything he has to say about early warning."

"Yes, well, send them to the herders. I'll be asleep."

"Hello, Casio," Gyro said, squinting at the plate.

"Hello, and good-bye, Dal Penne," Polon returned. Then the picture faded.

"Gorbie cause trouble? I'll see to him," Gyro muttered.

"Yes, Gy, but let's get some rest first," Dyann Penne replied, summoning Phant.

A short while later in Matted Plain, in a large, unadorned stone structure shaped vaguely like an upswept official's hat, the seven people of the Regional Godworship Council sat around a polished stone table in conference. All were dressed in magenta drapesuits, wholly unicolored, except for the old man at the end of the table. His suit was heavily braided with silver cords. Dully gleaming white disks hung around its bib. The seven read the lightboards in front of them in silence. At last the old man said, "You have scanned the report. I regard it as one of direst consequences. It confirms my suspicions that this whole droc plague craze was only a hoax on the part of a sworn enemy."

A murmur of assent went around the table. "We're dealing with a Dal family, though," a woman near the old man said.

"They nonetheless have to accede to the decisions of Godworship Council, as all do. Furthermore, we have never heard any dissent from Dame Penne, and her daughter, as I have it, is an advanced member in off-world services."

"That's so," said another. "But her treatment of her son does not . . ."

"It was an accident. She was attacking the Gorbie in quite justified outrage," another woman said. "The point is, what are we going to do?"

"I believe the Gorbie must be sacrificed publicly," the first woman said.

"You mean executed?" the old chairman asked, eyebrows raised.

"Exactly. He's done too much damage already," she returned. She still showed a slight rash from the strain C fever.

"It seems extreme. He could be incarcerated where no one would hear his views," said a younger man near the foot of the table.

"I would tend to agree with you," the chair said. "I have a proposal with regard to his . . . monster importation. It must be captured and shown for what it is—a ghastly genetic modification done by the Gorboducs to confute our theology. An experiment using, if it can be imagined, human genes."

"But is that really so?" the young man asked mildly. The others all turned to stare at him. "It's just a question," he added.

"What other explanation have you?" a jowly man across the table asked. "The theology is clear. It has been established by the facts for centuries now. Nothing has ever been able to confute it. Even what we know of the creatures in the Sea of Cruel Mouths shows it true. The Gorboducs themselves have shown by their behavior that they are perversions, not true humans, devilish creations. How could it be otherwise than that they would add to their perverse nature by their own perverse creations?"

"Perhaps," the young man said, "we could capture one of these creatures and have an anatomist we trust dissect it. The analysis and treatise would establish the truth of our theology. Such a person would have to be chosen with immense care, though."

The chairman's eyes narrowed. "That's a thought, Itle. I know just the individual, too. Not bad. But to our present problem. We need to act. We need a popular demonstration, a march to Potsherd Sump demanding the surrender of the Gorbie."

"He has fled."

"Yes, of course. Intelligence has given us everything. It doesn't matter if we get him now. What matters is that we sway opinion entirely in our direction. He's popular since this plague nonsense. But it's very easy to flip opinion over. We know this, don't we? In fact, it would be harder if he'd been forgotten."

"Don't you think we ought to clear all this with Central Church?"

"My dear woman, most of what I say has come from Choicity. I've been in conversation with them for over a tenthday."

"Well, if they ordered it, why are we even conferring?"

"They would like your concurrence, of course."

"Of course they have it," a younger woman said. "Let's not lose more time. Obedience is a chief virtue, no matter what the sacrifice."

That morning at Matted Plain Infirm, Leda Penne waited to see her son. The door glided open, and a physician emerged. He glanced at her, then looked down. "He's not in pain, but he shouldn't move his body much for now," he said. "You cracked his rib some."

Leda winced. "He got in the way as I was struggling with the alien," she said.

The physician raised his eyebrows.

"The boy may have given you a different version, but he's excited and—"

The physician turned and began to walk away. "But may I see him?" Leda continued.

The man turned around. "That's up to the boy," he replied. "He wants to be sure you won't hurt him again."

"I told you—"

"What you said does not accord with the facts as I know them. It is now my duty to defend the boy. Ah. You're angry again. Your son said that would be a problem."

"Dal Penne will have something to say about this."

"We all know Dal Penne is not himself, and Dame Penne has already conferred with me on the matter."

Leda turned away and almost began to leave but hesitated. "All right. What do you expect of me?" she asked softly.

"We will visually monitor your conversation, and if necessary, we will intervene. In any case, the infirm has filed a state abuse charge. That is routine and our duty. If you are found guilty, it will involve therapy before you will be permitted to resume your parental duties."

"I will fight that, of course."

"Your choice. I have heard the provocation. The Gorbie's wild claims. That may go in your favor. It must have been a shock."

Leda's jaw tightened. "Such filth!" she spit. "And my son attracted to him, wanting to protect him."

"But the Gorbie didn't resist you."

"He . . . no. He hurt Uji."

"Who tried to stun him. He didn't hurt you, though." Leda did not answer. "And if he had not fled, you would have killed him." Again she did not answer. "And as it is, you must have wounded him severely with laser fire sufficient to ignite the wall."

"What has all this to do with—" Leda began.

"Simply that your son goes over and over it. He almost saw his mother kill a man coldly, a person he holds to be honorable. You will have to be used to that idea, because you'll hear it from him, and if you flare up, we will remove you. Is that clear?"

"It . . . how dare you claim—"

"For the present, the boy is our ward. We don't wish him hurt further in our care—or after. Do not confuse Pell with your unfortunate husband."

"You think that? You've put that in your report?"

"It is your son's opinion."

"Rad abused me terribly. I . . . ."

"Your son said that, too. But your son has tried to love you, and now he fears you. It wasn't the Raider that did this. You have to realize that. In spite of everything, he seems to be a remarkable man—if he's still alive."

Leda whirled on him. "Oh, he's alive. He's like a plague himself. He'll turn up again. He's even turned our drocs against us. You should have seen them rearing up, ready to devour me."

"Before he came, the drocs were neither for nor against

any of us. Your son told me with great delight of talking with them."

"That's nonsense."

The physician reached out and touched her arm. "Please," he said. "You must see it's true. The evidence is all there. All it has to face is prejudice against it. Is it so important to be right in spite of everything? I've been told by one academician that the Raider knows more about drocs than anyone else on Landsdrum. The academics have the droc game now. They're playing it." The physician paused. "I see you've set your face against it. I won't go on."

"May I see my son?"

"Will you agree to our conditions?"

"Yes."

"Good day, then. Please be kind to him." He spun on his heel and strode away. Leda watched him go with a strange uneasiness. What if she were wrong? She did not like the feeling. An orderly slid the glider open for her, and she entered. Pell lay propped across the room. He was looking away.

"Pell," she said, approaching. He neither turned nor replied. "Pell, I'm sorry."

"You would have killed him," the boy said.

"He's an alien, an enemy. He—" She paused, seeing his profile change. "Yes. I would have. Everyone is reminding me of that. They all think I'm wrong—in spite of the horrible things he said."

"What if they're true?"

"Pell, not for me, but for your soul's sake, you can't say that."

"Everything else he's said has been true. And now he's hurt and out in the tangles, and everybody's going to be hunting for him. And I hear the Godworship people will be after him. What will he do?"

"I . . . he will get along."

"How? He can't."

"He has so far."

"But we—we weren't kind to him. We made him sleep out on the platform even in the rain. We got better. We gave him a fabric shelter. And now what is he doing? They'll hurt him. You'd hurt him, too."

"He'll just have to watch out for himself, Pell."

"How can he, all burned? I have everyone here to take care of me. He is out somewhere. Is it raining?"

"No." Leda saw the whole conversation somehow out of control. Irrelevantly, almost against her will, as though she meant her son, she said, "I'll help him."

Pell turned stiffly toward her on the bed. "You will?" he said. "How?"

"I . . . don't know. I'll think of something."

"Intelligence wants him. They want information about early warning."

"Well, he said he'd give it."

"You don't think they'd hurt him?"

"No. Why should they? They want their information."

"I mean after."

"They . . . I don't think they could. By law he's still father's . . . slave." Everything in her disliked that word, having seen convict slavery on Garre.

"But Dal Polon allowed that."

"He may still, you know."

"No. I think he'll lose his position now after what Umber said. About the animals. Being like us. Having a sex."

Leda jumped to her feet. "Pell, don't let me ever hear you say that again. Ever," she said.

Pell looked puzzled. "I thought it was true," he said.

An orderly appeared in the entrance. "It's all right," Leda said to the man. The glider slid shut.

"They think you're going to hurt me," Pell said.

Leda sat down. "No. I won't. But that's horrible. It can't be true. It's too ugly and obscene. I can't have you exposed to it."

Pell turned away again. "Everything else that Umber has said is true, though, isn't it?" he announced.

Leda looked at him bleakly, then covered her face with her hands.

Soon after she arrived back at Potsherd Sump, Leda heard the shouts and horns of the Godworshipers' demonstration. Some five thousand, racing their landrollers around the grounds, finally formed up in front of the house and began a chant: "Give us the Gorbie. Give us the Gorbie. Rid us of the Gorbie. Rid us of the Gorbie. Out with heresy. Out with heresy. Give us the Gorbie. Give up the Vandal. Give up the Raider."

Several Groundarmy hoverskimmers arrived to keep order, and independent crews mingled with the Godworship news crews to take impressions and convey them to the rest of the colony. A part of the crowd swarmed out toward the droc pans to see the rebellious drocs, but they were blocked by a line of Groundarmy soldiers, most of whom clearly sympathized with them. Banter passed between the groups.

Inside, Leda asked her mother to go out and speak to them. "No, Leda. I won't do that. A crowd can turn bad quickly. This one seems amused, but that can change. I have a strange feeling about this."

"Another of your feelings?"

"They're only half-convinced of what they're doing. A part of them already has decided Umber is right. This internal confusion can become fury."

Leda stared at her mother. "Oh, of course he's right, you mindless rock-oogling frump," Dame Penne added. "Isn't it obvious? I don't like the idea any more than you do. Ah, forgive me. I'm upset. All of this is too much. I hope Gyro is sedated enough. I've asked Phant to serve them all sea cakes and stem wine."

"What?"

"Yes. You forget. We have all the wealth from the water fences and droc worms. It may dent us, but it won't break us. And I've invited the Reverend Pio Kardeen to come at my expense and address the assembly. Here. On the front gravel garden—which Phant will enjoy raking out, because he will enjoy the occasion and his part in it."

"I can't believe this. So expensive."

Dame Penne laughed. "Only five thousand to feed. And, oh, yes, I invited the Peninsula Singers, with their orchestra. It isn't often one can entertain such an assembly with religious music."

Leda gasped. "Couldn't you find any more expensive—" she began.

"No, or I would have brought them. It is less than having

them break up the conservatory, burn the house, attack the drocs, drain the pans. They'll have their food, their preaching, their entertainment. They'll have done their bit for Godworship."

"And what if Kardeen whips them into a frenzy?"

"She won't. Not only is she a gentleperson—she's so deep into textual studies lately that she'll bore the rabble and interest the intellectual, but she doesn't whip up crowds into froth anymore. That is, any frothier froth than they are in. They're bubbles now. She may congeal them into a meringue."

"Is this a time for jokes?"

"Jokes?" Dame Penne turned to her daughter. "I'm furious. That pious rahnsucker, Chair Eisen, has thought this all up. He doesn't give dripping droc sweat for anything but his own position and the position of Matted Plain Synod in the Godworship Confederation. This has nothing to do with God or worship or truth or justice or prayer or spirituality or the principles of our planetary religion or common charity and decency. Now, if you can make yourself heard over that hooting out there, tell me. How is Pell and what are you going to do?"

"I . . . somehow I promised to . . . help the alien."

Dame Penne shrilled a long laugh. "How? What will you do now?"

"I don't know," Leda said, shrinking. "All of this is so unreal. My whole life has been unreal since I married Rad, but it gets more surrealistic all the time."

Dame Penne walked over to her daughter and put her arms around her. "Maybe you could go and find him in the tangles."

"In the tangles?"

"You're sturdy enough. It'll get you away. You'll prove to Pell you're trying."

"I don't have to prove to my own son . . ." Leda began. "All right. I do. Groundarmy is scanning the area already, and Lower Space is taking heat readings as well."

"Maybe they'll find him. I doubt it. Unless you burned him too badly, he'll avoid all that. He's no drooling dummy, you know. Listen, Kardeen has started. Now they'll be compelled to gather and listen. After all, they came out here because they're so religious."

"Oh, mother."

Umber had driven his hurt body all night, hoping to get beyond the search area. He lay in the shallow hole he had scooped in a gravelly bank, with a thick vine roof over him on which he had piled gravel. As well as he could, he reached behind himself to rub droc salve on the deep welt on his back to keep dirt out of it. He groaned and cried out with the pain, then held his breath as he heard the high whine of an approaching hoverskimmer. He drew well back under the low gravel roof of his shelter and lay still. The craft swept overhead and whined away into the distance. Once again he started reciting numbers in Gorboduc. It began to rain.

☐ XIX   In the Tangles

THE Matted Plain Godworship Council met again the next morning. Chair Eisen was both pleased and puzzled. "So great a gathering of the faithful and such hospitality to them by the Pennes is gratifying, but, somehow, little was accomplished. Still, we made our protest, and it was significant." He looked around, satisfied with his gesture. One young man, Itle, began a reply but thought better of it. The meeting soon broke up.

That morning, Uji, silent and straight-mouthed, drove Leda across the ford in the River of Good Intent, then north. She had him stop across the Darkeye Stream from the bank with the three stain lines in it. She scanned them for a time. "I did do an initial study of all that," she said to the drocherder. He did not reply. "The filthy Gorbie was right. Drive me on, please." Uji lurched forward. An LS hoverskimmer whined slowly by overhead.

Above the stretch of tangles, Leda asked Uji to stop again. She climbed up and stood on the top of the landroller, scanning the tangles, which stretched along the shore of Purple Lake, then, farther north, where the land flattened, fanned outward to occupy a vast area of land below the Vulftrok Mountain range. "That's a lot of territory," she remarked. Uji grunted noncommittally. "Uji," she said. "Don't be mad at me. I haven't done anything to you."

"No."

"What is it, then?"

"He called me a spy. The Gorbie."

"Why pay attention? You were good enough to him. You can't help it if he's—"

"I did spy. Dal Polon told me to. Dame Penne agreed."

"Then you only did as you were told."

"He knew it all along. It feels bad, you know."

"So you care about his opinion?"

"No. It rankles me that he knew it. That he could be able to have . . . contempt. I helped him."

"He causes trouble wherever he goes, Uji. Let it go."

"There was the droc plague, ma'am. He was right about that. We were lucky he came along."

Leda snorted. "How lucky? Look at me. I have to go try to find him because he hypnotized my son. How lucky?"

"It all adds up to luck, ma'am. Let me help you with that." He hefted her pack. "You going to carry all that?"

"Oh, Uji, it isn't rock samples. You be careful, now." She briefly clasped his hand, turned her back, and headed west toward the edge of the tangle. It loomed above her, rank and thick, almost vibrant, although its winter dormancy had almost arrived. Behind her she heard the high whirr of the landroller as Uji turned it to go back to the Sump.

After three days of picking her way west toward the shore and then north, she had found nothing. She felt a strange freedom, though, despite the entangling vines and the thick mud of the meandering streams in the tangle. It was like being adrift, free of trouble, like doing close examination of a planetary surface, in the old way, alone, far from Rad, from concerns.

Twice she encountered Groundarmy patrols hacking their way along. They were surly and rough, wishing to be home, seeing no point to such a primitive search. She felt uneasy around them and made sure she left them well behind before sundown. She pressed north in a late afternoon rainstorm, looking for a thick corkscrew vine on any slight rise to fasten her shelter to. At last she yearned to go home. Then she saw Pell's face as though it were in front of her. It disappeared and became a *platinus* leaf again. She shivered. It would be good to go home again. She knew she was punishing herself. Well, maybe I need a little punishment, she thought.

Not long after, a Groundarmy patrol lay resting near a muddy stream, angry with the whole chilly, wet manhunt. The men lay back on the scant matcreeper, staring up through the roof of vines overhead. One leaned up. "What's that?" he whispered.

His companion looked. "What?"

"I saw something—over there. Something small."

"Oh come on, there aren't any leatherarms this far from the lake, Decon—*Ahhhhh!*" He jumped up. Something scurried. "The Gorbie's monster. I saw it. Over there."·

"Where?"

The men held silence, gripping weapons. Soon the monster came hopping toward them, the front of its face wobbling. Occasionally it would stop and stretch itself upward, holding little arms against a light buff chest, staring at them with eyes nearly black. It also had what must have been ears, long as a third finger and, like the rest of the creature, hair-covered, except on the inside. When the sunlight caught those appendages and shone through them, they glowed pinkish, and the soldiers could see veins in them.

"Did you ever see anything so ugly?" one man asked.

"Hush," the field leader said. "It's coming. Walon, stunner at ready."

"Yes, sir," the man replied.

"Quiet, now."

The animal, used to people and wanting company, hopped

into the middle of the still group, sat up, then stretched forward, sniffing a man's walkboot, long whiskers fanned out.

"What do I do?" the man said.

"Grab it," another whispered.

"Not me," the man said.

Another man rolled toward it and reached out. Several others lunged for it. The small animal burst away, bounced over a thick vine root, flashing a white, fluffy tail, and was gone.

"I touched it," one man said, looking at his fingers.

"Crime, what was it like?" another asked.

"I don't know. Soft and warmish."

"Slimy?"

"No. Dry. Like hair."

"Maybe that's because it was hair," another said.

"Crimesloggers," the field leader said. "Will you shut it? All right. You people sit down and be still."

"What for?"

"For it to come back, droolylip. It came before."

"That was before we scared it, sir."

"We're not going to catch it crawling through these thickets. It's looking for its Gorbie. Let it come."

One man made a face at another, who nodded slyly back. Better to be lying around than slogging through the tangle. A third closed his eyes and soon began to snore. Somebody nudged him, and he jerked awake. He looked around and saw the others grinning at him. He shook his head, put it down, and closed his eyes.

After almost a measure they heard a scurry, and soon the small creature reappeared. It hopped over one man's outstretched legs into the middle of the group. The men did not move. The creature did a quick hop, turning halfway around. One man began to chuckle in his throat. The creature turned, lifting its ears and turning its head sideways to the sound. The man caught the field leader's glower and kept still. The creature thumped its long hind foot on the ground, turning its head. Then it crept forward toward one man's hand, stretching, stretching toward it, what must have been its nose wobbling, ears folded over its back.

The man did not move. The creature hopped forward and

hunched itself by the man's hand, then hopped over his forearm and nestled in by his elbow. It lifted its face toward him. In an easy motion, he brought the other arm around and picked the creature up.

It thrashed wildly as the others crowded in to see it. "Aaaah," the man said. "It's got toenails like teeth. Somebody hold its feet."

"All right, men, in this gearbag," the field leader said. "You, Ruar, touch up HQ. Looks like we've got our monster."

"Some monster," one man said. "It's like a toy."

The academy gained possession of the creature only by strong argument and the backing of the new Dal, Anel Boornten, who was an academy supporter. Godworship Council demanded that the monstrosity be destroyed immediately, then given a detailed anatomic study by Professor Oundesi, an elder. The former Dal, Casio Polon, contributed to the confusion by claiming that it must be *Sylvilagus* not *Marmota*, because its tracks differed so markedly from the ones the Gorbie had admitted were those of a *Marmota*. It could not breed, he claimed, so it ought not to be killed. "You can't examine the habits of a dead body," he said. The academy agreed. Not wanting to appear intransigent, the Godworship Council finally concurred, voicing the strong opinion, though, that the public not be exposed to its perversion.

But the public would not be denied, and after everyone had seen the holos, soon the Matted Plain Center sported small *Sylvilagus* dolls that could be bought for children. Godworship objected strongly, and through their influence, Groundarmy marched through the center and confiscated the furry dolls. After that they were objects to be coveted, shown secretly to friends, examined quietly in family groups, and buried again in private cabinets.

In spite of attempts at secrecy, word got around that *Sylvilagus* was a male, that he was affectionate in an offhanded way, and that he could be goaded to anger. At such times he tended to rush around and stamp his long, furry hind feet. He also yawned occasionally with his ridiculously small mouth and sometimes scratched his cheek with a big foot. He liked to dig and ate *platinus* leaves as well as corkscrew vine shoots.

Some of Umber's mysterious grass was given to him, and he ate it with pleasure.

So when a Groundarmy patrol finally lasered a *Marmota*, the people greeted the news with overwhelming curiosity and tended to mourn its death. It was turned over to Professor Oundesi for study.

After six eightdays heavy winter rains and some light snow began to fall. Groundarmy called off its search for Umber, assuming he must have perished in the cold. They had seen no fires. He had no food, though some had been found missing from a Groundarmy dropcamp. Perhaps, they thought, he had slept too close to the lake and a leatherarm had curled around him and drawn him into the water.

Then, as the drocs were brought into the leafheaps in their low barns, for winter, Casio Polon, musing in his study, suddenly saw his wall plate turn on and a message blink onto it, superimposed over the public drama there.

Dal Polon—Time to remove droc worm from designated droc. Soon leaves of worm shell split, drop away with thread stage of many young inside. This must occur only in lab. Threads saved, distributed to new centers, on mature droc, only on joint of large backplates, kept. Destroy any excess. Not good any droc forced to harbor many *Unipurp. quatrilob.*, especially over winter. All mature droc get small booster dose when removed from leaf barn. Remember, paralysis gland does not renew, nor do they retain immunity. All mature droc must be harvested next season. One exception each herd to teach young. That one must get frequent booster. Important to explain this to droc. It is for safety of young droc. They understand if explained right. Let Wahn teach how. This true all over Landsdrum. When droc under stress, sometimes reproduce in splash. Look for unusual mutants carefully among young. Think now the leatherarms from some former splash. Anatomy indicates that. Do not let any ridiculous fools stop the dissemination of this information. Vital. Umb.

Casio sighed. Things were hard with him at the moment, but he still had the earthbeast, and it was growing mightily in his horticultural houses. It only awaited the proper moment for introduction to the market. So Umber was alive. He had assumed as much. That would mean a renewal of the Ground-army search for him, but Casio suspected it would be only a gesture.

It would also mean Leda would drive herself out again on her search for the alien. Casio had seen her only once since her return. She had grown gaunt from her time in the tangles but seemed strangely renewed. She remained remote from Pell, declining to undergo either examination or therapy as requested by Matted Plain Infirm. Casio saw this as a punishment for both mother and son, but given Leda's nature, it seemed almost inevitable.

Casio tapped his stylus on his knee, smiled to himself and then recklessly inserted the commands that would superimpose Umber's message on every commercial screen in the district and hold it there for three hundred moments. They can't rescind that, he thought, as he dumped the source line and sent paths for the tracers to twenty-seven different possible points of origin.

Almost immediately his visiphone lit up. It was Dal Baats, angry. "What have you done now to discredit the party? How could you manage such stupidity?" Baats yelled.

"What are you talking about?" Casio said, astonished.

"What? The message! The message from the Gorbie!"

"What message?" Casio asked.

The next day two hundred Groundarmy regulars arrived and made a thorough search of the Polon estate. Umber, of course, was not found. When they finished, Casio Polon served them hot steam brew and piles of small cakes. They ate and drank with relish and left thwarted but satisfied.

Later, his visiphone signaled again. It was Dyann Penne. "You should thank me for the idea of feeding the inquisitors," she remarked dryly.

"Oh, I do," Casio said. "But for one thing."

"What's that?"

"These cakes were made of earthbeast root—*Grandaradix gentila*, as our despised exile has it."

"And you didn't explain?"

"No one asked."

"And if they have unscrambled this transmission?"

"I doubt they will have. But if so, the cakes are all successfully digested, I'm sure. How is Leda?"

"She left again this morning. Futile, I think. But it seems to be therapeutic for her."

"Yes. I hope she finds him. We need the early warning."

Leda walked straight north near the upper edge of the tangle, wearing a wintersuit and moving slowly because of her extra gear. The third day she saw a strange track, unlike any walkboot. She stooped and studied it. She was sure it was Umber's. He was wearing some kind of fabric on his feet, probably padded. But the track was old. She tried to follow it, but it pointed toward an area of low matcreeper and was obscured. Finally she gave up.

Ahead, where a jutting angle of the mountains nearly reached the open sea, beyond the arc of islands and peninsula that formed Purple Lake, Leda saw a chance to camp near a rock tumble high over the surf, protected from wind but in full view of a large area. She inflated her shelter and stooped inside, leaving the entrance open toward sunset, but in her fatigue, sleep reached her before twilight. She jerked awake in full dark, for a moment unable to tell where she was. She flared her pocket light. The shelter entrance was drawn closed. On the shelter floor near her an old *platinus* leaf was inscribed, as though by a knife point, with a message. Squinting, she read it.

You not safe here. Even this high leatherarms sense you. Move camp now.

She shook her head, then suddenly came awake. She fumbled for her stunner and, finding it, held it in her hand, scarcely breathing, and listened. For a long time she heard the light hiss of the wind and the dull crump and roll of surf far below. A flaw of rain pattered across the shelter. She grew sleepy again but fought it. Then she heard another sound, a slight scraping, as though of a toe on gravel. She held her breath. It persisted.

She should have moved immediately. She had never seen a wild leatherarm but knew them as oceanic predators with ropelike arms that sometimes stretched astonishing distances. At night they would rise out of the water and stretch landward through the tangles or across the mats and seek prey there. Even large drocs had been lost to them. It was easier in general to concede the shore to them.

She thought Umber was trying to frighten her away, but then the surface of her shelter dented in. The dent moved on the sheet as though someone had drawn a forefinger across it. Suddenly she jumped as a heavy thud outside jarred the ground. It was followed by the rolling and spattering of rocks and a slight scrambling.

Leda parted the entrance and shined her light out. She saw a length of leatherarm, crushed off, flipping and twisting on the slope. Then, as she watched, it slowly slid off the shoulder of the precipice and clattered downward in the darkness.

She crawled out of the shelter and stood in the wind, her nightsocked feet hurting with sharp pebbles and cold. She shined her light down the steep fall to the sea but could see nothing but the blinking lines of rain across its beam.

She sighed and closed her eyes, then yelled out, "Umber, Umber! Crime take you, you greasy Gorbie. Come and help me."

A gust of cold wind seemed to whip away her words. Almost shrieking, she yelled again, "Umber, Umber, Umber!"

"Not nice to call me names," a deep voice said quite close to her. She shined her light, and, squatting, the Gorboduc held up a hand against it. "Not nice to blind people with light, either. We move camp, all right? Not safe here even now."

Leda felt limp. She aimed her light at the ground and did not reply. "I'm glad you finally woke," Umber said in Onic. "I was getting cold out here. You pack first. I'll wait and help with the shelter. I have a good place for you. What creatures those leatherarms are! I'd like to examine one."

"Come inside," she said.

"Thank you. Not for long. The predator'll be back. He has

three more long front arms, not much brains, and friends. Pack quick. We can half deflate the shelter. We don't have to go far, but higher. Then I'll go. All right? You won't . . . hurt me, will you?"

"No," she said dully, stuffing things into her pack. She paused a moment, looking around.

"I have your lightpad," Umber said. "I need to work out the early warning. You must take it directly to Lower Space HQ. Give it to the commander alone. No one else must know."

"Why?" she began, then added, "Oh, all right."

They gathered her things and started up the slope in the rain, Umber carrying the shelter in his arms. She could see its gray shape ahead dimly. Finally he rounded a rock jag and threw his burden down. She set down her pack and sought out the air pump canister as he held the light for her. The structure rose, and they felt for the anchors and drove them home.

"Come inside."

"Must go."

"Come inside. I . . . please come inside. Please."

"You won't hurt me?"

"No. Come."

Only once they had crawled in and Leda had quickly unpacked and arranged her sleeper did she look at Umber. He had let his beard grow. She was momentarily startled, because Landsdrum men did not have beards, having them erased at puberty. His hair was combed and braided back as before. His cheekbones protruded more than usual, and his eyes lay in dark hollows. He was dressed mostly in pieces of Groundarmy issue with improvisations, such as his fabric-bound feet.

He saw her looking at him and said, "Groundarmy supply me well. Careless with many things. I have caches all over." He grinned. She looked away. "What do you want with me?" he asked. "To kill me? Please. It's truly important I not be killed yet."

She looked down. "My feet are soaked and frozen," she said irrelevantly. He slid down, stripped off her wet night-socks, and put her feet inside his coat against his undertunic. He rubbed her ankles and lower calves, massaging them upward to encourage circulation. "Had to do this once on

Klluum's north island," he said. "To an old biologist who had been out too long in search of a crawling plant known as *Etishus umbella*. Now. Please. What do you want with me? I'll give you the early warning. I mustn't die just yet."

"You keep talking about dying, being killed. Stop it."

"Tell me. I can't stay. They'll detect all the heat. At least they'll think you're out here with someone."

She snorted. "You can't go. Not yet. You have to give me back my son."

He looked at her, frowning slightly. She explained what had happened, honestly and fully, ending, "I know I wasn't rational. I lost my husband, you know. I loved him. Yet I hated him. He was so cruel. He saw in me a way of getting at the Dal system, shutting out most of the people from power. And yet I think he loved me in a kind of way."

"He'd be a fool not to."

She looked at him. "How can you say that? After all I've done? The trouble I've been to my family?" she whispered.

"You've been trouble, all right." He looked at her with a slight smile. "But you'd be easy to love. I say that dispassionately. Space has lengthened my life. Everything is temporary for the traveler. But even so, I have lost everything. So I'm free to do and talk as I please, not caring, except to stay alive for the moment."

"Why do you keep talking about dying? The forces won't kill you. Lower Space wants the early warning. You know that."

"They want it, though they aren't sure it exists. And they want to be rid of me because Godworship wants to be rid of me. I don't mind dying, but not yet."

"Are you warm enough?"

"Mostly."

"I'm going to get in my sleeper. Give me back my ankles, please. And thank you. You put my coat over you."

"I can't stay," he said, but he made no move to go. "What am I do to about Pell?" he asked.

"Come see him. Show him you're all right. Tell him you and I have made peace."

"Have we?"

"I have. I . . . did I hurt you much?"

"Lit my back on fire," he said. "Mostly all right now."

"Let me see," she said, rolling toward him.

"No need."

"Please. Let me see."

Umber rolled onto his stomach and loosened his tunic. She undid it and slid it up, exposing his lower back, muscular and shot across with a deep scar, the center of which was still wet, still flaking. She drew in her breath. "Wait," she whispered. "I have some spraycover." Rummaging in her pack, she brought out a small canister and used it to spray across the wound. Then she let it dry, testing its edge with her fingertip. At last she slid his tunic down, smoothing it carefully. She lay back and stared at the ceiling. "You must hate me," she murmured.

"No," he said. "No point in that."

She reached out and stroked his hair. "I'm sorry," she said, simply and clearly. "I never knew I'd say that to a Gorbie, but I am. I feel . . . small."

"I . . . It doesn't matter. I'm better now," Umber said. "But please don't leave Pell again and go off-world. He has missed you very much. He won't say it, and he fears your anger, but he needs you. If you have to go to a mine somewhere, take him."

"It's no place for him."

"Then it isn't for you, either. You don't have to be so hard on yourself. Pell thinks you went to get away from your husband. But you don't have to do that anymore."

"He told you that?"

"Not outright, but in a way he did." Umber rolled over and looked at her. He was suddenly struck by the beauty of her slender face, brown eyes set in dark skin, framed by fine, light hair. She caught his gaze, and neither looked away.

"I'm sorry about your back," she said again.

Umber shut his eyes. "No need," he said. "I'll work out the early warning on the lightpad and give it back to you as soon as I can. It'll take a while."

"All right. LS wants it badly. And please come talk to Pell. He wants to be sure you're all right. What I did was a shock to him. More than I could have imagined." She paused. "Now I can imagine it, though—now you're a person. I mean a real person."

Umber looked at her. "Nobody told me you were beautiful," he said, adding, "Except Pell, of course, but boys can't be believed on the subject of their mothers. I saw a holo, but then, it was only a holo."

They were silent for a time. Umber said again, "I have to go," but he made no attempt to move. Leda looked at him a while as he lay there, his eyes open, blinking but looking at nothing. Then she winked out the light. Not long after, she heard the long breaths of his sleep. He stirred and turned his back to her, murmuring numbers in Onic. She wormed over to him and put an arm around him. Then, as though released from anxiety, she, too, fell asleep.

☐ XX   Umber and Leda

LEDA woke to find Umber gone, her hand still over the empty coat. Dawn light stretched across the horizon, pale and dull. She rose and found at the entrance to the shelter another *platinus* leaf with Umber's incised scrawl. "Please don't go home. Need to work on warning plan. I find you. Erase this."

She carefully scraped off the leaf surface, her hand shaking with the cold, then returned to her shelter, gnawed on a dried droc cake, and drank tea heated over her smallfurnace. A Groundarmy patrol whined by overhead, arced around, and studied her camp from above. She stood outside in the wind watching them, shading her eyes. They cruised away to the south.

Later, leaving her shelter, she returned to her first shelter site from the previous night. She could still scarcely believe the leatherarm could reach that high, but a faint track still showed below and a stain remained where it had pumped out juices when Umber's big stone had crushed off its limb. She contemplated the cliff and sea with strange feelings, scanned the shore northward, then picked her way over the hogback and spent much of the day walking the hill crest and talus slopes up the coast. She turned back only in time to reach her shelter in early dark.

She took the shelter down and moved it farther up the slope. That night she slept uneasily, hoping to hear Umber return, but he never came. Yet in the morning she found another thick *platinus* leaf by the shelter door, incised with a message.

Take up shelter, pack, sight bearing 36.24, climb until you hit low cliff. Message ready.

Leda took the sighting. It would be a long walk on a raw, overcast day. She got out her glasses, stepped up the magnification, but still saw nothing of significance. Then she packed slowly and carefully, heaved on her pack, and started off.

The sun had crossed the meridian, and she was in light snow before she reached the low cliff where it broke into a tumble of huge boulders. She rested against one, broached a rations tube, and slowly sucked its contents, looking around. A short whistle shrilled, and, looking farther up, she saw Umber waiting for her. Then he stepped behind a rock. She sighed and slogged up the slope toward him. Reaching the spot, she slid in between the boulders and, stooping down, crawled in under an overhang.

Umber squatted there. He eased off her pack and said, "Good. I have it all here. Early warning and options for strategy. Presents for Pell."

She crawled forward behind him into the shadow, then into darkness. The gap in the boulders turned and abruptly ended in a small nest. She rummaged for her light and flicked it on. She could see that Umber had lined the cupped chamber with matcreeper hauled from below. On a ledge, rows of Groundarmy rations stood neatly lined up. A crack in the far wall was stuffed with a Groundarmy-issue sleeper, and another lay on the floor.

"One moment, please, Leda," Umber said, leaning forward. He felt along the edge of her open coat, found a tiny lump, and worked it up toward her armpit. There he popped it out through a perspiration grommet and held it in his hand. "LS tracer, I think," he said.

She studied it, a little bewildered for a moment. He opened it with a fingernail edge, stared at it, and switched it off. Then he placed it in her palm. She examined it in the dim light and thrust it in her pocket. Then she looked at him. He had trimmed back his beard.

"It keeps me warm," he said, rubbing his cheek. "You want a drink? Groundarmy tea? I want to explain the material on the lightpad."

"Let me rest a half moment," she said. "It's quite a climb with the pack. What of the patrols? I left tracks. There is snow, after all."

"No tracer. Same as Groundarmy issue. I managed to get one. It's on below, in the tangles. Went on two measures ago. Only two patrols a day now, one at night. They're going fast, looking for tracers. The whole tangle south of here is a grid of sensors. Like this." Umber held out a large, gleaming button in his hand.

Leda took it and studied it, then handed it back. Then she stretched out on Umber's sleeper. "Let me rest a little," she said. "I've been . . . under a strain." Umber grinned at her. She felt strangely relaxed and soon slipped into a doze.

She awoke to find Umber gone. Her chrono showed it was nearly dusk. She ventured out a mental forefinger, as though asking a baby's hand to grip it. What was she doing? Was it guilt or numbness—or a strangely luminous attraction? Well, she knew it was the last, mostly.

She seemed to draw comfort from this strange, rough alien. He was like the first swallow of a cup of warm cerre on a bitterly cold evening after a day in the deep mines. He seemed to enwrap, enclose, and surround her, though with a secret reserve—a kind of shyness, or withholding, or fear. She withdrew the mental finger, smiling to herself, contented in this bizarre circumstance, wondering. Eventually she heard him worming his way into the cupped shelter. He dusted his Groundarmy walksuit and said, "I took the tracks up the ridge to where there is no snow. Just in case."

He slid forward and lay beside her. She reached out and smoothed his beard. He smiled up at her. She leaned forward and kissed his forehead, then his cheek, the bridge of his nose, its tip, and finally his mouth. She pulled back with a slight giggle. "It tickles," she whispered, then leaned in and kissed him again, feeling his response, his mouth open, his arm coming around her. She moved against him, and his leg came over hers. "Oh, Umber, what are we doing?" she said. He did not reply, but his arms slid around her and held her gently.

They lay still for a time. "I'm worried about this early warning," Umber said. "If Landsdrum uses it, it'll have to follow through. You aren't a fierce people, you know."

"Uuhh," Leda said. "What do you mean?"

"Your monitor patrol picked us off all right. We were just going by—one old freighter. The Raiders will be professionals—ferocious, implacable, merciless, evasive, practiced, resourceful, tricky."

"You make them sound unbeatable."

"Oh, no. They can be beaten. The farther out, the better. They will be superior to you. Their weapons will be superior. But you will be defending a home, and you can bring to bear much greater resources. They'll be on a sweep. They've been elsewhere; they'll have had some losses, and they'll be in need of a rest. They'll see you as easy pickings—as I understand it, you were last time."

"Before my time. Yes, I guess we were. But since then we've put a section of our budget into defense. We've researched and learned from elsewhere. We've grown."

"But will the force not flinch? If there is combat, a lot will die. A lot will die well. But let a few ships turn and run, and they'll be through. Or missiles'll be through. Giving them tribute would be better than letting them win in a fight. Does Landsdrum have the nerve?"

"I don't know. I think so."

"They'll be ferocious but calculating. They enjoy combat, but not being beaten. They resent well, but they wouldn't mount a major expedition only for revenge. They'd want a profit."

"Umber, can't this wait? Is this for me?"

"Ah. I'm sorry. I've worked hard on it. I'm full of it. You can read the lightpad before you go."

"You?"

"I'm afraid of the Godworship people. Because of *Marmota*."

"You'll come to see Pell?"

"Yes."

"Then what?"

Umber sighed. "I'd come back if I could," he said. "I think somebody'd kill me, though. Maybe later. If Casio regains power. I miss the Sump, believe it or not. I miss Pell; we'd begun to be friends. I'd like to see the droc, Tistan, before it dies. And your mother. I found some new glazes for her."

"Would you come for me?"

"I . . . I barely know you, really. I see you don't hate me so violently anymore."

"That was . . . I was mixed up."

"I'll have to go sometime. To get back to Esstrremadrr. To take *Marmota* if I can. To be sure they know all I do about drocs and droc plague. How would that be for you?"

"Is that possible?"

"Barely. Yes, I think."

"What will you do there? How long . . . Will you return?"

"No. I will not return. They will kill me."

"Kill? I don't understand."

"I violated code by staying alive in the first place. I know that, knew it then. I did it because of the plague, and *Marmota*, and the grrrazz. I lived so long away, I acquired some of the Klluumian gentleness, I think."

"You'll go even though they'll kill you?"

"Yes. I must."

She shoved him away and glared at him in the dim light. He looked down, took her hand, kissed it. She began to cry quietly but persistently. "All you've been through and you want to be killed?"

"Leda, could I reasonably have allowed us all to die when we first came? Could I? I don't see how I could even in spite of everything."

"No. You couldn't. But you won't be thanked."

"I've been thanked. Tistan has thanked me. And the other drocs. And Casio and Pell and Dame Penne, and now you. To see the others alive is to be thanked."

"Even Groundarmy and—"

"Of course. Cannot a biologist respect life?"

"Why can't I get something permanent? I would . . ." Leda paused and shook her head.

"I'm a space person, Leda. I've left everything. I'd be permanent for you if I could."

Leda moved to him, put her hands inside his coat, then his shirt. They kissed lingeringly. "Leda," Umber said. "What if there's a child?"

"There won't be," she said. "Shut up. Come here."

☐ XXI   Early Warning

LATER, Leda sat propped up against Umber, sipping tea and reading the lightpad, scrolling through it slowly, going back, frowning, moving forward again.

"This is more than an early warning system. It's a plan for alternative defense strategies," she said at last.

"Uuhh," Umber said, coming out of a reverie.

"They're really that bad, then," she said.

"Yes. They're professionally nasty."

Leda questioned him at length about numerous points in the text. They revised some passages for clarity. Umber explained some of the mathematics while smoothing her hair.

"Umber, I'm truly sorry about your back," she whispered. He kissed her ear. She threw the bottom of the sleeper over them, lying back, and finally she drowsed off. Umber stared at the rock over his head in silence, blinking in the darkness, listening to her breathing.

A measure before dawn he roused her. They packed in silence. He gave her some small carvings he had done for Pell. "You will come?" she asked.

"Yes. I said so. For a time. Leda, from what you know of this shore, is it subsiding or perhaps rising?"

"Very slowly subsiding. Why?"

"I was wondering about who brought the drocs. Or what."

"No one has ever found remains."

"No. I gather no one has really looked here. But they have elsewhere, and no one has come up with anything yet."

"Maybe God dumped them here, plague and all," she said, smiling.

"No. Too poor a plan for God, I think. What if it were an amphibian, a swamp creature?"

"You mean it would have stayed in the shallows?"

"In its ships or in the shallows, perhaps. If I have to hide away from the Godworship people a while, I might as well spend my time looking."

"You'll come to the Sump first?"

"Of course."

After a lingering embrace Leda set out before sunrise, tramping west to the edge of the tangles, then south along them. When the LS patrol came over, she took the bug Umber had found and switched it on and off. They arced around, hovered, and settled near her. She went forward as an officer stepped out and said, "Take me to LSHQ please."

"What do you have?" the commander asked, hands behind him.

"I'll tell the CO," she replied.

"Give it here," he said.

"No. To the CO," she said.

"Would you prefer we took it?"

"Would you like me to erase it here? Now?" she countered.

"Why this?"

"You don't know what I have. You may surmise. Part of the plan is its secrecy. You picked me up. You took me. Your crew will know that. No more."

"You mean if we lose, the Gorbie won't be blamed."

"Why don't you drink droc sweat, you fatskull?"

The man raised his eyebrows. Standing aside, he said, "Very well, come aboard." She walked by him, holding her finger on the dump key of the lightpad.

She kept her finger there until she was ushered into the office of Admiral Uprye, chief of Lower Space Command. She handed him the lightpad, and he inserted the tap and transferred its contents to his storage.

"You may erase it now," he said, grinning slightly.

"Yes. When you check to see you have it," she said.

He checked. "Very well, we have it," he remarked.

"I'll wait to see if there are any questions," Leda said casually.

He looked a little surprised. "Very well," he said. "Out there." He gestured toward the outer room. She nodded and left.

For over two tenthdays people passing in and out saw her there, still muddy, her clothing rough, her hands scratched and her hair beneath her field cap smoothly combed and beautifully braided behind. Then Admiral Uprye stepped out, glanced at her, and said, "Come in."

She returned and sat. "This deceleration pulse. You're sure it exists?"

"Umber says it does. He wanted you to try it out from behind the sun."

"We will," the admiral replied. "We will. This is extraordinary. For a Gorbie, too. He must have reasons." He looked at her. She smiled. He held out his palms. "Even other reasons, perhaps."

"He thinks you should keep the whole thing full secret. And not, of course, diminish any other warning systems you have."

"He thinks there are agents?"

"No. Not yet, he says. But most of all he stressed the actual fight, if there is one."

"Yes. I read his training suggestions. Most dramatic. Hard on the trainees."

"He thinks we have it too easy."

"So I gathered. So I gathered. And he's still too afraid of Godworship to come in."

"Yes. And he wants a code so he can reach you at any time."

The admiral raised his eyebrows. "I'm sure that can be arranged, too," he said.

That afternoon Professor Okdal Oundesi presented his first public lecture on the structure of *Marmota*, which he and his team had been studying at length. The description of his study was almost entirely factual, a comparison of muscle groups, skeletal structures, and internal organs. Surprisingly enough, it was watched by a large fraction of the population of Landsdrum.

By the time the lecture was half-over, probably a third had switched to entertainment holos, but the others stared in silence as Oundesi unfolded the results of his examination.

Finally, he summarized the findings of the lecture, riffling through the diagrams he and his staff had made, saying, "As we have found, the similarities between *Marmota flaviventris* and our own species are remarkable, striking, certainly showing a closeness I have seen nowhere else among species I have known. Clearly they are variations of the same theme.

"Some differences, whether of tooth formation, here perhaps dependent on differences of dietary habit, or hair covering, so much more complete in the case of *Marmota*, or of the rotation of muscles, such as the downward positioning of the latissimus dorsi or the forward placement of the pectoralis, or of hundreds of other details, remain, if one were to compare us to *Drocii quatrilobus*, or any other local species, almost incidental.

"Naturally, we have been asked to comment on our notion as to whether *Marmota* is a created species, a monstrous offshoot of humankind purposefully designed. It is of course premature for us to speculate about such matters. Probably we should leave such speculations wholly out of our work. Suffice it to say that if *Marmota* is a designed species, the design has been accomplished with astonishing intelligence, equipment, and sophistication such as I am wholly unaware of. I would hate for Landsdrum to have to pit itself against the massive abilities any such designers have at their command. We would be in no position to hope to match such masterful technology. For example, even the adaptation of the vertebrae to the horizontal posture of *Marmota* suggests a greater aptness than the same structure does for our vertical one. It is a brilliant solution—absolutely stunning.

"As to *Marmota*'s sexuality, the one specimen we have looked at, a female, has its reproductive equipment, insofar as we have been able to ascertain it, in working order. If *Marmota* has not reproduced, it will fail on this planet, as *Sylvilagus* will. If it has and we have a chance to examine some other examples, living, I hope, we will arrive at more advanced conclusions. Thank you for your patience. Further lectures will deal with other aspects of *Marmota*'s physical makeup."

Professor Oundesi turned from the projection, gathered his materials, and walked out of the studio into a storm of newspeople. He continued to walk through them, unblinking, as they clawed at his sleeves and shouted questions at him, jostled, mobbed, brayed, and finally blocked his path.

Stopped, he silently handed the materials he was carrying to an assistant, reached into his pouch, removed a tiny canister, aimed it at the woman who was shouting into his face, and sprayed. She collapsed. He stepped over her and continued, lifting the canister again when the way was blocked with clamoring and threatening newspeople. This time one knocked it from his hand and the rest mobbed him, refusing to let him pass until he answered their demands. Elderly, inclined to be frail, he fainted and was kicked and trampled in the sweep of the crowd.

Later, from his bed in the infirm, he was to learn that he had violated the civil rights of those who had accosted him. He smiled sweetly through his bruises at that news and said nothing.

The Godworship Council quickly announced that Oundesi's lecture proved that *Marmota* was a created species and that the methods of its creators were so diabolical that Landsdrum would have to redouble its efforts to root out the species. They were unready for the widespread derision that this announcement brought.

☐ XXII Interlude

SHORTLY after she returned to Potsherd Sump, Leda went to a hearing over the custody of Pell. The harmony between the mother and son was so obvious that the questioning was short and peremptory. The physician who had initially examined Pell was there, looking serious and official and finally suspicious and a little bewildered. Clearly a storm had passed. Leda wore her hair in a Klluumian braid. She looked rested and quietly radiant. Even Pell seemed caught up in her glow, reflecting some of it. It was a strangely muted session.

Leda left with Pell and returned to the sump. She found her mother combing Gyro's scant hair. "Well," Dyann Penne said. "That's it, I see. Now I trust I can turn over to you the management of the droc worm distribution. We've already had a message from Urrget for some."

"Urrget! Crime on a cookie. Already? Mother, I'm a geologist. I—" She caught her mother's fierce stare. "All right. I'll arrange it. I ought to stay here for a while anyhow."

"A while?" Pell asked.

"If I go, you go, all right?"

He smiled. "All right."

"Now, on another subject—" Dame Penne said.

"I don't know when he's coming, mother," Leda replied. "No one's patrolling anymore now they have the early warning information. The sensor grid is still out in the Arc Tangles. It looks as though Oundesi's lecture cooled the Godworship people some. Although . . ."

"Yes?"

"I don't know how it'll go down when spring comes. Umber says the marmots are merely hibernating and will come

139

out again in spring. He assumes they've reproduced. He hopes. He thinks the one they dissected was a young one."

Dame Penne gave a nervous laugh. "So, Pell, want your hair combed?"

"No, it's all right," he murmured.

Eight days later, Uji signaled Dame Penne. She touched off her wrist tickler and turned to the monitor to see his solemn face. "Your Gorbie's back," he said. "He's communicating with the big droc."

"Thank you, Uji. You are to mention this to no one, certainly not to Casio or Boornten. Is that understood?"

Uji swallowed. "Yes. I understand."

"You haven't already, have you?"

"No."

"Very well, then."

Umber was still massaging Tistan's ridges when Pell trotted up behind him. The Gorboduc grinned up at him. "Hello," he said. "You're all right?"

"Yes. You look thin."

"Was thinner. Things are better now. Come talk to Tistan."

Pell stooped in the entrance of the winterbarn and squatted by Tistan. The droc gently waved a limb at him. The boy took it and touched a series of plates.

"You're learning," Umber remarked.

"Wahn's been teaching me."

"How is he?"

"Fine. He's at Isa teaching droc vocabulary and grammar according to your little instruction list."

"Good. I imagine he's learned some things I didn't know by now."

"Ask Tistan if it believes in God."

Umber paused, frowned quizzically at Pell, and hesitated a moment. "I'm not sure I know how," he said. He touched a question on the droc's limb, then asked it, "Question what you signal thing all things made?"

Tistan held its arms very still for a time, then signaled, "Ask different path."

Umber pondered and tried. "Question friend ask what thing made droc, person, pan, water, food, all?"

Tistan signed a new series of touches on Pell's forearm, then repeated it on Umber's.

Umber shrugged. "I don't know that one," he said. "Maybe it's God."

"Ask it how it knows about God."

Umber rolled his eyes, then touched out, "Question Pell asks how you know (new sign)?"

The droc paused a very long time, then signed, "Droc not feel. Droc think. How droc know (new sign) think first. Necessary. Fallingwater color. Droc receive. You receive. All receive."

Umber signed, "Thank you." He said to Pell, "That must be the sign for God, then. Only don't tell the Godworshipers."

"I'm a Godworshiper."

"Yes, and so am I. In my way. But not a fussy one. The council might either declare the whole idea blasphemy or decide that if drocs can think about God, they mustn't be eaten."

"I . . . find it hard to think of eating them now that I've talked to them."

"Yes. But they accept it. Receive it, as Tistan says. In his long history, man has eaten many beings he had much closer relationships with. As far as I can see, drocs are fatalists."

Pell frowned slightly. "You're talking so much better," he murmured.

"I've been learning. But it seemed no use to let you know," Umber replied with a slight smile.

Tistan signed, "Question what say?"

Umber replied, "Friend question you happy kept by us?"

Tistan's reply was immediate: "Yes, happy know you, happy be here not not be here. No, not happy not free. Receive both yes, no. (New sign) decide. Happy here not not be here because of plague. Thank. Know must die warm time. Receive."

"We thank, sign good-bye," Umber returned, rising.

As they walked down the berm, they could see Uji watching from the droc station. Umber dropped his eyes. Though Pell protested, Umber began his droc work immediately, raking a pan to prepare its renewal, examining the winter dryrest conditions, hand pruning rows of seedling *Platus platinus* in the nursery, until Uji presented himself and said, "Dame Penne wants to see you."

Umber looked up. "Thank you," he said.

"You look thin," Uji added.

"Had a hard time."

"You well now?"

"Yes. And you?"

"Yes."

"All right. Good-bye, boss."

"Good-bye."

Uji watched him walk toward the potshop.

As usual, Dame Penne kept Umber waiting while she added incisions on a wet flat slab dish. He stood with his hands behind him, watching. At last she dipped her hands in a pot of water and wiped them on a huge rag she kept at hand. Then she turned and looked at him steadily, her mouth tight.

"I trust you will be more pacific than at our last meeting," she said.

"Oh. Yes. I hope so," he replied.

"Sit."

"Thank you."

"A strange outfit. Steal it from Groundarmy?"

"Yes."

"And the worksuit? Where is it?"

"Used up. Had a big burn in the back and fell apart. Made a carrybag out of it."

"For the things you stole from Groundarmy?"

"They threw them around. Just had to pick them up."

"You will change to a proper worksuit immediately. And resume your kill collar. It won't be activated."

"Thank you."

"Only because I fear the Godworship conservatives would try to find a way to trigger it off."

"Yes."

"Your status has not changed. You are still Dal Penne's servant."

"I understand."

"Know why?"

"Perhaps he wants a slave."

"No. If you aren't that, you have no status. You haven't been relieved of the Matted Plain Council's decision about your fate. Besides . . ."

"Yes?"

"How else will I keep some order with you? You've turned the whole island on its ear—the whole colony. It just keeps up. Your arrival. The plague. *Marmota* and the grass. Your obscenity about other sexual beings. Your temporary escape —yes, yes, I know the reason. Talking with the drocs. Now Pell tells me they have a sign for God. Can you imagine how that will go down with Godworship Council?"

"Yes."

"Where is it going to end?"

Umber drew in his breath and sighed it out. "There are big things and little ones," he said.

"Give me a big thing."

"The Dark Sector Gorbies will come. Maybe you can't beat them. That seems big enough."

"Do you think we can?"

"Yes, if Lower Space puts its whole mind to the problem and the populace backs the cost."

"A small thing?"

"I just heard from Pell that Dal Polon plans to market his earthbeast soon."

"So he will. Many people have already eaten it, including me. Delicious. Easier to raise than drocs. Solid nutrition, too. Obviously he'll prosper from it—and so will all of us. Now, anything else?"

Umber sighed. "That should be enough for now," he said.

"Are you sure?"

"Dame Penne, have you ever been off this planet?"

She jerked back slightly. It was the first time Umber had ever asked her a personal question. She put herself on guard. "No," she said. "Why do you ask?"

"Oh, I was wondering how much older I am than you. It doesn't matter. It's all very odd. If I'd been here all the time, I might almost have been your grandfather."

She looked hard at him. "That much travel?" she said.

"That much."

"Well, I'm glad you weren't. I wouldn't want so prominent a nose."

Umber touched it. "It's not fine and delicate, then?"

"No. It's a relief you're finally learning to talk. I wearied of that 'Me go feed droc' lingo."

Umber grinned. "If that all, me go eat?"

"You go eat. Then go to your platform. Pell has made it comfortable for you with an inflated shelter and some furnishings. You understand, I'm sure, that we have to maintain the status quo to satisfy the conservatives."

"You say, I do," Umber said, rising.

Dame Penne smiled at him slightly, wryly. "Good day," she said. "In the morning I'd like you to examine the seed drocs. Uji will direct you."

"Me do," Umber said, wryly grinning, and turned to go.

Late that night, as Umber dozed, the small communicator in his shelter clicked on and he heard Dame Penne's voice say, "Return to the potshop now, Gorbie. You neglected to tell me something."

Umber sighed, slid into his worksuit, and dropped to the ground. It was deep night and overcast, without the usual flare of stars. He crouched a moment and looked around. Something was odd. Was it more still even than usual? Hearing nothing, he rose and headed for the shop.

He found Dame Penne sitting there in a nightrobe, a cup of hot brew steaming next to her. Her expression was severe. "One thing you neglected to tell me about," she said without preliminaries. "A big thing."

"Yes?"

"Why be coy and pretend? My daughter, my unstable daughter. First she almost kills you, and now you and she . . . you have . . ."

"Yes. We have."

"I can bear all the other violations of code, honor, custom, religious truth, but this is too much. I cannot possibly permit it."

"I know," Umber said simply.

"Why did you?"

"You never forbade it."

"I never imagined it."

"Surely. . ." Umber began, letting the statement die.

"I trusted you. You should never— Well, I know Leda and how complex she is. She says it has erased Rad. And that she loves you. But still, you should never have permitted such a thing."

"I don't get to do much permitting, you know."

"You should by all rights have told me."

"You can't forbid a thing that's happened."

"But I could forbid any repetition. You still want to leave, after all. You may find a way. I can't have my daughter going to a Gorbie planet. You must understand that."

"No. I know."

"Besides. It isn't only wholly unseemly, inappropriate, dreadful . . ."

"Yes? Worse than all that? Your daughter with a mere Gorbie beast."

Dame Penne leapt to her feet. "That's just it. A Gorbie beast." She turned her back and began to pace. "You know what Godworship says about Gorbies—they aren't real people. They're the devil's imitations. Many believe that, will continue to believe it. What if there's a child? You think I want my daughter to have a child that's half devil in the minds of some? You think I want a grandchild of mine to be responsible for bringing down another stated truth of the established church? How the child would suffer for that! A walking embodiment of something loathsome." She seemed to deflate and sank back down.

At that point a sudden explosion and burst of fire came from outside. Umber rushed out and looked toward the droc pens, his face flaring red from the distant flame. It was his platform, the quick blaze already dying back.

Dame Penne came and stood beside him. "What next?" she asked. "You'd better go and put it out. I'm going to call LSHQ."

"LSHQ?"

"Obviously you'll be of more use to them alive than burnt up. In the coming conflict."

Umber looked at her for two moments, then trotted back to douse the blaze.

As he finished, Pell and Leda ran up. The three stood together in the dark, surrounded by drocherders. "You're all right, then?" Leda asked.

"Yes. Fit as spit. Whole as a pipe. Right as a hand."

"Umber, this is no time for jokes," Leda said.

"No. You're right. I could've been fried droc feed by now."

"What did you lose in there?"

"Sleep. The other losses are the Dal's."

"Umber, why are you so happy?" Pell asked.

"Happy? To be alive, after all this," Umber said.

"Here comes security," one of the drocherders said, turning toward an increasing engine whine from the southwest.

"No," Pell cried out. "It's Lower Space. What do they want?"

"Me," Umber said. He looked at Leda in the dimness. "Their prize Gorbie expert."

"I don't understand," Leda said.

Umber chuckled without mirth. "I think I do. I'm to go to a place of security to protect my information as a resource."

"They can't. Mother won't let them."

"I think she may," Umber replied, taking Pell's hand and hers.

□ XXIII A Devilish Degeneration

In spite of what he had said, Professor Oundesi did deliver his second lecture, but only over the holos. His audience was not as big this time, but it was still huge, even though his title was "Some Genetic Observations Concerning *Marmota flaviventris*."

Oundesi's presentation was dry and technical, much of it having to do with genomes, genes, chromosomes, and known and unknown codes. As he ended, he made the subjective comments that everyone had been waiting for, saying, "As you know, our populace has been extremely curious as to what all of this means. That is, how does this strange creature bear on us? To me there are some interesting facts about its DNA sequences, especially the interspersed ones that may well have nothing to do with current behavior. As we have said, some of these nonfunctional codes are identical to those found in humans. A number apparently are not, though further investigations by our team are necessary to be certain they are nonfunctional. Here we are either breaking new ground or rediscovering old.

"The entire somatic cell coding differs considerably from that of humankind, but not entirely. Oddly enough, we have been able to examine the sequences of *Sylvilagus* as well, and again we discover some of the same coding as in humankind as well as some of the same as in *Marmota*, though the similarities seldom are in the same sequences. As an appendix to this presentation, I have summarized the facts of what our investigations have discovered.

"All of this is extremely suggestive. Either the creators of these devilish imitations of humankind, these degenerations, have been diabolically, remarkably clever and lavish with their efforts in planting nonfunctional DNA sequences to confuse this issue, or else humankind and these creatures, as has been suggested, have a common ancestor, and they aren't devilish imitations. That is, the nonfunctional sequences once had a purpose but no longer do, yet the codes remain. Such questions are not ones to be answered by me but by much wiser heads. I apologize, too, for whatever in this study will have turned out to be premature. I am sure further study will revise some of our conclusions. Thank you for your patience."

Oundesi turned and left the studio. At Godworship Council headquarters, the watchers sat stunned. "We have been betrayed," the chair said flatly. "Betrayed. How could he have done such a thing? Bood, prepare the papers necessary for his arrest."

"I think that's impossible," the council attorney replied. "He clearly said he left the conclusions to be drawn to wiser heads. Yours is the wiser head, and you must supply the obvious conclusion."

"He should have."

"In his position that would have been unwise."

"Unwise? Why? He's a lifelong devotee. He has advanced in rank."

"But the vast preponderance of the evidence he presented supported the Gorbie's surmise."

The council stared at its attorney in shock. Bood shrugged. "Didn't it?" he asked.

"The point is," Tadi Stats said, his thin hand shaking, "that he selected the evidence. He could have selected the evidence that favored the truth."

"How do you do that?" a young council member, Burcc Dezan blurted out. "Don't you use the evidence at hand? Isn't the conclusion of that evidence the truth?"

The chair stared at the arced ceiling, musing. "For a long time now, the Godworship Councils of this colony have held it together, have held it to its purposes of unity, survival, devoutness, singleness of purpose. If that is lost now, we as a colony are in for a very bad time. No matter what faults your theology may have, it behooves you at least to support the prosperity of the colony."

"Then Oundesi left you the solution. You are the wiser head. All you have to do is to state the conclusion."

"From the evidence presented," the chair intoned in exasperation, "that is clearly silly. The fault lies in the evidence."

"That's a preposterous thing to say."

An older woman, Gian Dok, asked for the floor. "For some time now I've listened to the objections of our young friends, Council Member Itle and Council Member Dezan, and I've concluded that this discussion shows Member Dezan is simply too young to be included in such momentous deliberations. It is said that the novice goes too fast or too slow. I would say the novice also goes too blindly. I think, quite frankly, that he was elevated too precipitously, and I would like formally to request a vote on his continued suitability as a council member."

The council fell into silence again. Council Member Itle

hung his head. Without calling for any discussion, the chair said, "I'll call for a button vote on this issue. Is that agreed?" The young man made no reply. The vote for his ouster was unanimous.

After the vote Dezan silently rose, bowed slightly, and left, his face held stiffly. Gian Dok spoke again. "To have voted against himself! Either that shows contempt or a remarkably sudden self-knowledge. I think we're going to have trouble with him."

"No," the chair replied. "Not with what we know about his wife." He tapped his fingers. "Isn't it obvious that the real issue is the Gorbie? Since he's come, everything has been churned and scrambled. He needs to be . . . excised like a tumor."

"Not with the impending attack," Council Member Danan said, rubbing his bald head.

"Who knows if it's real? He might have cooked it up," another member remarked. "The cost is immense. The whole new cathedrals project will be sacrificed."

"The danger is real enough," Dok said. "I was a small child during the last Vandal raid. Before his lifetime, surely. It's real. But this proposed cost is far too great. We absolutely must fight it. After all, there are priorities."

"Surely the Divine will protect the faithful. The projected buildings prove our devotion to Her," the chair intoned.

"But God is large and might wait. The Gorbies won't. She wouldn't want us unprotected. Remember the story of the man in the flood," Tadi Stats said.

The chair snorted. "That's a stale joke," he said. "We've worked too long to get this project approved. We've even got them to agree to borrow from the Gorboduc tribute fund."

"Let's glue our lips shut about that. There'll have to be some compromise. The danger is certainly real. I'm sure we can give a little if they can," Gian Dok mused.

"I'm surprised," the chair returned. "It's all the Gorbie. He's up to something."

"The Gorbie's out of reach," Dok spat out in disgust. "Lower Space has taken him from the Pennes. Who knows where he is?"

"We'll have to find that out," the chair remarked. "Then we can deal with him."

Umber had left aboard a LSHQ hoverskimmer the same night his platform had been blasted. After a meeting with Admiral Uprye, he went with a crew to Doublewedge Island to enhance the space scanners. Umber had little to do but advise. Much of his time was his own, and as winter weather gentled to spring, he wandered freely on the island, down its precipitous headlands to the shore, wearing a Landsdrum shocksuit to discourage any leatherarms. He prowled the shallows in coves where the high Landsdrum surf did not reach, examining tidewater creatures, mostly tiny, mostly botanical. The planet was extremely rich in native aquatic organisms, as its atmosphere had led him to suspect. He found a miniature creature he was instantly sure was another product of droc splashing, though strangely enough, his probing of the tapes of Landsdrum species did not include it.

He had specimens sent to the academy, with a false address, naming the organism *Drocina oundesi*. This caused a minor stir, but though the mystery of its origin was not disclosed, the species was listed under that name after study.

Umber also finally took the time to master Westsector grammar. He had resisted it at first, finding a more primitive speech useful. Clearly that time was over.

On the mainland spring brought the whistle of marmots in the Crescent Vine Tangles and the Arc Tangles beyond. The people of Matted Plain showed little horror over the survival of *Marmota*. In fact, marmot observing became a favorite pastime, and in spite of the objections of Godworship, laws were passed to protect them. A pair was captured and brought to the academy for study. Another pair was sent to Choicity for their study and diversion.

As spring slowly turned to the drier Landsdrum summer, the Doublewedge Space Ear was completed. Tested, it showed Umber's claims to be correct. A sudden electromagnetic deceleration pulse was detectable from beyond the sun. Umber warned the LS technicians not to expect as loud a signal as they received from their own craft but to look for repeats. He warned as well that they should monitor the whole sky even though the Raiders liked to use the cloak of the sun.

But detection was alone no solution. It was of little use to learn you were going to be overrun, as Umber remarked to Basecommander Stallard. The man rolled his eyes.

☐ XXIV   Hot Wind, Hot Air

As summer deepened and hot winds blew up the coast from the wider southern section of Northisland and across the narrow strait to Doublewedge, the base, with its big push over, relaxed slightly. At first, few noticed Umber's persistent absences, until base security decided to check on it. Monitoring, they found him bent over several large lightpads, sketching on each in succession, using a mathpad as well. They could tap that, and found calculations obviously both of an engineering and a financial nature. Records showed also he had called in a number of historical, economic, governmental, and engineering reports from LS Central. The Doublewedge officers murmured about this in puzzlement.

At last, Basecommander Stallard announced himself at Umber's quarters. The Gorboduc touched the slider command and rose to meet him. Stallard found Umber a little frowzy, and his dayroom in complete disorder. The commander drew himself up and glanced around with military disdain.

"Busy," Umber said, following his eyes. "Will clean it up. Later."

"Busy with what? Aren't you satisfied with the tests?"

"Oh. Yes. It's . . ."

"Yes?"

"You have contingency plans, no doubt. About defense. Assuming you won't get the money needed."

Stallard frowned. "Of course," he said. "Right down to surrender, of course, though this time that won't happen. They'll give us the money. They have to."

"But if they don't . . . I have this feeling. Governments seldom do."

"This seems so clear."

"I've examined some records. There are pacifists. There are those who would like merely to give a tribute."

"We still have people alive who remember the last raid, Umber," Stallard replied, still glancing around.

"Ah. But no majority. I was trying to recall a component of a system I once heard of. A primitive one—but effective at times and not at all expensive."

"Yes? We won't have time to engineer an entire new system. Not if we're to be ready."

"Maybe not. It would deprive Landsdrum of the use of a big patch of space, too. On the solar side. Maybe it's impractical. Maybe I'm just using time. But it keeps me occupied, as well."

"May I see it?"

"Of course. It doesn't mean much yet. It's a system of chaff-missile buoys. Old technology but still hard to stop. The trick is connecting them with hypertense wire, and providing many dummies. Overloading the automatic trackers of any oncoming vehicle. They are inert. They just sit there like asteroids until any tremor in the whole system activates them and sets them scanning and self-launching. They're so compact they're hard to detect. Here, sit down."

Umber patched his pad into the wall display, and riffled through his sketches, explaining each to Stallard, who leaned back and pulled at his lower lip. When they had looked through the diagrams done so far, the basecommander said, "Huh. Send me copies, please."

"I will. Let me finish them first, please. This is all so rough."

"Is this a Gorbie system?"

"No. I assume Esstrremadrr knows of it. We sent it in a databurst. But it is really Ostirnian."

"Don't know them."

"I met one once. They lie toward the galactic core and are

basically peaceable. They also get raided by the Gorboducs and tried a system like this."

"Did it work?"

Umber sniffed lightly. "No. Wasn't big enough. The raiders went by it. Never knew it was there. They took their tribute, did their damage, and left. But then they sent back a plague missile, and the buoy field took it out."

"A plague missile?"

"Sometimes they'll do that. When a colony seems to be prospering. So when they come again the recovery may be underway, but the colony won't be strong enough to resist."

Stallard whistled to himself. "They might do that here then?"

"They might. They mustn't get the chance."

The two talked for a time, and as Stallard rose to go, he remarked, "Oh. Leda Penne and her son are coming to see you. I almost forgot."

Umber held in his emotions. "They are?" he remarked mildly.

"Yes. Being from a Dal family, they can. They'll be quartered with my family, but they can visit you." He stared at Umber.

Umber looked directly back with a slight smile. "And you suggest I clean up," he said.

"That, too," said Stallard.

As summer advanced, Leda and Pell did come to see Umber, but the Lower Space officers seemed to see they had little time together. Something always seemed to come up. Still, walking with them near the coast, or on the high, rocky ledges, Umber was relieved and happy. Pell contrived to leave the two alone. Umber thought the boy was amused by the novelty of his mother and the Gorbie liking each other, but one afternoon, as they sat on a high outcrop, with Pell below throwing stones far out, to see if he could reach the surf, Leda remarked, "He wishes you were his father."

Umber felt a surge of stinging despair, remembering Alaynnr, but as he absorbed this, looking down at Pell, it ebbed away, and he was washed over with pleasure at the thought. Leda took his arm and squeezed it slightly. As Umber turned toward her, though, he felt a slight entrapment, a reserve, thinking of a long list of numbers he had to remember, which he could not let die here.

"Umber, what is it?" Leda murmured.

"So much. So much," he replied, looking down at Pell's shining red hair.

At midsummer, as the legislative business of the colony droned on at the Palace of Social Union in Choicity, everyone could sense a crisis slowly coming. The expense of defending against the Vandals was mounting, shoving at the barriers of the budget.

Two days before the annual budget meeting, at which all negotiated positions finally came out in the open for debate, Dal Polon stopped by Potsherd Sump. He found Dyann Penne idle in the manor house, lying on her day bed. She extended a hand in greeting when Phant admitted him and motioned for him to sit. Gyro Penne sat nearby, picking at the edge of his sleeve.

"And your beauteous daughter?" Polon began.

"On a trip with Pell," Dame Penne replied with a vague wave.

"It's hot," Polon said.

"Surely not in here," she said.

"No. Outside. And in Choicity."

"You are going to the meeting? Even though Boornten has your place?"

"To observe. It's allowed."

"Of course. So how do you read it? Will Godworship manage to cut off defense funds?"

Polon sighed. "They're divided themselves. They lost a cathedral in the last raid. At West Reach. They want to be defended. But they want to build more, too. It seems they'd worked out some deal to borrow from the old tribute fund . . ."

"I thought that had been dispensed."

"No. The Pacific party has managed to keep it in existence —in a huge storage facility to be ready if needed. Of course it wouldn't satisfy them, the dirty Gorbies."

"I know. Somebody told Umber about it, and he said they would treat that just as extra."

"Perhaps he's just cynical," Polon remarked absently.

"I think not. And I suppose those sleazes from Southisland want to kill the whole thing."

"Of course. They are so scattered they think themselves invulnerable. Except, of course, from droc plague."

"And I understand Boornten is skeptical about the whole thing. Thinks it is some plot from our pet Gorbie and his friends."

"Oh. Yes. Quite so. I think he is truly doubtful, but Gian Dok has gotten to him, too."

"And no doubt, Lost Mountain feels it is all too much bother."

"Yes. Dal Tuhl is against it as he is against everything. And Choicity is for it because they expect to build most of the ships and weaponry and they have the most to lose. Except for the workers, who just hope everything will work out and don't want to be taxed."

"What does all that mean? They won't get the funding, will they."

"No. Not enough. There isn't enough. We still have hull contracts. We may convert some of them, but Inidis has committed ships to a nine year journey here to get them, and we can't ignore that."

"What if they ran right into the middle of a raid?"

"Little chance. But if we didn't have the hulls, we'd have to agree to deliver. It would be dead loss."

"No," Dyann Penne said. "It would be dead loss if we didn't have the means to sustain a raid. But tell me, did Lower Space pad the budget enough so they can take a cut?"

"No. They couldn't, with all the watchers."

"That doesn't look good, does it."

"No," Dal Polon said. "No."

As the two friends had predicted, when the budget report was made at Choicity, the Convening Director had trouble keeping order. As usual, though, he assigned Orators to each point of view and held the discussion to a reasonable time limit. The 386.2 billion unit budget for initial building of the defense system proved impossible to sell. Both the Statists from Southisland and the Pacifics opposed it. Even the Defensists had to balk at some of the expenses. It meant debt. After nine days of arguing, the Convening Director announced that Social Union had grudgingly approved only 191.2 billion for Vandal defense.

"The funds aren't there," the Statists claimed.

"We might as well not spend any, then," the Defensists retorted. "Just give it to the Vandals and let them maim us."

"We must not forget the force for good of Godworship," Boornten rejoined.

"Perhaps if we give them what they want, they won't hurt us," the Pacifics said.

After the vote, Admiral Uprye sat slumped in a chair at his desk and stared at the wall. An aide entered and cautiously said, "Sir?"

"Not now, Rayn," the admiral replied. "They've just taken the whole center out of the plan. The Gorbies will penetrate our initial Tchatoo squadrons. They will probably go through our Whank vessels, with some losses. Then the needle ships will be absolutely needed to distract and destroy to set them up for the launch platforms, with two systems behind that. Necessary redundancy. It all made such sense. Now what do I do? Cut out a system or two? Or cut back on all of it? The whole thing is silly, foolish, the drivel of enchanted money-pushers. Don't they know what they're up against."

"Sir," Rayn said.

"It's not as though this were all fun and parties. We've been accused of overblown perquisites, padded retirements, luxurious expenditures. Don't they know how hard I've worked? How hard? And how much we've done already?"

"Sir," Rayn said.

"We even have the early warning system in place and working. It does work. But what's the good of early warning when you can't do anything about it? Does it give us more time to commit suicide? Of all the stupidity, the crime-sniffing, manure-caked, droc slimed, rank and rotting stupidity..."

"Sir," Rayn repeated with emphasis.

Uprye didn't answer. He stared. Finally, he turned and noticed Aide Rayn standing there, a lightpad held carefully in front of her. "Yes, Rayn," he said, absently.

"Sir, we have a complex message from Doublewedge Island. Something about a different defense system."

"What?"

"A different defense system, sir. To replace the needle vessels."

"To replace the needle vessels? After all our design expenditures? Of all the crimethick . . . a new system now that we've been cut in half? I can't believe—"

"Apparently much cheaper, sir."

Admiral Uprye seemed to come out of a stupor. "Cheaper?" he asked. "Where is this from?"

"Doublewedge, sir."

"Then it's from Umber, isn't it."

"I don't know, sir. It's something about stationary chaff-missile buoys. An interlocking system."

Uprye extended a hand. "From Umber. I'd better look at it. But we'll still have to cut out at least thirty Tchatoos and twenty Whanks. I can't believe it. Crime. Crime on a candy."

Aide Rayn winced slightly. Uprye glanced up at her. "You object to my language then, Rayn," he said flatly.

Aide Rayn shut her eyes. "I looked at the material before you got back," she said. "It's been tried once. At someplace called Ostirn."

"Did it work?"

"No. Only a little. Stopped a plague missile."

"A plague missile?" Uprye muttered, already becoming absorbed in the text. Eventually Aide Rayn bowed and left, glancing back at the admiral's gray head, bent over the lightpad.

☐ XXV   Local Raiders

As summer neared its end, a ship landing at Truncated Mountain brought word of a droc planet on which all the colonists were dead, and a ship from it adrift with a dead crew. They brought holos in evidence. Repeated on the public news, these gave a collective shudder to the colony and enormous relief for having been spared.

Umber was informed by the LS field officer on Doublewedge Island. He only shrugged. His idyll was tiring. Leda and Pell visited when they could, but it was not often enough for Umber. They slowly had grown to be his family—not merely his convenient local family, but a truly functional one, in which the three together had rhythms of intimate easiness with one another. Leda had gentled. He had come to see that her anger had been as much frustration as anything else. Each time the LS transport lifted off with them, a strong wave of loneliness spread over Umber. It seemed worse than his first several fiftydays on Landsdrum, because then he was alone, wholly alone, and knew it, so braced his barriers against it. Here he was softening, wishing to stay, wanting some pastoral domesticity, even though he knew that was impossible for him.

The station staff had families with them. While he was welcome, and often played an evening game or two of Ourdoo with them, he remained alone. His biological prowls began to increase his restlessness rather than providing the relief of distraction. No matter how often he shook off the feeling, he missed Leda and Pell deeply.

The long Landsdrum year waned toward its autumn, and though the spin of the planet was not severely tilted from its orbit, the orbit itself was slightly elliptical, increasing the impact of the seasons. Leda and Pell seldom came in the winter. Umber quietly recited his numbers each day, continued his researches, and did his best to bide his time. He even attended Godworship ceremonies, but feeling strangely unwelcome there, he reverted to the more private, and satisfying, contemplations he had learned on Klluum. This brought him temporary islands of peace, ones almost as gentling as being with Leda and Pell, or lying quietly with Leda, his face buried in her hair.

The long Landsdrum year once again warmed, and dried, and while Leda visited more often, it seemed not often enough. And yet Umber had a strange foreboding—of the kind he had learned to trust. The defense system was going well. The chaff-missile buoys, fairly simple to construct, were ready to be deployed. A surge of local prosperity in Choicity brought about by defense work had given the population center a feeling of well being. Even Admiral Uprye seemed pleased.

There were dissenters, of course, especially from the Godworship Councils, who felt this push was too protracted, too absorbing. The cathedrals project had been cut back long enough, and now that the old tribute resources had been thrown into defense, they seemed to feel even more abandoned. Where had all this change come from? Increasingly they identified it with Umber. Some went as far as to associate him with anti-God for all his disruptions, the strange, obscene creatures he had brought to the planet, and the plague they were sure to disseminate sooner or later.

Then suddenly, as summer once again ebbed toward autumn, and the year approached its 650th day, Leda and Pell vanished from Potsherd Sump. Matted Plain Security and even the Groundarmy failed to find them. This event deeply troubled Matted Plain. Somehow, they thought, the Gorbie was involved in this, though he was assured he was elsewhere and continually monitored.

When this crisis was six days old, Dame Penne requested Admiral Uprye to call on her. This was unusual, even for a Dal family, but in her request was the remark, "I gave you our Gorbie, and now I need your help." He came.

Once they were settled in the Penne receiving room, the

admiral, restless, preoccupied, waited patiently. Dame Penne looked at him and said, abruptly, "I need my Gorbie back."

"That's militarily undesirable, Dame Penne, in spite of our present preparation, I regret to say. What's the problem?"

"Leda and Pell."

"How could he help?"

"He's helped much so far. Besides, he's fond of them. If he gives it his whole mind, he may discover something."

The admiral pondered. "It's doubtful," he said.

"Not in my mind. Give him to me for twenty days. Then you can have him back. You owe me that. It was my idea you take him in the first place."

"I don't see how we can."

"Besides . . ."

"Yes?"

"I got this message yesterday." Dame Penne touched the recall code, and the words TRADE FOR GORBIE came up on the monitor.

"You can't trade him. Not now."

"No. But I'd like to see what he could do."

"You will keep him safe?"

"As safe as he's willing to be."

Again the admiral pondered. Then he grinned. "We'll get along. I won't tell. All right. Twenty days. You shall have him."

"Thank you, Admiral. Now, I won't ask any more of your time unless you'd like some tea."

The admiral rose. "I'd like that, Dame Penne, but I must be gone. I do have one question. What do you have in mind? You can trust me. We need to get along."

"I'm not sure."

"Is it Godworship, then? You think they have your family to get at Umber."

"How did you surmise that?"

"It's the current word in some circles."

"Yes, I think that."

"Hmm. You've got to be careful with Umber. We can't lose him now."

"I'll be careful," Dame Penne replied, knowing she was lying.

The admiral rubbed his jaw. "It's odd how untouchable they are. Well. Much to do. Best of luck with the Gorbie. You'll need it."

"Yes, I know. Good day, Admiral. I'm in your debt."

"No. The debts are even, maybe, but I still have the better of it. Remember, take care of Umber. Good day."

The admiral spun on his heel and strode out to his waiting hoverskimmer. Dame Penne watched him go and touched the code for Casio Polon. His face came on the screen surrounded by huge leaves. "Casio," she said abruptly. "I need you to come see me immediately."

"Immediately? I—I . . . all right. May I clean up first?"

"No."

"That immediately?"

"Yes."

He saw her serious face and said, "Coming."

He arrived sooner than she had expected, still in a worksuit. As he walked into the receiving room, she said, "Busy with the earthbeasts, I see. I won't keep you, but I warn you, I'll need some time."

"Time is what I have little of. But Leda . . . has she returned?"

"No. And I want all of your time right now."

"Well, you're frank," he returned.

"Yes," she said, leaning forward and motioning him to a seat. "I've sent for Umber. LS has agreed to let him come. It has to do with Leda and Pell."

"Oh, Dyann, you can't know how—"

"Never mind that. I want you to help. I know your ability in nosing around in records." She watched his slight smile. "I have a theory. No one else is helping much. You have to swear secrecy."

Polon rolled his eyes and said, "Of course."

"Who else but that crimeriddled Godworship Council would have taken my family?"

"What?"

"They know, well, they surmise, the Gorbie would look for them. They're right. I've sent for him to do exactly that."

"Isn't that playing into their hands even if you're right?"

"Of course. And as much as Umber's done, I'd gladly poke

him down a hole to get Leda and Pell back. But that may not be necessary. I'd like to put him on it. Look at all he's managed. He has a way."

"And me? What use have you for a deposed Dal?"

"Your skills. I want Umber to have plans for all the God-worship facilities and all the residences of all the council members."

"Great holy crime stiffs, is that all?"

"No need to swear about it. Yes."

"You swore. When?"

"By tomorrow."

Polon clapped his palms to his forehead. "Is that all?"

Dame Penne grinned slyly at him. "For now," she said.

His shoulders sagged. "Let's not start that again. You know she has no use for me."

"She's learned."

"And Umber?"

"Umber. We meet him at every turn—when we need him and when we don't want him. Umber may die for Leda. And Pell. Now. I'd sacrifice him. He's going to die anyhow."

"I don't understand."

"He's told us. He does love my family. I know it. And they . . . have a fondness for him. But he has chosen and said he has. He's going to go home to die if it kills him."

"A bad joke."

"It's on Umber. Gorbie honor."

Casio hesitated, then asked, "Are you saying he dallied with Leda?"

"I don't know. She with him, I think. He's human, in spite of all the myths."

"You want me and Leda . . . after that?"

"I'm old. Why can't I be outrageous? Yes, I'd like that. Our families are both Dals. Leda's first choice was a disaster. Now her second is an impossibility. Now the third, if I can bring it off, is an outrage . . . for you. For her it would be a miracle."

"You use everybody, don't you?"

"If I can. At any rate, you'll need to get at snooping for plans immediately. Umber'll be coming."

"I didn't agree to." She smiled. "Mind if I change first?"

"No."

"And go home?"

"Of course not. Be comfortable. You can send copies directly. As you find them. Coded."

Casio Polon stood and sighed. "You're something," he said, stooping to embrace the old woman.

"I try to be," she replied.

At LSHQ, Umber, still in a shocksuit, sat with the admiral, who sketched out what he knew of Dame Penne's request. "You are to take no chances. I want you available to do the monitoring when something happens."

"I'll know when they come. Leave me a communicator. I'll contact you immediately."

"You'll know? How? By telepathy?"

Umber smiled. "I can't tell you. But I'll know. My fear is that with all the other garbage out there, and the slightness of the signal, they may miss it. I can't find a way to augment it without augmenting everything else. They have to look for a fairly regular pulse. Small but repeated."

"So you've said. But you'll know."

"I think so. And I'll let you know."

The admiral looked at him quizzically. "Very well. My aide'll give you a communicator. The hoverskimmer's outside. My regards to Dal Penne."

"Thank you, Admiral," Umber said, bowing slightly, spinning, and striding to the slide door.

At Potsherd Sump, Dame Penne outlined the problem as the first of Casio's plans began coming in on the monitor.

"Why do you want me to do this?" Umber asked. "What about security? I still don't know your people. I don't . . . All right, but explain, please."

"They don't want Leda and Pell. They want you. They hate you. You've disrupted their little world, and now that Oundesi gave that last lecture, they have no idea what to do about it. It's a trap, and I want you to step into it."

"What will they do?"

"Kill you if they can. If necessary, you may die. It wasn't Leda's doing. Nor Pell's. You owe them their lives."

"You mean these moral paragons may kill them?"

"They're in a corner, getting up their courage to fight their way out."

Umber pondered. "You have no idea of the cost of what you're requesting. All right, let me look at Casio's plans."

"What's that ridiculous outfit?"

"A shocksuit. For leatherarms. Whacks them with a good charge."

"Change it. Put on a decent worksuit."

"When I get a break, please."

Umber spent the whole night at the monitors, staring, coding, calling up additional information. In the morning Casio Polon showed up and looked over his shoulder.

"What's all that?" he asked.

"The figures? Likelihoods. I'm doing three analyses—for if they're very stupid, very smart, or somewhere in between."

"They're very stupid, in an oddly smart sort of way," Dyann Penne murmured from the daybed she lay on. She had never left Umber.

Casio and Umber discussed the matter at length. The options kept crossing at the residence of Gian Dok, on the prominence near the center of Matted Plain. "It's the most fortresslike," Casio said. "She's a conservative. She herself is clever and determined. The chair wouldn't want to be associated with such an operation. If it goes awry, he'll disclaim it. The house plan shows it has a likely room. One entrance, easily defended, underground, unused."

"Bad," Umber said.

"Don't back out now," Dyann Penne murmured.

"I don't mean that. I mean if I fail, they die."

Dame Penne sat bolt upright. "I—you mean . . ."

"Of course. Godworship covering its crimesoiled butt, if you'll pardon me."

Dame Penne looked grave.

"Does Gian Dok have any children?"

"A daughter and two grandchildren, as I understand," Casio Polon said. "Why?"

"Then we'll make a trade," Umber said.

"You can't do that!" Casio cried out.

"Besides, they'd come search the place. Rip it all apart. Gyro is in worse shape and—"

"Any more conditions?" Umber murmured. "I save them. In an impossible place. Get killed. Get them killed. All to play by some kind of rules? Besides, I wouldn't bring them here."

"Not my place!" Casio yelled, standing up.

"No," Umber said. "Right there." He pointed to the diagram of the Matted Plain Godworship Temple. "See? Under there. Where I'd have put them. Harder to get in than Dok's. Well, not there. Up here, where only a fool'd put them."

"I know nothing about this," Casio said.

"Nor I," Dame Penne said. "Get on with it, Umber."

"Tonight. If the Doks live in Matted Plain. I need some rest and some more information." Casio sighed. "No. Not from the system," Umber added. "Just from some common directory."

"I'm good at this," Casio said. "They'll never trace it."

"Not a matter of tracing. A matter of knowing about an inquiry. They'll watch Dok's. They'll even watch the temple."

"Then why are you breaking in?"

"Because they'll be watching the wrong place." Casio and Dyann Penne exchanged glances. "Oh, yes. Please summon a security contingent after I leave—for round-the-day protection. You've received another threat, and you want to be secure. Dal Polon? You, too."

"That'll be too obvious."

"Yes. But it'll be a message. And it'll prevent the places from being torn up."

Dame Penne held her head. "This is almost too much."

"It'll be worse," Umber replied quietly.

☐ XXVI   Tit for Tat

WHEN Council Member Dok's grandchildren disappeared, the flurry of security searching was immediate. They were nonplussed when it was discovered that Potsherd Sump had been under security guard since before the event. Security made its own surmises, as it had earlier, but it was forced to play by the rules.

At their meeting in the morning, the Godworship Council examined its options. The chair kept interrupting, saying, "The brazenness of it all. The utter deviltry."

At last Gian Dok herself said, "That isn't helpful. It wasn't brazen. It was obvious. The Pennes know we did it. We now know the Gorbie was summoned. He did the simplest thing. We need to ask where the children might be."

"He's killed them," a member murmured.

"No. Likely not. The Pennes want their own back. Of course they won't get them."

"What?" the chair exclaimed. "They don't know who took them, do they?"

"The Pennes do, don't they? I want my grandchildren back. And I still want to get rid of the Gorbie. And of course we can't free the Pennes. They'd make too much trouble."

"This has gone too far," another member said.

"In the defense of Godworship, nothing is too far," the chair said. "I agree with Gian Dok. Now, what do you suggest?"

"We have our own security force. Where might he have them? Out in the tangles? Unlikely. He has to be able to produce them for a trade. Then they must be nearby. Correct?"

"Yes, yes," the chair said, holding his head.

"What suggests itself, then, is that they're in one of the

places in the city plan file—the ones they tapped. We expected the tap. The fact we couldn't trace it proves to me they did it. We have the list, don't we?"

"Yes, but as you suggested before, the likely places have been guarded."

"Then we must examine the unlikely ones."

"All of them? This has gone too far. We were only going to eliminate the Gorbie threat," an old woman said.

"We're in it now. We have to see it through. Faith isn't always simple. It's being done for Godworship," Gian Dok remarked dryly. And for my grandchildren, she thought. And for the fact that that commoner, Dyann Aket, married into a Dal family and has ruled the whole operation out there with her common ways all these years.

That night Umber was drowsing in the temple attic near the two Dok children when a shadowy figure slid the entrance and saw them. He pressed a silent alarm and stepped forward, covering the Gorboduc. Nudging him with a foot, he said, "All right. On your feet, crimescum. Elsen, bring the binders."

Another figure stepped forward as Umber stood groggily. "Wrists out," the first man said. As the one called Elsen moved to put the binders on, he touched the shocksuit and kicked backward with a shriek, collapsing. Umber slammed the first man under the nose with the heel of his hand as he swept his weapon aside.

The Dok children, soporific with sleepdrug, sat blinking in a semistupor as the men struggled briefly. As Umber tied them, he could hear distant shouts and approaching feet. He lifted the children into a corner, tousling the boy's head.

"What's happening?" the child asked.

"A little trouble," Umber said, readying his stunner and crouching near the crawlway.

From outside a voice yelled, "Elsen, Bruk. You found him?"

"Who's that?" the boy said.

"They're in there," a voice called. "We know you're in there, Gorbie. Give up now."

Umber stayed quiet. Behind him a small portway opened,

and a wirestunner lanced out and took him on the hip. He screamed and slumped down.

"All right. He's down. Come on in," a voice called from the port. Eight men swarmed into the low room, freeing their fellows and the children and stooping to bind the limp Umber. The first two were slammed back by the shocksuit. Another, a veteran, reached inside the collar and shut it off. .

"Are you all right?" one asked the children.

"Oh, yes. We're fine," the girl said sleepily.

"What'd he do to your arms?" a man asked, pointing to the diagrams on their forearms.

"Oh, he was teaching us to do droc talk. We were going home as soon as Grayma frees the Pennes."

Three men whipped around. "What? What'd you say?"

"We're going home as soon as Grayma frees the Pennes," the boy replied.

The men looked at each other. "What's this?" one said.

"I don't want any part of this," another said.

"You're in it. Tie him good."

"It's all a lie," a third said.

"Not so sure," the veteran said. "I've heard the rumor. To get rid of this Gorbie. Will you look at the size of him."

None of them saw the last man, who had crouched in the entrance, slip away. He stole down the stairs and dodged into a room when he heard more people coming. Once they had passed, he lifted the corner of his cuff and said, "This is 16849, Chief. They've got the Gorbie. He told the children they could go home when their grandmother freed the Pennes. They're in the top of the temple. They're bringing him down soon."

He received a soft beep of acknowledgment, stepped out in the hall, and continued down. Three people came running up the hall. He raised his arms and said, "They have all they need. Not enough room for more." The four turned and walked back to the lifts together.

Later, in the basement, Umber lay bound on the floor, his possessions laid out on a bare table. Four Godworship Council members stepped in the door. Gian Dok stood, hands behind her back, and regarded their captive. "So this is the famous

Raider," Gian Dok said, smiling slightly. "Not very ferocious-looking now, is he."

She turned to the things on the table: a stunner, some fine-line, three toys, a handpad, a vial of sleepdrug, and a small black LS communicator. She examined them each in turn, and as she touched the communicator, Umber grunted behind his gag and shook his head.

"Oh? I'm not to touch this, then?" She turned to a security man. "Take this and leave it outside LSHQ. I see it's theirs."

Umber groaned and shook his head again. The man slipped it in his pouch. "That bothers you, eh?" Gian Dok said. "Let me tell you something that will bother you more. Your stupid effort has failed. You are now expended. Your evil is snuffed. Your heresies are at an end. And your beloved paramour is to be sacrificed to the good of this planet, this society, this true word of God. Now how do you feel?"

Umber regarded her impassively. "You, take off his gag. I want to hear his reply," she said.

The security man removed it. Umber stretched his lips. "The box," he said. "It's backup. Keep it by me. If the LS Space Eyes don't catch the Raiders' pulse, I will." He looked around. "Though maybe not down here," he added. "Just don't press the signal."

Gian Dok held out her hand for the box, took it, and examined it. She put her finger on the signal and smiled. "You'll have half of LS in their ships," Umber added. "Expensive."

"You don't have that kind of power," she said.

Umber shrugged. "All right, go ahead, then. It's your economy."

She gave it back to her security man. He set it carefully on the table. A buzzer sounded outside. A man stepped in and said, "They're raiding the chair's house! What do we do?"

"They? Who?"

"Men in black."

"Nothing," Gian Dok said. "But back off and take holos. It's the Pennes. They've made another nice mistake." She laughed lightly.

Another buzzer sounded. Another man stepped in. "Now it's Chee Danan's."

Suddenly Gian Dok looked grave. "What is this, Gorbie?" she demanded, glaring at Umber.

He shrugged. "Looks like tax accounting time, kidnapper," he said.

"Give me that weapon. I'll settle this now," Dok demanded, holding out her hand toward a security woman. She hesitated a moment, then passed over her hand weapon. Dok pointed it at Umber, frowned, and asked, "How do you make it work?"

"The button on the left. Move it forward."

"Here. You do it."

"No, Council Member. I'm sorry. There's been no trial."

Gian Dok glared, moved the button on the left forward, and aimed the weapon at Umber. The security man to her left gently but firmly took it from her. "There's been no trial," he repeated.

"How dare——" Gian Dok began, then turned, saw the box on the table, and pressed the button on it. "Your allies. The military. It might have figured. Now they'll be busy. You. All of you. You may leave. I'll handle this."

"Do you have the Pennes?" a security man asked.

Gian Dok gave him a wild look, raised the security woman's handlaser, and discharged it at Umber just as another security woman knocked it aside. As the laser pulse hit Umber in the thigh, he yelled in pain, writhing in his bonds. His yells mingled with others, growing louder in the hall. Three God-worship security people moved to bar the sliding door. One looked and fired a laser weapon out the entrance, then was blown back in, his arm nearly severed at the shoulder. Another hesitated, then moved to the door, looked, and dropped her weapon.

Seven men in black body-armor marched into the room, three with full laser packs.

"You. You can't do this. This is God's house," Gian Dok shrilled.

"Against that wall, all of you. Aymes, signal the field leader. You, Gorbie, you all right? Don't worry. We found the Pennes. They weren't in her place. Only a trap there. We lost three people. They were at her daughter's, within short measures of the grandchildren."

"They all right?" Umber asked through gritted teeth.

"Dehydrated. Filthy and knocked about, I hear. They'll recover. You—your leg?"

Umber passed into shock and did not answer. More people in black filed into the room, filming holos. They sprayed Umber's wound, gave him relaxant, hoisted him onto a roll-chair, and left two guards at the door, heavily armed men who stood silently and did not reply to the clamor of the Godworship captives. A wrist tickler alerted one. He flipped a sleep-bomb into the room, and both left as the Godworship people rushed the closing slider, coughed, and collapsed.

☐ XXVII   Never to See Any Stars

IN the morning Matted Plain was aware that something very unusual had happened. News had it the Pennes had reappeared and were in Matted Plain Infirm, dehydrated, exhausted, and showing signs of abuse. Their chamber was under military guard. Neighbors had noticed the raids on Godworship Council manors, but the sudden announcement of the resignation of eight council members took everyone by surprise. Choicity sent a large flight of Groundarmy hover-skimmers, fearing civil disruption, but they turned around when only partway up the long shoreline.

Umber lay in LS infirm, though the public did not know it. The laser pulse had seared his thigh deeply. He was fretting at his immobility, feeling drained, when the admiral showed himself into the chamber and sat by his bed.

"Thank you, Admiral," Umber said. "I didn't know you would help."

"Dame Penne told me enough to show me we'd lose a military asset if we didn't help."

"What are the legal aspects? It must be a real tangle."

"It's been put under a military cloak. Groundarmy, LS, Seaforce, and HS commanders have all agreed. Not that this was easy. The threat helped. The substantiality of your aid also helped."

"Admiral, put your hand on my head, please," Umber said, gesturing. "Right there." The officer did. "Feel the slight ridge?" Umber asked.

"Yes. I remember the reports. The scan showed no implant, though."

"No implant. But a neurological alteration. My whole body is an antenna, specifically focused on Dark Sector pulses. I am a backup. That is, if pieces of me don't keep being burnt off. I realized how seriously I took this when they had me in that crypt. I knew it would mask the signal. Now please tell no one. If Esstrremadrr learned I had revealed this, they would kill me on the spot. Automatically."

"I had suspected something of the kind. Thank you for your trust."

"If there is a raid this year, I suspect it'll be soon. They like this season. Sometimes they have to land and direct their plunder. They hate it and exact a penalty. But they need the drier time for what they call 'raking a planet.'"

"They do this to you?"

"No. We're too close to them. We just send the ships. They even maintain an agency on Esstrremadrr, a resident wound, bleeding off our resources."

"Nice."

"It's truly vital they don't land here, that they capture no one."

The admiral frowned slightly. "Of course," he said.

"More than of course. They have drocs, you see. We've messaged our people about the plague. Only one of the other Gorboduc planets is a droc planet. I'm hoping, trusting, my compatriots will find a way to let them know. There are no *Unipurp. quatrilobae* in that region of space." Umber shook his head. "I'm also hoping our message got through and was understood. We put it in the center of a blurt of biological data. I doubt the Raiders would be interested."

"You mean . . ."

"Exactly. The drocs could win the big victory for all of us.

I hate it. So many innocents. So many drocs, too. So much side damage to a whole biological system—at least I assume the Dark Sectors have one."

"I don't understand."

"No one I know of has ever been there—even knows where their home is. They live in a huge dust cloud—or behind it. The crews we have to send them never come back."

"How huge?"

"About point three two five light-years across."

The admiral whistled.

"You know, they probably never see any stars," Umber mused.

☐ XXVIII   Pulses from Behind the Sun

UMBER recovered rapidly in spite of the fact that he had no medical help other than the cleaning and spraying of the wound. On this third day in LS Infirm, the entrance slid open and Leda strolled in, looking pale and drawn. She sat down and smiled. "You don't look so good," she said.

"You do," he replied.

"Are you coming home soon?"

"I doubt it. I don't think I'd be safe there. I think they mean me to return to—"

"Doublewedge?"

"Yes."

"If you go, I go, too."

"Your mother?"

"Fiddles with pots. Pell will come, too." She took Umber's hand.

He smiled slightly. "I've been lying here thinking . . ." he began.

"Yes?"

"Doublewedge is offshore, steep-sided. Not good droc territory. Yet there was a droc splash derivative there, the one I sent the academy, the one I named *Drocina oundesi*. I doubt it could've come from the mainland. The organism is unknown elsewhere."

"So that's what you've been thinking about."

"Other than you, I mean."

"Oh, yes, of course. The area's a well-known rapid upthrust. I don't know much about it."

"Let's assume it has risen some. There are plateaus—small ones, of course. If they were droc swamps . . ."

"I doubt it came up that fast, according to your timetable for plagues."

"If it did, it might be a natural place to look for the remains of the original migrants—assuming they settled there and brought their own local droc resources."

Leda laughed. "You mean assuming the drocs splashed as you believe, and the island rose rapidly enough, and the droc derivatives didn't get there on their own, and there were migrants, and they left remains, we might find something."

"Well, if we're there, it'd be something to do waiting for the Raiders."

But they never had the chance. LSHQ asked Umber to go alone, at least at first, and on the hoverskimmer going over Umber's body suddenly jerked stiff and trembled. He shuddered, stood out of his harness, and lurched toward the pilot. "They're here," he croaked. "Not the force. Some advance softener. Get the admiral. It's out off this hemisphere, coming fast. Get the whole defense up."

The planetside warning system had picked up the signal, but it was not what Umber had described. They were puzzled and hesitating. His message came, and the low space missile buoys were set and tracking. They picked up a radar-obscure object coming with incredible speed for an in-system vehicle. Rapid trajectories showed it was aimed at the high desert east of Choicity. The LS umbrella buoy system sent chaff missiles out to meet it and took it in a shower of intense light some 20,000 kilospans up, east of the Choicity horizon. But people in the city caught the flash and glow.

"That came in well off the sun," Umber said over the communicator. "Its deceleration may have masked their own first one. Did anyone catch anything?"

"Yes, a directional blip," a voice said.

"Listen for another, about mark eighty moments," Umber replied. "They've got ships in at least two directions." They paused a short while, then Umber's body jerked again. "Did you trace that?" he asked.

"We have five directions, the sun being the weakest," a voice said, reciting the vectors.

"It's from the sun, then—the main attack, I think," Umber said. His body jerked once more. "Ahhh. Another pulse," he said. "That may be the last."

The hoverskimmer arced around and raced for LSHQ near Choicity. Squadrons A and E had already launched for the sun in two wide arcs around it, shortly followed by B and F. Each contained ten class-five Tchatoo cruiser-weight vessels. C and G squadrons, twenty similar vessels each, soon rose from East Cruelmouth Base, followed by H and D, heavier Whank ships, in a closer cone to Landsdrum, outside the chaff-missile buoys in stationary orbit at forty million kilospans out.

The heavy I squadron, fifty vessels, ringed the planet at thirty million kilospans, while J and K, consisting of lighter particle-beam platforms, stood in disks behind them on the sun side at ten and five million kilospans. The inner orbit of sixty medium platform and launch stations lay at two hundred and eighty thousand kilospans out. Lower Space had gleaned as much colony wealth as they could for the venture. They were confident the Dark Sector Raiders would be surprised.

Umber was not. "They've seen it all, calculated it all," he mused to the hoverskimmer pilot. "Their announcement a while back was a calculation. They based it on the last two raids, I surmise. But they have a plan for whatever you throw at them. That is, unless A and E bypass them and head for the captive ships. But that's a long shot. It's up to the steel of Landsdrum character now."

"Don't sound so doubtful about our steel," the comm officer said.

The hoverskimmer landed at LSHQ, and Umber and his

escort dashed inside. As he arrived in command central, forty Raider vessels came around the sun, astonishingly near to it, in two close-formation pods. Squadrons A and E were not halfway there yet, so the option of driving the enemy into the sun was lost. But the defenders were well positioned, containing the Raiders within their cone.

Enlarged scans of the Raider vessels showed them to be heavy, armored, and awesome, coming in at 0.18 lightspeed, and shielded. As they watched, the Raiders launched their first missiles, small drone vessels that locked onto the lead squadrons. The two Raider pods never swerved.

Five ships from A and E squadrons arced toward the Raiders, their own beams lancing out at the Gorbie drones, which glowed within their shielding, then burst, one after another.

"Tell them to beam the fragments," Umber said.

"Yeah, we learned that one," an officer replied.

Waiting and watching was nerve-twisting. Sweat poured down the face of one man stationed at a scanner. He blew droplets off the tip of his nose every few moments.

Beams from the lead Raiders made the intercepting lead squadrons pulse and glow blue, then burst in a shower of fragments. But half of each squadron continued around the sun. The Raiders paid little heed to them, though they followed them with beam weapons, destroying one.

"That's eleven of ours," a monitor intoned. Several officers glared at him. Then B and F squadrons split, and half of each arced in toward the Raiders. All ten ships sent their beams toward the second vessel in one Gorbie pod, holding them there in spite of incoming drone vessels. Finally pieces fell away from the Gorbie, flashing on the enlargement screen, and then, in a huge, white glow, the vessel disappeared. The one behind it ran into some fragments, and partially caught fire as internal atmosphere vented from a hole in its skin. Soon the glow ceased. The ship maintained course.

As they watched, all ten attacking ships of the second Landsdrum squadrons glowed and blew apart. Squadrons C and G seemed too wide and too slow to stop the onrushing Raiders, but at that point the two pods of attackers ran into the buoy field. The admiral held his palms to his forehead. They seemed to be slicing right through unscathed, the clusters of small missiles glancing from their shielding. Umber stood, hands folded, staring.

Then, in quick succession, the east pod lost four huge ships in blinding explosions. The west pod swung toward G squadron, hitting them straight on in a fury of fire. But they, too, lost a ship to the buoy field. Their drone-vessel fire, supported by beam weapons, decimated G squadron, winking out eighteen of the twenty vessels without a loss, but C squadron, concentrating its beams, took out another of the east pod's ships before its last wave of drone vessels went through the squadron, disintegrating four more ships.

Behind the buoy field, the I squadron, made up of fifty heavy vessels, met the oncoming Raiders with powerful beam weapons, taking twenty-two quick losses themselves but blowing apart three more ships of the east pod and five of the less damaged west group. In the middle of its passage through the I squadron formation, the east pod began to veer off to join the other pod. Even so, they closed on the array of beam platforms, which caught and returned the energy of their beams, holing another Raider from each pod.

"They're running," the admiral said.

"Yes, but we have the other signals," Umber said. "Is there a summary of those ships?"

"Three pods of two, four, and three, lighter vessels, all on the other side, separated," a monitor intoned.

"I suspect they won't join battle but will hang around and try to punish us later."

"Punish us?"

"Damage the planet with something. They like to win. If L squadron holds its place until they can be chased, they ought to be controllable."

"Damage the planet?" an officer asked.

"They're not good losers. If they can spread a disease or fungus or otherwise weaken you, you'll be an easier target if they come back. Now maybe I squadron could follow them. We've got the lead squadrons out there and may not get them back. The Raiders have lost seventeen ships. That's more value than they could manage to take from this planet unless they won everything. They know that won't happen. They're a long way from home and in no shape for any more adventures, except chance encounters. If our lead squadrons catch any of their captives, we can up the losses. But they won't be grateful. From here on Landsdrum has to be alert for a damaging weapon."

"And we can't send them one."

"No reason why not if you want to."

"Too far. And didn't you say no one knew where their planet was?"

"True. But it could home right in on their particle track. Not yet, of course. It will happen, though. Unless . . ."

"Unless what?"

Umber paused. "Unless it isn't necessary," he murmured, smiling.

Out toward the sun the battle had not yet wholly broken off. The two pods of big Raider ships managed as tight a turn as their speed would permit and accelerated for a point west of the sun. The Landsdrum I squadron followed, along with tag ends of the others. A stationary buoy conveyed information from behind the sun. Squadrons A, E, B, and F had found another pod of Raider ships behind the sun, twenty smaller and lighter vessels. And far beyond them they detected a flotilla of 183 cargo ships. Enlargements showed them to be captives.

The four Landsdrum squadrons, already moving fast, set out after them while the Gorbies got under way and pursued. At HQ it was impossible to discover exactly what was happening until I squadron swung wide of the sun and could report directly.

It looked bad for the Landsdrum forces. In spite of their maneuvers, their pursuers slowly focused beams on them and took them one by one. The main attackers, once around the sun, began to overhaul them.

From behind, I squadron managed to destroy another huge attack ship, but the Raiders, too, concentrated fire behind them and exploded one after another of the large Whank-class vessels. Suddenly sixteen of the smaller Gorboduc ships dissolved in fire nearly at once. The fleeing Landsdrum squadrons had dropped homing chaff behind them, missiles so small they went almost unnoticed in the fury of the chase. The four remaining from the pod swung wide and continued the pursuit.

The captive ships remained well ahead, getting under way when the last of the first four Landsdrum squadrons vanished in a blue flash and I squadron broke off its pursuit. One surprise remained. After many ponders, nearly a whole tenthday, the Gorboduc ships slowed to gather up their captives, but those vessels, still well ahead, began to blow apart. The dying Landsdrum squadrons had sent missile swarms ahead of them, tight and fast nuclear warheads that caught and vaporized the hapless captives one after another until I squadron counted eighty-nine destroyed.

The Raiders seemed in no hurry to leave, and as I squadron held position, they occasionally concentrated beams on one or another of them, but the distance was too great and interference too easy to allow them any more kills. The LS ships returned the beams. They also destroyed several incoming missiles, fast and narrow, and warned the J platforms of several others sent around the other sides of the sun.

At last, after three Landsdrum days, the Gorboduc fleet began to get under way on an outward heading. Umber, who had never left command central, was skeptical. Then I squadron received a voice message that said, "*Rrregatz choo daaiee vvog rrrahnn togg mak sseynnn. Flagooot, shagg flagooot. Sahll fohgg tahh pah. Doohh deee mahhh. Mahhh.*"

"What's that mean?" they asked Umber in HQ control.

"Essentially it says, 'Don't think you've gotten away with this outrage.' The next is just a bit of name calling. Then it says, 'You shall fully take pain. Heaped on you is our contempt. Contempt.'"

"How should we reply?" the comm officer asked.

Umber shut his eyes and sighed. "I see no need to. I wouldn't say anything. But keep monitoring the high orbiters, send out scout followers, and maybe some miniature deep space torpedoes. When we know they're gone, maybe it's time to send a force against the orbiters. I doubt they'll stay there too long, but it would be better to chase them than let them try something."

"Like what?"

"A disease missile, or a cloud of them. A smallbomb cloud of *Platus platinus* parasite. Some nice thing."

"No more attacks?"

"Not sure. But look at the economics. What did they gain? Nothing. Their losses are not only great, but their chance of raids is lessened now. The distance home is so huge, they have to garner what fuel they have. They used up a great deal of energy and ordnance. I know of no fuel sources close to here unless they chance on some stray vessels and lock on them. But that isn't much help. Their problems will be greater when you message all the planets you can think of with the situation and their departing vector."

"Our trading circle is behind them," an officer remarked.

"Stick your trading circle. All the planets."

"Some are hostile."

"Tell them anyway. Full information. Remember, if the Raiders lose every ship, they'll be that much less likely to come this way again. With the economics of space raiding as it is, it's hard to justify a distant punitive expedition. It really is easier to stay home and build an economy. Their cultural personality has blinded them to that. And you've ruined this whole expedition already." He smiled wryly. "Just the way you ruined mine," he added.

"Sometimes I wonder if you've helped your own people at our expense," Admiral Uprye remarked, frowning at the list of casualties.

"I'm sure I have in a way," Umber returned. "But more weight will fall on them now. Esstrremadrr will have to help make up this loss."

"They won't thank you for that."

Umber shrugged. "They're going to kill me anyhow. They can't do more than that."

"You still think so? For your not dying in our attack."

"That, plus look at all I've told you."

"Umber, I still have the feeling you haven't told us everything," the admiral said.

Umber chuckled a little in his throat. His head swam with

fatigue so great that everything seemed fogged in the upwelling mists of an Uuvian swamp. He wanted to collapse but fought it off. The orbiting Dark Sector ships had not yet been chased off.

☐ XXIX   After the Raid

As Umber had suspected, missile clusters fell from the remaining Raiders, which maintained three high orbits around five hundred kilospans out. All the clusters were caught and destroyed, and when the L squadron platforms held energy beams on one of the ships for a long period, its monitoring was confused enough so they never saw an old-fashioned torpedo coming. The ship vanished in a flash visible from the Landsdrum surface.

The remnant of I squadron, freshly resupplied, began closing the gap between themselves and the remaining invaders, and at last the Raiders got under way. Joining together, forming into a pod, they accelerated rapidly in the wake of their main body, sending one final message: *"Choo llandzdrrumm daaiee u duk' k nuz laask rragourrr nuz—skwull uflazz."* This Umber translated as "You, Landsdrum, think about our curse until our return, unutterable ordure."

"Surely we should reply," the duty officer said with a weary smile.

"All right," Umber mused. "Say this: *'Choo oillezz nogg djjuuya nuz. Sssayll judd ya noikjudd.'*"

"You say it."

"No. It has to sound amateurish." The officer made Umber repeat it, then he transmitted, *"Cho awlez nog d-juya nuz. Sayl jud ya nokjud."* Umber laughed.

They waited a time and then received a long series of angry shoutings that Umber described as a tirade of empty blatherings, adding, "He thinks you have a filthy accent, too."

"What did we say to them?" the officer asked.

"We said, 'Go with our blessings. Travel well and heal.'"

"We said *that*?"

"It can be taken as an insult or a blessing. They took it as an insult, quite naturally. They also must think you are learning Gorboduc better, though, and this may put them off their guard some. All in all, Landsdrum acquitted itself extremely well."

"But the losses, the losses," the admiral murmured, leaning near the entrance.

"Yes, but the gains outweigh them," Umber returned.

"All forty ships of our lead squadrons? Twenty-two of C and G? Thirty-two Whank-class ships?"

"Their personnel losses are greater. You took out more than half their combat ships, more than a third of the captives they've traveled billions of kilospans to get, and left them to limp several light-years home. You've hurt the chances of future raids on their way home. You made them expend a huge store of energy and a large number of intricately designed weapons systems. You hurt their pride and their economy. You've warned their enemies."

"And we lost over six thousand highly trained, fine people."

Umber shut his eyes and smoothed back his hair. "You might have lost that many just in their intimidation. I understand they killed more last time."

"Yes. But what of their vengeance?"

"There is that. But how do you mount an armada for vengeance when it's a mere gesture, at enormous expense, at so great a distance? The Raiders are good haters. But they know a fine fight, and you showed them one. They know if they come back, you'll be better. They have no respect for weakness. My people don't, either. If they ever meet me again, they're going to despise me as a coward."

"Probably that won't happen," the officer said.

"Perhaps," Umber said.

Shortly after, the mop-up patrols caught a message from a drifting hull—one of the captives. Umber advised against any gullible move to take the wreck in tow. The LS force watched from a distance, assigned a monitor, and went about their work. Distress calls continued for over twenty days until the monitor became impatient and its officers asked permission to board.

"Send a drone lander," the admiral replied. They did. It locked on the underport, opened to the ship, and vanished in a quick flash.

Subsequent distress calls apologized for the accident in Molod, a common trading language in the galactic center, claiming the Raiders had mined all the entrances. The callers seemed more and more desperate. "When droc smells bad, don't eat it," Umber said, but eventually the monitoring ship again asked permission to investigate.

The admiral had anticipated that and sent a listening hookup out on the next shuttle. Launched, it locked on the hull of the drifter, bored in, and eavesdropped. It heard conversations in Molod. The monitors were excited. The talk dealt with everyday matters: worry about survival, getting home, having enough food, the intentions of the Landsdrum watchers. Again Landsdrum requested permission to board from the admiral.

At control central, Umber listened to the conversations and made a face. "They have the Gorboduc 'r,'" he said. "It's a setup. Converse with them. Use the term *waison* so they have to repeat it. If it comes out rr*aison* or even r*aison* they are Raiders. You'll see."

"What does it mean?"

"It means 'calculation.' The transmission should be such that they have to use it in their reply."

The command pondered that for a time, got a board of linguists from the Choicity Academy, and relayed a broadcast. After collecting the data, five or six agreed that not only was the Gorboduc "r" present but there also was the tendency to impart emphasis by holding sounds. That was foreign to Molod.

"I'm going to offer them captivity if the whole command agrees," the admiral said.

"No," Umber said. "It would only harm you. Never trust a Dark Sector Gorboduc, except that he'll hurt you."

"What about you?"

Umber smiled. "No, I won't hurt you—though I have disrupted you. But I'd rather have you not trust me than trust them. Here's an idea. Send another drone. Tell them to disarm one of the remaining ports. Tell them physicians, medical supplies, food, and survival supplies will be on board. Say that we will take no Gorboducs but that others will be brought planetside. But have no one aboard, and make the drone highly explosive. If they touch it off, they'll go up, too. They'll blow it up if they think they can kill a few more of you."

"Sounds expensive."

"You can't have them sitting out there, or soon enough they'll send a databurst with so much information about you in it that you could make an almanac out of it."

The officers regarded him, pondering. Finally they agreed, sending a small drone masterfully conceived to confuse the drifters, with chatty conversation aboard they could monitor as well as feasible answers to all queries from the wrecked ship.

Acceptance signals winked from the aft port. They locked on, and two suited figures could be seen in the air lock. The Landsdrum lander requested that they remove the vacuum suits. They said they had to decline because the atmosphere was too poor. The lander said they would return when it was improved. The figures begged and pleaded for consideration. The lander said it would need more information. It asked where they were from. They replied that they came from Ostirn. They had been captives for over eleven hundred Ostirn days. Now all the Raiders on board had died, and they yearned to be free.

The lander asked if the Gorbies were really such *sstaaksh nooggglutzz rrenallld ffownk-ez* as they seemed. One figure stiffened and replied, *"Zzannndurrrx sskutzburr,"* leaping from the air lock and surging back in with an instant borer. He slammed it against the lander hull and pushed back out of the air lock again as it fired its charge through the heavy skin. The whole lander, along with the derelict ship, erupted in a huge mass of silent fire. It died away in a scattering of spinning fragments.

"So much for that," the duty commander, standing safely off, remarked. "By the way, what did all that gibberish mean, anyhow?"

"I don't know, sir," the comm officer replied. "Something the Gorbie cooked up."

"We wasted another lander, I see."

"Got rid of a problem, too. Helm, pull us back another forty kilospans or so."

"Aye, sir," the helm replied, still straining to see the nearly empty monitor.

At control central the whole incident was replayed several times. The command officers seemed relieved at getting rid of an ambiguity. One turned to Umber and found him pondering, his eyes brimming.

"What? What is it?" he asked.

"I don't know. Only the one was a Gorbie. The other—I think was a woman. I'm sure she was a captive. I think she had been one a long time. I doubt she was from Ostirn. Her lilt was like somebody from one of the Uke planets, from here maybe eighty degrees from the galactic core. They are reputed to be a gentle people, out of the way, returned to an agrarian life. The Raiders must've sliced through them like a shovel through mud. I wonder how many others there were."

"So you think we made a mistake."

"No. No. But it's so sad."

An officer shrugged. "It's all pretty sad," he said. "I lost a brother and three cousins out there."

"It has to stop," Umber said, almost in a whisper. Later, alone, his heart still heavy with what he had seen, Umber found himself wondering for the thousandth time where his honor had gone. There were the numbers, and he went over them all again to be sure of them, but that did not relieve him. He had reached a point at which he felt that no perspective on honor would justify him. He yearned for Leda and Pell and the simple stability they offered, but as he did, he seemed to see Dame Penne looking grimly at him and knew she would be wholly justified. He had endangered his own people immensely. A record of death by hard torture might avert Raider anger, he thought, and then his body shuddered at the thought of it. At last he shook his head and forced the whole question out of his mind. But of course it came back and burned in his thought with the hard fire of the whitest stars.

☐ XXX   Cold Pastoral

SPRING had become summer, and Wahn was teaching Pell more about talking to Tistan, with Umber watching, when Leda came up. Umber smiled at her and remarked, "Pell will be on his own soon. He's a natural."

Leda brushed some dried mud from Umber's sleeve. "Mother wants you," she said. Umber looked pained. Leda smoothed his hair. "Do all Gorbies' ears stick out?" she asked innocently.

"Mother!" Pell said.

"Only mine. All the others have ears fused to their heads. What does she want?"

"What you'd expect," Leda said, tugging at his arm. "We knew she'd bring the whole thing up."

"I'm in such a false position," Umber muttered.

"Don't say that. How do you think that makes me feel? Well, don't hang back. Come on."

Pell watched them go.

Inside the receiving room Dame Penne was waiting, hands in her lap. She motioned to the seats opposite her. "Umber," she began immediately, "I understand that Lower Space offered you a commission and that you turned it down."

"I had to, Dame Penne. I'm an officer in our own force."

She regarded him. "Then it's settled in your mind that you

aren't going to stay—even though you . . . hang about with my daughter."

"If they come for me, I have to go."

"To die, you say."

"Yes."

"And death is preferable to you than Leda."

"When do we get our preferences? We play with what we're dealt."

"There's a demand that you be more than Gyro's servant."

"Yes. I've heard."

"I suppose you can't be a citizen, either."

"No. Perhaps a resident alien? I was that on Klluum."

"This is not Klluum. If you are to be with Leda, there has to be some legal and moral provision for it. If you leave, what'll she be?"

Umber looked at his hands. "I think I should withdraw."

"No!" Leda cried out. "How can you push us around like this? Did you think I was a good little celibate on the mining planet, mother? Does anyone? Am I to have no say in how I'm being hurt? Can't I take care of myself?"

Umber and Dyann Penne stared at her. "Well?" she asked.

Umber stood and faced the entrance. "It can't be to your honor in this society at this time in this situation to . . . be my lover. I can't marry you because I'm quite certain I will leave. I—"

"To die," said Leda.

"Yes. Home-staying Essttremadrrians marry for life. Space-faring ones aren't held to that. It's not as though we met in the first rush of youth and passion. We know what we have to bear, to meet, to what degree we can enjoy."

"You've never said you loved Leda, Umber," Dame Penne said with a severe mouth.

"I didn't at first. She seemed possessed, wild. I feared her. I suppose I began to love her when I had to sit out in the rain and dark because she had camped where the leatherarms could get her. She seemed so sturdy and yet so innocent."

"What's this?" Dame Penne said in a flurry.

"Oh, mother. It isn't anything. He saved me from it. Got

me to move camp. No man had ever done anything like that before. It was the way Rad was supposed to be."

"Huh," Dame Penne snorted. "And your father? What did he—" She paused and thought. "I suppose not," she ended lamely. Then she added, "And what of Casio—his standing offer? It may not stand forever, especially. . ."

"Especially if I am seen to be cozying up to the Gorbie? I can get along without that. What a dull relationship that would be."

Umber looked at her warily. "Casio?" he asked.

"We were children together, even though he's older. He always thought I'd marry him. Father wanted it. I wanted some adventure, not the stuffy politician's life. Rad came along. I thought—" She laughed ruefully. "I was mistaken," she said flatly.

"Leda, your father is dying," Dyann Penne said flatly. "No, I know you think he has been for a long time. He really is. The Dal electability will pass to you."

"Who wants that, mother? I'm a geologist."

"Pell may want it. You have to maintain it."

Leda rose to stand by Umber, hanging loosely on to his dark braid. He rolled his eyes at her. "Dame Penne," he began. "On Klluum they have a quality they call '*korsayn*,' a way of seeing, a way of knowing. You have that to some degree."

"You have it, too," Dyann Penne replied.

"Some. I know somehow they're even now coming for me."

"I know it, too."

"What are you two taking about?" Leda remonstrated.

Umber looked hard at Dame Penne. "I will do what you think is decent, proper, and—"

"And what you want to do," Dame Penne finished, sighing.

"You two are deciding my fate as though I were some droc!" Leda exclaimed.

"Leda, my dear, we're both deciding to do what you want," Dame Penne said.

"Tell me what I want, then."

"Umber, for now."

At that point Pell wandered in. "Umber," he began, "teach me to talk Gorbie."

Umber whistled. "Pell, I had hoped to spend my remaining time on one last mystery."

"Who brought the drocs," Dame Penne said. "Gorbie, can't you leave the Godworshipers one last myth?"

"We don't have to tell. It'll help the puzzle. Suppose, for instance, they didn't all die of plague. Suppose they planted the drocs in passing for a food supply if they were to come again."

"Umber," Pell interrupted.

"Yes?"

"Will you teach me Gorbie?"

"Say 'zzdakmaal sog dur kluud roon pahh.'"

Pell repeated it, and Umber laughed. "I'll work at it. I really will," Pell said, taking Umber's wrist.

Dame Penne shot him a look. Umber rolled his eyes and said, "All right. I've already committed so many remarkable acts, I suppose that won't matter. The Landsdrum academies ought to know my language anyhow. We'll start soon."

"Tistan wants you to eat some of it when it is killed," Pell said hesitantly.

Umber frowned. "It told you that?"

"Yes."

"Like us, it wants to go on living somehow," Umber said, a little sadly.

That night Leda found Umber moody and pensive. "What is it?" she asked, kissing his ear.

"I'm afraid. Not for me. I may mess it up. Going from the luxury of you to . . . hard Esstrremadrr treatment. Will I handle it? Eventually, it'll be worse than anything yet. I have to make them hold off a while."

"What? I don't understand."

"What if they kill *Marmota* on the way home—or it dies of neglect? The loss. The information I need to convey. It's so much."

"I'm sure you'll manage it."

"Don't. It's not just talk. I have one sure hope of remaining alive—claiming my right of tribunal."

"Why not do that?"

"I'll have to do that."

"What's the matter, then?"

"I'll lose. It'll make the death harder. I have to die well, or they'll write me off as a useless coward."

Leda stared at him in the dark, then moved closer to him, placing her cheek against his beard and kissing his ear. "Oh, Umber," she murmured. He did not reply, but after he began drifting off, she felt him twitch and heard him murmuring numbers in his sleep.

As summer advanced, Umber devoted himself to teaching simple Gorboduc to Pell and a small group of academy linguists. Leda noticed how much time he spent hardening his body, supervising the management of the *Unipurp. quatrilob.* colony, and simply thinking. Occasionally she drew him away for a game of Ourdoo, sitting close to him, leaning against him until they forgot the game in the pleasure of closeness. Sometimes Pell leaned on them, his head between them, musing on the movement of the polished white counters.

The time came to terminate the old drocs, all of which were susceptible to the plague. They could not hold immunity any longer, and their bodies seemed almost to generate the type A microbody. Tistan had a final conversation, got them to renew a promise to eat some of it, and held its forearms up willingly to be lifted onto the terminating rack. Its final message was "All things in right time." The old droc was now famous, and after the whole family and all the herders had partaken of it, the rest was given out to a crowd of interested people from Matted Plain.

Umber managed a trip to Doublewedge Island for more specimens of the miniature *oundesi* droc. Leda found him studying one of them closely as it lay in a shallow tank of seawater. "What now?" she asked, leaning on his shoulder.

"You thought this wasn't a droc splash?" he asked lightly.

"Well, you're the biologist. Doesn't look much like the original."

"It talks the same way. Look." Umber demonstrated, using a stylus tip and a finger. The small animal replied. "It's simpler. Doesn't have much vocabulary. But please remember this if any question comes up."

"Umber, if you keep talking about being gone, I . . . It makes me sad."

Umber turned and embraced her. "Worse than sad," he said. As he held her, his body jerked and trembled.

"What?" she asked.

"Only a chill."

"No, it's more."

"A deceleration pulse. No, not the Raiders. It's different. It's Esstrremadrr come for me."

☐ XXXI   Obduracy

UMBER rolled out of bed and into a worksuit as Leda touched in the code for the duty officer at LSHQ, Umber reciting it to her as he closed the suit. The officer's harried face appeared, looking over her shoulder and back at Umber.

"It's Esstrremadrrian," Umber said. "Come for me, I surmise."

"They've said something, but I don't understand it."

"Play it over, please." Umber listened as it was played back and said, "It's just numbers, a recognition announcement. Can you send it a normal landing beam? I'll talk to them if you wish."

"Before the landing beam, we want to know their intentions. They've made no previous trade announcement."

"Let me talk to them, then."

Clearance was obtained, and the comm officer said, "Go ahead, Umber."

"*Zzazdruk hool mantinnuntt,*" Umber said. "*Foornikrrut a Llanzzdrrumm Sahk Noot Noot Wwworg.* That's, 'State your intentions. Welcome to Landsdrum, Five Eight Eight Seven.'"

The Esstrremadrr reply said that they would state their intentions when they arrived. Umber replied in Gorboduc, "This is Commander Umber Trreggvethann, Esstrremadrr Expeditionary Probe Six Two Three One. You will not arrive unless you state your intentions now. Landsdrum is unable to grant clearance to a warship on other terms."

The reply came in a deeper voice. Translated, it said, "We have come for you, traitorous slime, to peel your skin and fry you."

Umber told LSHQ their stated intention was to come for him. The duty officer gave him the navigation coordinates and clearance, and Umber said, "Very good, Five Eight Eight Seven. I've been expecting you. I have information and a small cargo for Esstrremadrr. Follow the coded beam at the prescribed speeds, please."

The deep-voiced reply indicated that they would come as and how they pleased.

"That will not accomplish your purpose, Five Eight Eight Seven, since Landsdrum Lower Space Command would destroy you, a useless waste of Esstrremadrrian equipment and personnel."

"We are not all gutrotten cowards who let ourselves be taken," the reply came.

"No doubt you are right," Umber replied. "But if you are intent on dying uselessly, why not fly into the sun? All Landsdrum will watch your courage, as will I. And then I must wait longer to regain my honor."

"You have no honor," the reply came. "However, for the pleasure of seeing you scream and weep, I will follow the beam and speeds."

"Very good, Captain," Umber returned. "I will await your arrival. May I speak to the biology officer, please?"

"No," the voice replied. "We will let you know who you may speak to and if you may speak."

"Very good, Captain," Umber said. He turned to see Pell standing in the entrance, wide-eyed.

"Will they really do that to you?" the boy said in a near whisper.

"Perhaps," Umber said. "They aren't pleased. They are always frank. I violated the code—more codes than they now know. Just remember that it is a standard military announcement from a standard military mind. No matter what they do, I will be the gainer from having known you and your mother."

"I can't let you go," Leda said.

"I must. LS is bringing them down at North Cruelmouth Base. If I'm not there when they arrive, they'll put me down for a true coward."

"I'm going, too."

"I'd rather you didn't. It might be nasty."

"I will." Leda embraced Umber, crying into his shoulder. He returned the embrace, and Pell came into the chamber and put his arms around both, burying his head between them.

North Cruelmouth Base lay on a small promontory jutting out into the Sea of Cruel Mouths, well south of Choicity in a dry, desolate terrain deeply cut by erosion, rough and wind-blasted. Umber waited in the control station as the black oval of Esstrremadrr's 5887, a deep-space patrol and mapping vessel, escorted, settled on to the pad with a heavy roar and swirl of dust. The ship had followed the prescribed navigation commands to the letter. Umber had read the standard quarantine order in Gorboduc from the military manual as they had approached. He recited to them Landsdrum landing expectations and general protocol. For this he received only acknowledgments of the messages.

The ship was put down on the farthest landing pad, isolated. Still, as Umber told Lower Space, the device they no doubt had activated would take out the entire complex if the vessel were attacked.

At last a large landroller went out to the ship with a crew, a base officer, and Umber, still in his white worksuit. The hatch swung down, and two men in deep purple landwar suits marched down the ramp and stood at the bottom. They were tall and heavily muscled. Another man, even larger, then came down the ramp in landwar armor and stood on the pavement. He saw Umber and glared at him.

"Landsdrum has asked me to welcome you, Captain," Umber said in Gorboduc. "I am here to await the commands of Essrremadrr and to present it with the remaining specimens of our expedition. Landsdrum has also requested that if possible, communications be conducted in Onic, since that is the language most usually shared by members of our cultures."

The captain looked at Umber a long moment, then strode up and struck him heavily across the face with the back of his armored glove. Umber reeled, then came back upright. The captain struck him again, this time knocking him down. Again Umber stood up. As the captain stepped forward again, the Landsdrum officer stepped between them.

"I'm sorry," he said. "Your treatment of your countryman may be appropriate for your country, but it is not for ours. We will not condone it."

Umber translated. The captain replied, "Then I request you to release him to me for discipline according to the laws of Essrremadrr."

Again Umber translated. The duty officer responded, "We release him to you to treat as you must when you leave our space, only under the condition that he not be harmed while he is under our jurisdiction. We have found him to be a good person. He has benefited us in numerous ways and no doubt will benefit you similarly, given the opportunity."

The captain replied, "We are an honorable people. He has not acted with honor and will be so dealt with. However, since we acceded to your demands to retrieve him, we agree to your terms and request that he come aboard our vessel."

"Agreed," the base commander replied. "We also recommend that you take with you the specimens he suffered so much to rescue. In spite of our initial reactions, they have already benefited us greatly as no doubt they will you. If it troubles you that they came from him, he has given us to understand that they are the results of a whole series of expeditions by many cultures. It is his opinion, though not ours, that four of the specimens come from a planet of origin from which all humans radiated. Taking the specimens would give your scientists an opportunity to evaluate those species."

The captain regarded him coldly. "I will give you our view of that matter later," he said.

"During your stay you may have the freedom of our base and, if you wish, a tour of Choicity. We also recommend, if you agree, that you meet with some of our governing citizens. You may also trade for fuel or other materials you may require. But we do not authorize unescorted travel off-base. We also trust that if Umber is taken aboard 5887 now, he may be visited before you leave."

"I will also give our view of that," the captain said. "Now please release our . . . citizen to us."

Umber had tried hard to convey accurately the tone and content of all his translations even though his face was bleeding and swelling from the captain's blows.

"Very well," the base officer said, stepping forward spontaneously and embracing Umber hard. "He is yours, Captain."

Umber and the base officer saluted. Umber turned, nodded to the captain, and walked up the ramp. The captain and his men followed, and the ramp whined up and snapped shut.

"Sir, you have blood on your coat," an aide said to the duty officer.

"Crime on a crutch. Shut up," the man replied. "Back to the roller. Now, now."

The 5887 was not a big vessel. Umber was escorted to the one room of any size in it, the command and navigation center, where much of the crew awaited him, all stern-mouthed, all silent, all dark-haired and blue-eyed like Umber. He swept the room with his eyes. "Now," the captain said, arcing his fist again and knocking Umber down. Umber stood up. The captain knocked him down again. This happened three more times. Umber's face streamed with blood, but as he stood again, he said in a clear voice, "That's enough."

"Enough! Enough!" the captain shouted, swinging again. Umber caught his arm, twisted, threw the captain across into the console, and kicked him hard as he fell. Three men were on him instantly. One screamed and dropped. He threw the second into the third, turned and grappled with a fourth, and as the captain staggered up, flung the man into him, knocking him down again. At that point a stunner made him crumple. The captain, reeling, staggered over and kicked him.

"*Ygaah stooff,*" another officer shouted, and the captain whirled at him. It was the intelligence officer. The men glared at each other. The officer had just asked him who was the coward. The man added that he would like to have something left to interrogate, adding that maybe Umber could teach them how to fight, especially when somebody was fighting back. The captain glared at him.

"When we are home, I will settle this. I promise," the captain said.

"Well, have enough sense to get us home and we'll see about that," the security officer returned. "You dented the console. Not you. Only your armor."

"I'll see to you, too," the captain said.

"If you don't, I'll challenge you," the man replied.

Umber, who lay dizzy and bleeding, said, "It's a wonder anybody survives in this service with all your threats." The captain whirled and aimed a kick at him, but several men held up their arms, and he desisted.

"Lock him up," the captain said. "Prepare to depart."

"The specimens. You must take them," Umber said.

"I don't take any advice from a proven coward who violated the basic code he swore to—not to give or take quarter to any enemy."

"The specimens were gathered by loyal service people," Umber replied. "They will enrich both us and our trade. They have nothing to do with my treachery. Esstrremadrr deserves them. Stupid poses would impoverish us more than the Raiders."

"Take him away," the captain said.

"Besides, you cannot kill me until you get me home," Umber added.

"I agreed with these slime I wouldn't kill you in their area, but in space I am in command."

"I helped them defeat the Raiders. Landsdrum did defeat them. The Dark Scum may eventually find out, maybe from the captain who acts so much like them. If they don't have me for vengeance, it will fall on Esstrremadrr. You have all heard it in case he chooses to kill me in space."

The room fell silent. The captain almost choked. "You . . ." he began.

"When? When?" the intelligence officer asked, wide-eyed.

"Not long ago. They came with 60 ships and 183 captive vessels. They left with losses of 38 ships and 89 captives. They never touched the planet."

"I—this is—unbelievable treachery," the intelligence officer said as the captain beat both fists on the console.

Umber laughed, showing his bloody mouth. "Treachery? Yes, treachery to the friends of those blood suckers. Not to a true Esstrremadrrian."

"Who are you to tell us about a true Esstrremadrrian?" the security officer yelled. "You must have told them how to detect the deceleration pulse. You must."

"You can kill me only once," Umber said with a shrug. "To sacrifice a planet just to hold that secret, which you never use to any advantage, is stupid."

"It's not our planet, you drooling idiot!" the intelligence officer shrieked.

"That's why they've always beaten us, why they hold us as a planetload of foolish slaves. They're all our planets. Every time they savage one, they beat us. Every time they lose, they weaken. It's time to resist them."

"And be crushed. Who are you to advise us, to determine the course of our history?"

"Somebody has to," Umber replied. "Somebody other than a lot of heavy-muscled, posing shouters."

"If you don't take him away, I'll kill you all!" the captain yelled.

"See?" Umber said. "He's going to lift ship himself with a load of corpses. Security," he said, "I have a lot of information for you, and for intelligence, if there is any intelligence on this slopbucket. Now, where is the brig?"

After Umber left, the captain daubed his bleeding face. The intelligence officer began to laugh. He slapped his leg. "Not what we expected, eh? But the slob's guaranteed himself a harder death than I can think about."

"Deserves it, too," the captain said.

"Maybe. We'll see, Captain," the security man said.

The next day 5887 received a request for a visit to Umber. Surprisingly, it came from Burcc Dezan, now the head of the Godworship Council for Matted Plain. After some argument, it was agreed he could see Umber in his tiny cell. Dezan arrived in his robe with its chair's decorations, walked up the ramp, and finally stooped into the tiny room.

"They've hurt you," he said in greeting.

Umber chuckled. "And I them," he returned. "What can I do for you?"

"Just one question, really. You—you really don't think that we came from a home planet and that other beings are sexual, do you? It seems so obscene, so harmful to worship. I mean, I need to hear you say you tricked us yourself. You are going. It can't matter to you to tell the truth."

"You need to hear me say I tricked you?"

"Yes."

"Will that change any facts?"

"It . . . since all your upheavals, I've been . . . dizzy. I find it hard to head an organization it is difficult for me to see clearly."

Umber pondered. "May I say something in preamble before I answer?"

"Yes, of course," the young man replied, earnestly nodding.

"Esstrremadrr has a religion of sorts. It's more of a code of behavior. It worked well for a long time in disciplining us. We live on a hard planet. But in essence it's a very limited religion, absolute, rigid, and in a way cruel. I've been on several planets. Each one has its own version of deity, and some have several. When I got to Klluum, I lost whatever vestige of Gooll, our home religion, that had remained. It was washed away in the beauty of Klluumian perceptions of Being. One of its pleasures is that it is free of rigid mythologies. It has an elaborate concept of the deity, or Being, and a code of conduct based on kindness and love. I see similarities between some of its ideas and some of Godworship."

"Similarities?"

"Yes. You are good people. You get caught up in holding to the idea that God put the drocs here or that there are no other sexual beings and forget the main point. Many people pray. Some of us are better at it than others, because some of us just pray for stuff to fatten us. I imagine the Raiders even pray for victory in battle. Other people pray to know what to do or to be better or help or not to hurt or to know more clearly or to be healed or to know what they are and what is really true."

"What are you saying?"

"Two things. Never give up on your Godworship, and yes."

"Yes, what?"

"Yes, *Marmota* is real. We didn't make it. Him. Her. It is sexual. So are *Bukloe daktyloid*, *Sekale sereal*, and many thousands of other species. But it doesn't matter."

"Of course it matters."

Umber put his hands on the young man's shoulders. "No. It doesn't. That's what went wrong when the council tried to kill me. They focused on the myths rather than on the point. Sometimes one has to say, 'We made a mistake.' But never give up on Godworship. Make it ride with the times, with the facts. You don't want to be left with nothing. Everywhere I've been, the intellectuals scoff at notions of deity. And most people pay little attention to it. But they all benefit from its order, its perceptions, and maybe even from the possibility that prayer is, in some sense or other, answered. That's really what Gian Dok was after. She got it confused, though. She thought it was important that people were the only sexual beings, when that simply isn't so and has no importance whatsoever."

Dezan stared at the wall. Umber found himself looking closely at the white beads on his robe. He looked more closely. "Those look like Ourdoo pieces," he said, pointing.

Dezan shrugged, still pondering. "They're the same as the old ones. New Ourdoo pieces are white plastic in imitation."

"Where are they from?"

"I don't know. I hear all the old ones came from Truncated

Mountain when they cut it off for the space base. All from one area. They're rare and so valued."

"May I look at them?"

"Yes, of course. You really mean it? About sexuality?"

"Yes. I do." Umber summoned the guard and asked for a powered hand glass. The man brought it without a question, and Umber leaned forward and studied the white beads carefully. They were clearly organic.

"They come in different sizes, and a matched set like this is extremely rare," Dezan said, a little proudly.

"They're bonelike," Umber said. "Some creature that used to live on the mountain, I suppose." He paused and chuckled a little. "Interesting," he added, giving the glass back to the guard. "Well, I wish I could tell you I only said those things, but they are true enough, I think. Remember that it doesn't matter, though. Please. But other things do— honor and love and truth and mercy and joy and peace. Things like that."

Burcc Dezan sighed. "Go well," he said, standing and stooping out the entrance.

Umber pondered the bony beads, trying to memorize the structure he had just seen. At the sump he had been sure the Ourdoo beads were just plastic. After a time, he asked to see security.

When Urrdi Inntegg, the security officer, came, Umber asked, "Did Esstrremadrr get our message about the droc plague? I need to know."

"Droc plague?"

"It's too much to suppose you'd remember unless something happened at home. Do you have the text of our databurst?"

"Yes," Inntegg said coldly.

"Please search it for the droc plague. We buried it in a lot of biological information. It's vital."

"Explain," Inntegg said, folding his hands.

Umber did at length. Inntegg grew more and more serious as he saw its implications. Finally he said, "I'll check."

Umber touched his arm and asked him with hand signs not to tell the captain.

"Why?" the officer asked.

"Do the Raiders raise drocs?" Umber asked mildly.

"I don't know," Inntegg said, slowly catching the implications of Umber's concept. "You really hate them, don't you?" he said.

"Not hate. Do you hate a disease or wipe it out?"

"Huumm," Inntegg said, closing the brig door.

The captain did not raise ship immediately, needing fuel and still arguing with his officers about the specimens. The next day Leda was allowed to see Umber. She was nearly as tall as the Esstrremadrrians and with some effort squeezed into the brig with him. "They hurt you," she said, kissing him.

"I hurt them, too, when I'd had enough."

"You did? I saw the captain. He did have a bruise." She giggled slightly. "You got away with that?"

"He has honor. He would never bind someone and beat him. That would only prove his weakness."

"What will become of you?"

Umber smiled slightly, his mouth still swollen. "Something bad, it's likely. But it hasn't happened yet. Listen. I think I've just learned something." He began to laugh. "You know the pieces in the Ourdoo game?"

"Yes."

"Burcc Dezan came to see me. He had some decoration like those pieces on his chair's robe. I got a look at them. They're bony—some kind of bone I know nothing of."

"Of course. Mountain bone. Ours are only plastic. Real ones are rare. What are you laughing at?"

"I don't know. But they aren't from any creature now on the planet, are they?"

"No. I don't know. Why—you mean . . ."

"Yes. One possibility is that they come from whatever brought the drocs. Right under our nose. Something, anyhow. They aren't here now. They aren't old enough to have fossilized. I wish I could stay to look into it."

"Oh, Umber, I want to go with you."

"We've been through that, Leda, my love. It's a long journey. We get there. I die. You are left. Not good, I think."

"I can't stand this."

"There's no other way. It has to be stood. I told you from the beginning."

"But I thought it wouldn't happen."

"I *sent* for them, Leda. Before I knew you. It had to be done. Can you think what the earthbeast will do for us—that alone?"

"You've said."

"How is Pell?"

"He's here, trying to get permission to come aboard."

"He could practice his Gorboduc."

"He only wants to see you," Leda said, beginning to cry. Umber took her in his arms and held her hard.

"Gggratz blassn," the guard said.

"Time to go, my love," Umber murmured into her neck. Leda pulled away slowly, her eyes closed, kissed him, and turned through the brig door, nodding at the guard, her face streaming. The man looked at her impassively.

Later, when the security and intelligence officers reviewed the transcript of the conversation, Inntegg said, "What do you make of that?"

The other shrugged. "They're lovers."

"Did you know our scan showed she was pregnant when she came aboard?"

"No. Does he know?"

"No. I think not."

"Don't tell the captain. Don't tell anybody."

The two looked at each other. "No," Inntegg said. "This is very complex. Maybe we could learn more if the boy comes in. He seems to know some Gorboduc."

"The traitor has even taught them that."

"True. But it might be nice to be able to converse with other cultures in our own tongue."

"Against regulations."

"To please the Raiders, though."

Pell was allowed aboard that evening. His conversation with Umber was mostly silences. When the guard announced that his time was up, Pell hugged Umber and cried. Umber asked the guard to show the boy the command room. The man grunted. "I wish I could give you something, Pell. But you have something more precious than I can give you—the legacy of free people. We've never had that—yet."

"I wish you could stay," Pell returned.

"Who knows, young one. I may be back," Umber said with a slight smile. "I may see you one day on Klluum. Be brave now, as you always are." He kissed Pell on the cheek and ruffled his hair.

"*Ggratz blassn,*" the guard repeated.

"*Daw, brrak theenn,*" Pell replied. "*Vvogll trresz, maga.*"

The man chuckled slightly and said, "*Brrakll, vaann issu. Suunuk choo krruk stukeen.*" Pell shot a glance behind and saw Umber grinning broadly at him.

But after Pell had gone, Umber's smile failed. He stared at the curved wall of the brig a long time, then shut his eyes and seemed to wilt. "So, then," he whispered aloud. "I haven't been true after all. What garbage you are, Trreggevthann. How many loyalties did you think you could manage?" He hugged his arms across his chest and shuddered. Soundlessly, his lips formed the shapes of "Leda." Standing as straight as the room would let him, he braced against the cold wall and stretched hard and long, his arms trembling. Then he lay back on the short bunk and curled up still and silent.

Much of the night, Leda sat in the window of the watch room looking across the wide array of landing pads toward the silent, dark Gorboduc ship. Occasionally she sobbed quietly. Pell, who had been sent to a bunk in the crew quarters, left it toward morning and padded quietly, barefoot, down the polished corridors, past the sensors, which explored him briefly then shut off, and came to his mother. They looked at each other bleakly, and the boy put his face against his mother's shoulder and wept.

Not long after, Casio Polon arrived, he too walking quietly. He stood back somewhat, hands behind him.

"Casio," Leda murmured, looking up.

"Your mother sent me. She said he would be gone soon."

"Mother? How did she know when?"

"She is the one who knows things, remember?"

"She and Umber, too."

Casio chuckled ruefully. "And me, sometimes, too," Pell said softly.

"You, too?" his mother asked with a tight smile. "What do you know?"

"I—I feel I will see Umber again . . . sometime."

"Perhaps so, little one," his mother said with a long glance at Casio, who kept his face blank.

"Not here, mother. On Uuvia or someplace."

"Are you going there, then?" Casio asked.

"Sometime. Maybe. Somewhere. I feel it."

"It's a good thing to feel," his mother whispered, and began again to cry softly. Casio came behind her and put his hands on her shoulders. She paid no heed to him but gave herself up to quiet grief.

Early the following morning the Esstrremadrrian captain asked to have the specimens brought aboard and commanded that Umber be responsible for their care. Not long after sunrise they requested clearance and lifted ship, escorted, rapidly diminishing from view.

Leda and Pell watched from traffic command; Casio Polon, in his Dal's coat, for he was again a Dal, was standing with them. Both the Pennes looked blank and dared not touch or even glance at each other.

"What he did to us," Casio said. "We'll never be the same."

"No," Leda said, tight-lipped. "Casio, you will need to marry me now. Very soon."

Casio shot her a long look, then went to the window and stared into the blank sky. He turned and laughed ruefully. "So," he said. "That's the last gift of the Gorboduc Vandal. All right. I'll take it. Such as it is, strings attached, I'll take it."

"He's not a Vandal," Pell said.

☐ XXXII A Long List of Numbers

As 5887 cleared the Landsdrum system and set out homeward, the captain summoned his officers to command and navigation. "I've reviewed information about our traitor. His evil is greater than we first thought. Damn, I want to kill him off now before the Raiders find us with him and kill us all, and as captain, I desire the ship's council to take the matter up."

"Captain, we need to learn much from him yet. And to kill him now would invite Raider revenge later," Subcommand Inntegg said.

"To kill him now would also save him," the captain returned. "I gather it was a fair fight. But Dark Sector won't see that. We can fire him out an air lock. It's not like their tortures."

"It's so summary. And so uncalled for. He's not a coward. We've seen that already. He has the highest clearances. Don't be stupid. Let the planet decide. And what if he appeals to Esstrremadrr judgment?"

"How would he?" the captain asked, swinging his big arms. "He knows he'd be condemned. He violated the code. It's simple enough. Those bastards shot down an innocent ship passing through the system. He volunteered to be their slave, helped them in countless slimy ways, even consorted with their women. It's enough to make a decent man gag."

"Captain," Urrdi Inntegg said. "I've reviewed what he said to the local religionist. He's been to other planets. As an agent. You can't just fit in unnoticed and also keep your rigid beliefs. It defies human ingenuity, even ours."

The captain snorted. "Then we should not have agents.

Always seemed yellow to me, sneaking around."

They discussed the matter, shouting and threatening at times, at some length. Finally they decided to bring Umber out for further general interrogation.

He glided into the room with his guard, still in his dirty worksuit, its blood spatters nearly black. "Well, Captain, want another round?" he said.

"Shut it. You will speak when spoken to. There are more questions. I for one cannot fathom why somebody with all your training caved in so fast."

"The specimens aren't enough?"

"Esstrremadrr does not compromise. We never did. We never will."

"You came to get me. Wasn't that a compromise?"

"Orders."

"We serve the Raiders. Isn't that compromise?"

"I'm asking the questions."

"Then I'm requesting your security clearance before I answer."

The captain let out a roar and pushed off across the room toward Umber but was held back by two officers. "He has the right to ask. It's in the orders," the security man remarked.

The captain relaxed a little and said, "Get on with it. There's the console."

Umber moved to it and rapidly put in a series of numbers. "Class Q," he said, musing. "That goes for everybody?"

"Yes," Inntegg replied. "Except for intelligence and me. We are Y."

"Well, I'll tell you some. First there's the droc plague. The specimens of *Unipurp. quatrilob.* will save us a lot of trouble. Fortunately, we sent our message. And fortunately, Esstrremadrr has a fairly slow revolution period. We have some time."

"Coward, you just told a whole planet about droc plague, I understand. And you want security from us?" the captain shrieked.

Umber smiled. "Maybe Dark Sector has some drocs," he said.

The captain paused and let that sink in. "Huh," he said.

"You may hate them worse than our other enemies. But at least they speak our language."

"What is language? Words? They speak the language of death. I've been in other societies now a long time. Every one is better than ours. We've been infected by them, the Dark Slime. We could well speak more of the language of charity, generosity, even, if you'll pardon the expression, kindness."

"Just give us the information, Commander Trreggevthann," the intelligence officer said.

"There is another reason," Umber said hesitantly. "*The* reason, really. I've carried it so long, it's hard to realize it might be the right time to tell it. Maybe to security."

"You've seen the clearances," the intelligence officer remarked.

Umber was still at the console. He strapped himself in and spun the chair toward them. "You remember we sent out probes some time ago—explorations looking for a new home."

"Eight," the intelligence man said. "We've accounted for seven. None succeeded. The Raiders killed off three. As far as we know, there were no confessions."

"We got a message from one about five Esstrremadrr years ago. Very faint. They were dying."

"It would have been code."

"Yes, 1,317 numbers. I memorized the numbers. I have said them over every day since then."

"Numbers. You gave our secrets to the enemy for numbers?" The captain shook his head.

"I worked them out on board, using my clearance. They found a planet. It has a complete biological community, a decent rotation period and size, a stable sun, a benign atmosphere, much water, minerals. It is off the travel routes. Best of all it's so far from the Dark Sector, they'd never find it—or if they did, we'd be very, very strong."

"It sounds like a banquet in the sky," the captain said, chuckling. "How long did it take you to make this up? Was it last night?"

"Earlier," said intelligence. "We've heard him mumbling numbers every sleep time."

"We named the planet Andwikk, after the family of our communications officer, who received the message."

"My cousin, you unspeakable pervert," the captain said.

"It was also the family of the commander of the *Roog*, the lost vessel."

"Another cousin, more distant," the captain muttered.

"Huh," Umber remarked. "They were good people."

"Commander, stop sparring and give us the recognition code. I will match it. Move away—over there."

He replaced Umber at the main console and touched in some codes as Umber glided to the other side of the room and stood facing the gauge-covered wall. "Recognition code is eighty-two numbers as follows," Umber said. Then he recited them in a slow monotone.

"They match exactly," the intelligence officer said, staring down.

"Of course," Umber said.

"Give him the rest, then," the captain said.

Umber turned, gripping a pull bar. "I didn't go through all I did, violate my own honor, suffer indignity and injury, live with strangers, compound my code violations, put up with provincial stupidity, and nearly die in several ways just to hand over the code when I don't know what will happen to it, especially when the commander of this vessel is aching for a chance to execute me. No. You know I have the numbers. I'll put them in a Z-clearance security box, but I'm afraid you'll have to take me home before I recite them."

"You'll just die there."

"Of course. It's right that I do. Maybe they'll let me go back to Far Cloud for a moment."

"Might have known he was a Far Clouder," the captain muttered. "And what about the woman? If you had such a bad time, how come you found a hot-bodied lover? Eh?"

"Yeah," Umber said. "They welcomed me and said, 'Here. Here's a woman for you to idle your time away with until your friends come for you.' And that's all I did."

"There was a woman," the captain said. "I suppose you deny it. And she—"

"Captain!" Urrdi Inntegg shouted.

"What?" Umber asked. "Because she came to the brig?

Loves me? Do you think she'd have made me swerve from bearing these numbers? Never. Nothing would. It's too good a chance. Too good. For all of us."

"It looked convincing to me," the captain remarked.

"So. You'd have me make it unconvincing?" Umber said.

"Commander, I'm going to change the subject," Subcommand Inntegg said. "What was your clearance?"

"Z," Umber replied.

"To think they gave a weakling a Z clearance!" the captain roared.

"Where in Far Cloud were you from? Green Rock?" the intelligence officer asked.

"No. Sound of Water."

"The one the Raiders removed in their punitive strike."

"Yes. With my family. All of it but me."

They all looked at him in silence. At last the captain said, "All right. You go home. You have the freedom of this ship and duty with the rest. You take care of the crawlies you brought on board. I won't say welcome, but you're here. Your helm watch will commence in sixteen time measures, relieving Dzzannun. Rrraggh will issue you a uniform. On board you are only a subofficer. Agreed?"

"Agreed," Umber said. "Thank you, Captain."

"You will still die at home. No way out of that."

"Yes," Umber said. "No way."

At Potsherd Sump, preparing the last of her things for the move to Polon's estate and for her wedding, Leda found in her slide cabinet a *platinus* leaf incised with a message in small, careful letters from Umber. She read it, closed her eyes, and read it again.

Dearest Leda,

I feel like someone who has closed a large, ornate, beautiful door on a light-filled interior full of people and love, and now I stand outside in the dark and cold wind. Suddenly space does seem a vacuum, and the distance I will be from you impossibly immense. There will be no other like you. I bear your scar in heart as well as body.

To be human is to feel the agony I feel in leaving. But to be human is to struggle to grow strong again in spite of it. Stay well. Stay happy. You remain radiantly beautiful. Help Pell be a man. You have the strength to be complete.

>   All my love,
>   Umber

She looked at it a long time, then sighed and with her fingernail peeled up the corner of the drying leaf skin, then pulled the surface away, carefully shredding the skin, then the rest of the thick leaf. She dropped it all in the waste tube, dusted her hands over the tube, then put them on her stomach and stood musing. A cloud moved from in front of the sun, and the new light struck a patch of grass, *Sekale sereal*, growing in one of her mother's hand-thrown pots near the colonnade window. The green of the grass and the deep blue of the glaze on the pot went well together.

Leda sighed and smoothed back her hair. There was nothing to do but get on with it. Dame Penne would be waiting with Pell and her father. He would be sitting like a bundle, wrapped well for travel although the day was warm and the distance not far, not far at all.

About the Author

A native of New Jersey, Paul O. Williams holds a Ph.D. in English from the University of Pennsylvania. Following three years of teaching at Duke University, he settled in a tiny Mississippi River town, Elsah, Illinois, where he taught American literature and creative writing for twenty-two years at Principia College. He used the background of this area as the setting of the seven novels of the Pelbar Cycle.

Currently he lives in Belmont, California, with his wife, KerryLynn Blau. He has two children, one a newspaper photographer, the other a U. S. Marine. As well as writing science fiction, he teaches and writes poetry, essays, short fiction, and reviews.